L'elfe qui a Apprivoisé un Géant

The Elf Who Tamed a Giant

(This Ain't No Fantasy!)

A Color of the Rainbow Story

Book 1

Raj Lowenstein

www.rajlowenstein.net

Published by Raj Lowenstein

ISBN: 978-1-964452-36-4 - (sc)
ISBN: 978-1-964452-37-1 - (hc)
ISBN: 978-1-964452-38-8 - (ebook)
Library of Congress Control Number: 2025901335

Printed in USA

Acknowledgment

As always, thank you to my family. RJ for his support for these many years. My children and grandchildren and I'm not forgetting my sweet puppy of 13 years, Eli! I couldn't do this without you all.

A shout out to MR for her help.

This M/M Romance contains graphic language and sexually explicit material and is intended for adult readers.

TYLER ET JEAN-PHILIPPE

Fuck! Fuck! Fuck! Fuck! Fuck! I screamed in my head as I looked for a place to curl up and die.

The voice in my head was calling me every obscene name it had on file.

Tyler Hawthorne Braxton, you are the stupidest son of a bitch in the world, it told me.

"Yeah! Yeah! Tell me something I don't already know," I said through bloodied lips.

I'd always played outside the lines. It was the one thing that made me good at what I did. But this time, not only had I been outside the lines, I wasn't even on the page. To make matters worse, I hadn't told anyone, not my handler or captain, about the meeting. It was supposed to be the most insignificant meeting with the most inapt member of the gang I had infiltrated.

Boy, had I been wrong!

I had been beaten by four men bigger than I was. I was stabbed before being thrown into the trunk of a car for an indeterminate time - being unconscious messed up one's sense of time and place. I vaguely remember being tossed out of the trunk, kicked a dozen more times, and abandoned to bleed out. The fact that I had been semi-conscious had probably kept me from getting a bullet between the eyes.

I didn't know where I was or how bad I was bleeding.

Everything hurts. Everything! Even my fucking hair!

I thought I had been stabbed twice. Hell, what did it matter?

Through my hazy vision, I thought I saw a building. It looked abandoned. I needed to get inside. Maybe someone, a squatter or someone, would find me and call 911. At least if I was out of the cold, I might have a chance.

The little voice still calling me names also reminded me it was supposed to get far below freezing tonight.

Happy fucking Halloween, you stupid dick! Your life sucks! The voice in my head laughed.

****

I had missed the last bus to the old industrial part of the city where I stayed. I was cold, tired, and wet to the bone. My apartment, what I called an apartment, had heat. It was a small Franklin stove, but I had gathered enough wood and papers to warm the one room.

The owner of the building, a former john, had taken a liking to me. Even though I didn't have to service him often, the man let me have this space in the basement. Only the top two floors of the five-story building were used, and the entrance into the basement was secure and locked.

I was safe.

I was almost at the door when movement caught my attention. I froze, not knowing what the danger was. My keys were already in hand, but I didn't think I would have time to unlock the door before someone that close could grab me.

There was a body lying against the building. The movement had been an arm raised. Maybe to get my attention, maybe not, but I couldn't just do nothing. Despite how life had treated me, I wouldn't turn my back on someone if they needed help.

Cautiously, I moved to the body. I touched the colossus of a man's pulse point. There was a pulse.

Okay, now what? I had no minutes left on my phone, so calling 911 wasn't an option.

"Help," the faintest of a rumble spilled from the man's blood-covered lips.

Damn, okay. Get him in the apartment.

That was easier said than done.

I'm one hundred fifty centimeters tall...almost. I weighed forty-five kilos...maybe. I'm tiny, but I did have muscles. You don't live on the street for long unless you can fight off the attackers, and there have been too many to count.

"I'm going to move you to my apartment," my voice sounded like a young teenager. Despite living in America for almost seven years, my accent was still heavy, and my English sucked.

The giant's hand moved slowly and touched mine.

****

An angel, a fairy, or an elf was at my side. It was trying to move me. The cold snow had already stopped, and the feeling of being inside had made it to my muddled senses.

It hadn't been easy, moving. There had been a board…maybe…lots of starts and stops. The elf had rolled me and apologized for hurting me…I think. But then they seemed to drag me into an enclosed space.

My angel spoke words that were not in English, but I liked the smooth sound. When I opened my eyes again, there was light, dim and far away.

"I need to see where you hurt," The purr of a voice came from somewhere near my head. "I'm not going for help, but I can."

****

I put my clean comforter on the floor, then carefully rolled the man onto it. I then rebuilt the fire in the stove and ran hot water in the tub, throwing in a few wash towels. I would have to strip the man to see where the blood was coming from.

I just hoped the man didn't die in my space. It was all I had.

It took thirty minutes to get the man out of his clothes. I took the rags from the hot water, sat next to him, and, starting at his head, began to clean him up. The man was tatted up, which was the first thing I noticed. I have some tattoos of my own, but whoever the artist was who had done the ink, that guy was a master in the craft.

I took another thirty minutes to wipe the blood off before reaching for the first aid kit. Using its contents, I put butterfly bandages on the man's face, over the cuts on his brow, cheek, and the bridge of his nose. There was one stab wound on his side. It looked like someone had tried to gut the man, but from either luck or poor stabbing skills, the knife seemed to catch the side of his torso and go right through.

I hoped there were no significant organs there.

Whoever worked the man over had done an excellent job. I wasn't sure, but I thought there could be broken ribs. The man's nose was busted, but I couldn't see any other damage.

Since the man was out, I applied antibacterial cream over the cuts and opened my sewing kit. After sterilizing the needle on the stove, I darned up both sides of the knife wound.

After about forty minutes, I stood and looked down at the naked man. I took him in. The sight of him was amazing. He looked like he was into some rough stuff, and I wasn't, if I could help it.

Yes, the guy was hung. Even in his flaccid state, that was clear. So, standing over him and gawking at his dick was just plain rude, but I needed to know if there was more bleeding. I hadn't dragged the man, and it had taken over an hour to get him from where I had found him to my apartment to eye-fuck him.

Finding a dry face towel I covered the man's junk out of respect, I told myself. Then I stood back and waited to see if blood oozed from another spot.

When there was no evidence of more wounds, and before I got out of my wet clothes, I put back on my coat and followed the trail from where I had found the man to the door. It was snowing heavily now, so I was confident that any traces of the man or my movement would long be erased before the morning light. I took fifteen minutes to spread out the place where blood had tinted the snow red and the path to my space.

Returning to my room, I hung my coat behind the stove to dry and stripped off my clothes. Since the room was warm, I moved around naked and arranged my clothes to dry. I'd take a hot bath and remove the chill I was starting to feel. I couldn't afford to get sick. There were no clean clothes, utilities, food, and, more importantly, no lessons without my job.

I had worked the streets from when I was barely fourteen until seventeen. Then, the owner of an agency heard about my unusual looks and sought me out. The agency had clients who wanted the unique and the exotic. Although height and weight-wise, I was the size of an eleven or twelve-year-old, I was clearly a man.

My mother had corn-silk blond hair and pale skin. My father, not the man whose house I was raised in, had OCA type 1, a form of albinism. I was hairy, but the hair on my body, chest, arms, legs, face, and head was almost translucent, like my birth father. I also had his ice-blue eyes and my mother's elfin features.

The agency sold me as one of the Elves from *The Lord of the Rings* movies. I fit the description to a T. I had even allowed the owners to modify my ears with plastic surgery so they were shaped to a natural peak.

I had made good money. The agency had made much more. I had shared a decent apartment owned by the agency with other boys who worked for them. However, I had still been a whore, and I had wanted more for my life than that.

I left the agency when a john, Bernard, had offered me this apartment.

The apartment had been critical for me in turning my life around. I got a dishwasher job in a restaurant about ten miles from this place. I had gotten a mailbox with Bernard's help. Bernard came two or three times a month to 'collect' rent. Bernard's fees were often brutal, taking me days to recover, but they were worth it. My life improved, and I had no one to be grateful to but myself.

I threw the only other blanket I had over the man and left him to sleep. After draining the tub and cleaning it with the balance of my bleach, I refilled it with hot water. The tub was big enough to sit in with my legs under my chin and was positioned between the toilet on one side and the kitchenette on the other. A sink served both the 'bathroom' and 'kitchen.'

There was a microwave I had found on the street, and under the three-foot counter was a dorm-sized refrigerator. The room was ten by twelve. It was tiny but clean, warm, and safe. I had spent money on the new full-sized mattress pushed up against the wall opposite the kitchen and bathroom. A low coffee table served as a dining table and desk. Two floor lamps lit the room. It wasn't much, but it was home.

I would have to do laundry tomorrow. Luckily, the laundromat was only a twenty-minute walk. If the snow stopped, I could take care of it. Otherwise, I would have to wear the same outfit for the next several days. I was off for a few days before working a seven-day week, so being in the same clothes for a day or two wasn't a problem.

After my bath, I dressed in heavy flannel pajamas and thick socks purchased from the local thrift shop. Next, I cooked soup on the Franklin stove and made half a sandwich. I took the food, moved to sit on the bed, and watched the man. The blanket rose and fell with his breathing. I needed to keep him hydrated, I knew. There wasn't any way to keep ice, but the water was good to drink. Even if I poured the water into his mouth, that might be enough.

I cleaned up and then did just that. Using a straw, I got enough into the man to hopefully keep him from dehydrating. I hoped that would be enough if I did that every hour.

I set the timer for an hour and a half, turned off the lights, and curled up in the dark. My last waking thought was I hoped I hadn't just brought a killer into my home.

****

I opened an eye. I was warm but uncomfortable as hell. Not only from the beating I half-remembered but whatever I was lying on was hard. With one hand, I explored my body. I was naked, but someone had cleaned me up. I found bandages across my nose, brow, and cheek as I explored my face. After further examination, I discovered someone had sutured up my side.

There was enough light in the space for me to see. Carefully, I sat up and studied the surroundings. There was a Franklin stove, its chimney leading out between two filthy high-placed windows. Clothes hung on hooks near the pipe that carried the smoke out of the space.

In front of me was a kitchen/bath area. There was no furniture, but everything seemed clean. A beat-up-looking guitar hung on the wall between the 'kitchen' and the one door in the room. An additional scan showed nothing else on the wall: no photos, paintings, or a calendar.

I turned to look behind me.

A low table was between where I lay, and a mattress shoved against the wall. A kid was on the bed with their back to me. A sheet was pooled around the kid's legs, and they were curled up in a ball as if they weren't warm enough. Their hair was long and braided into a thick ponytail. In the dark, it glowed like moonlight on snow.

I turned back to the stove. There was a stack of wood. Apparently, the wood was scavenged from the neighborhood, but enough to keep the small room warm for several days. I moved slowly so as not to wake the kid or damage my body, and I added more wood to the fire. After that, I moved to the kitchenette with practiced stealth and located a sharp knife, which I palmed and returned to the makeshift pallet.

The task had worn me out. I was just about asleep when an alarm sounded in the area near the head of the mattress.

"*Merde*," A feather-light voice said before I heard movement. The voice wasn't that of a child nor precisely the voice of an adult.

I kept my eyes closed, my body relaxed, and I waited, ready to strike if needed.

After a moment, the kid kneeled next to my head. The voice was whispering but not in English. French, maybe, but I wasn't sure. I felt a smooth hand run over my forehead, down my cheek, and then the press of the kid's head as they seemed to listen to my heart.

"*D'accord*," the voice said and placed something on my lips. "Must for you drink water."

I allowed the slow stream of water to filter through my lips and soothe my throat.

"*Bon!*" Definitely French. "Now, you sleeps, yes." There was a gentle caress on my cheek, and it took everything not to lean into it and smile.

There were more whispered words and the sound of someone getting into bed.

I allowed myself to relax and was soon asleep.

JEAN-PHILIPPE

I woke twice more to put water into the man and keep the fire going inside the stove. When the morning light filled the room, I was exhausted but got up again to check on the man.

He seemed to be okay. There was no fever. The last time I watered the man, he had accepted almost half a cup. If the man stayed in the same condition, I would buy more minutes on my phone to call 911 this morning.

Stepping around the prone body, I moved to the toilet and pulled the shower curtain around for privacy. After relieving my bladder, I washed my hands in the sink and made coffee.

Almost everything I possessed had been picked up off the street or in a thrift shop, including all my kitchen supplies and guitar, everything but the mattress, which was new. I even found a French press coffee maker at the thrift shop.

I put a tea kettle on the Franklin stove and added a piece of bread for toast.

I was used to being quiet. Before being kicked out of my home, being noiseless was the only way to not get noticed. Then, on the street, it was the same. At home, it was just a beating. On the streets, it was worse. Best to be as invisible as possible, and that meant keeping quiet.

With a cup of coffee and buttered toast, I turned my attention to the man on the floor and froze.

His bloodshot eyes were half-open, and he was watching me with caution.

I stepped away as far as possible, backing into a kitchen corner. There was no way to get to the door. I sat my coffee on the counter with my toast and held my hands up.

"*Je ne t'ai pas fait de mal. J'ai aidé.*" I shook my head and then repeated, "I no hurts to you. I helped." *Please don't kill me! Please don't kill me!* I added to myself.

The man just stared. He moved to sit up. I stepped toward him, lifting my arms to show him I meant no harm, "Please careful. I no know you have inside hurts. I to call 911, no have time for phone. I go now if you wants."

The man continued to get up slowly, and I noticed the knife.

Tears started to roll down my cheeks. *This was it, I'm going to die now, and everything I was trying to become was for nothing.*

"Come here," the low growl of the man was terrifying. I shook my head. I knew my eyes were wide with fear. "Come here!" the man repeated, and I did as I was told this time.

The man's hand shot out and took my arm when I was close enough, pulling me to him. He was well over 60 centimeters taller than me and maybe 60 kilos more in weight.

It would take nothing for the man to snap me in two.

"What is your name," the man asked as he moved us to the mattress and sat down.

"Jean-Philippe. Many say Pip." Why had I told him that?

Still not letting go, he pulled me closer. There was a moment of surprise on the man's face when I was close enough for him to see the white stubble on my face.

"How old are you?"

"Please, no hurt me. I only wants help." I didn't answer the question. There was no way to get out of the man's grip unless I hit him in the side of his face. That was indeed suicide by giant. "*Vingt-et-un.* Twenty-one."

"Did you move me?" The man asked.

I nodded.

"How?"

"I dragged you." I thought maybe by being friendly, I could stave off the inevitable. *Perhaps I should offer to go down on him or maybe let him fuck me. Would it keep me alive longer?*

"I'm not going to hurt you. Thanks for helping. I need to lay down."

The man said and moved to the mattress. He placed the knife on the floor at the head of my mattress. He shifted to his uninjured side and pulled me down with him. With one strong arm, I was held against the man's chest. There was no way to get out from under his arm.

Maybe if I slept, I would have enough strength to escape.

When I woke, I was curled face-first into the man's warm, tattooed chest. His arm was still securing me, but I thought I would be able to slip away.

I was wrong.

"I was surprised you slept." The man's voice rumbled over my head. "I need to pee, and I need your help getting to the toilet. Will you do that?"

I looked up at the man who was smiling down at me. It wasn't a smile that sent chills down my spine. I had seen many of those when I worked on the streets.

"Yes. *D'accord*." My eyes shifted to where the knife had been placed, "You lets go firsts."

"Promise you won't run." The man's voice was gentle in its tone. He followed the direction of my gaze, and he added, "I didn't know what I was up against."

I nodded, and the man relaxed his hand. I tried to keep my eyes up and away from the man's naked body. My own body threatened to go full mast if I didn't keep my mind away from that.

Wow, that was messed up!

"Where are my clothes, Jean-Philippe?" The man asked as I helped him to his feet and led him to the corner.

"I take thems off. Make okay you okay. Sorrys. There," I pointed to the pile of clothes near the door, "I go to clean. I have no to fits you." I said, turning my back so the man could take care of his business, but then he grabbed my arm again so I couldn't escape.

"Have toothbrush new if want. I makes coffee. Somethings. I no go do something you no want. I keep secret. You want, you fuck me, whatever. Please, no hurt me." I started to cry. There was no way this wasn't going to turn dangerous.

The sound of the toilet flushing and then the water running in the sink was the only sound behind me as I waited.

"First of all, I'm Tyler. I'm not going to hurt you, and I am not going to fuck you. I just need a day or two to recover before I head out. You don't need to call 911." Tyler's voice was soothing as his hand lightly touched my shoulder.

I slid to the floor crying while my arm was held over my head.

Then Tyler let go.

I knew Tyler had moved back to the bed, picking up the blanket off the floor as he passed. Lifting my face, I watched Tyler cover himself up and lay watching me.

"I'd love a piece of toast and maybe some hot tea if you have it." Tyler finally said.

Tyler's voice was as deep and dangerous as Tyler was big. It should have scared me, although currently, everything was freaking me out a bit. His voice simply sent delicious chills down my straight spine.

I prepared toast and tea for Tyler before warming up my coffee and eating my cold toast. Once both were done, I gathered the cups to wash.

I needed to get dressed. Since there was no privacy, I took out my clothes for the day and turned my back to Tyler, stripped out of my pajamas.

There was a hiss of breath from Tyler, which I'd expected.

Tyler would ask about the scars, tattoos, ears, and albinism. Everyone always did, especially as most people assumed all albinos had pink eyes…I wasn't a rabbit! I would tell him. There was nothing I could say other than I was gay, which could bother Tyler. I was sure Tyler had already figured it out since I offered to let him fuck me.

Tyler didn't seem like someone who had had a charmed life. But trust was a hard commodity for people like me.

When I turned around, Tyler was asleep.

I wrote a note as best I could for Tyler and left with clothes and a bag for some groceries. It had stopped snowing, and even though it was just below freezing, I walked the twenty minutes to the laundromat to drop off the clothes. I didn't really have the money for the wash and dry service, but I didn't want to leave Tyler all day alone. I'd return after four for the clean clothes.

I was back two hours after a quick trip to the market.

Tyler was sitting up on the mattress and reading one of many books lying around when I stepped into the room.

"You see note?" I pointed to the paper that simply said, "***I go food. Cloth to clean.***" I was proud of my neat handwriting but not much for my writing skills.

I unloaded the bag of groceries into the small pantry and fridge. Once done, I glanced at Tyler, who was watching me. I straightened up and faced the man. "I fix soup or sandwich for eating. I buy chicken to tonight. You eat will help heal, but I no doctor." I laughed.

"Soup is great, thanks," Tyler said but continued to watch me.

"You have question, ask. I no to hide. I questions first. Some peoples looking you. Snow thick night last, I go to clean outside. I think blood covered away." I didn't look at Tyler as I opened the can of soup, poured it into a pan, and carried it over to the Franklin stove.

"No. Not really. You're safe."

"*D'accord*. Okays." I stirred the soup and, once it was hot, poured it into an extra-large mug and took it to Tyler, who was sitting up.

"Why are all the books meant for little kids?"

I glanced over and eyed Tyler. "Good to learn."

"You illegal?" That was a weird first question, I thought. I had been asked that before. I knew what the question meant.

"No. I born America, my parent no. Student for university. I have six weeks moving back for France. Thirteen when I arrival to America. French my language." I returned to the kitchen and pulled a Coke out of the fridge.

"Who used a whip on you?" That was the question I had expected.

"How time?" was my answer.

I had been beaten from time to time by johns, and each time I had to 'pay' the rent to Bernard, but those marks weren't the ones Tyler was asking about. The first and the most frequent had been my father. When I looked up, the expression on Tyler's face brooked no messing around. "My *Père*. My father."

"How long were you on the streets?"

I looked up into the man's face. Tyler was good. He couldn't be a cop. Not with how he was dressed and all the tattoos. "You asked why?"

Tyler smiled crookedly, "Because you offered yourself to me without hesitation. That seems like something someone who worked the streets would do."

I shrugged. "I like eat. I like places for sleep. I gotted new job year agos. I have, hmm, I make sex for man he give me here." I looked around the room, puffed up my chest, and straightened my shoulders, "I work restaurant. I washed dish. I have class quickly, soon." I was proud of that.

Tyler smiled, nodded, and offered me the empty mug. I cleaned it with the other dishes.

"Will you come sit over here with me?" Tyler asked.

I moved over and sat next to Tyler.

"You said you have to have sex with the man for this room, right." Tyler's voice had a hint of anger, making me flinch.

"No big things. I safe. I warm, dry place." I lifted my chin, defying Tyler to say something different. Tyler only wrapped his arm around me and pulled me against him as he lay down and went to sleep.

I slept for an hour or so. When I woke, I headed to get the clothes at the laundromat. It cost me most of my spare cash, as the place I took them didn't ask questions about the blood-soaked clothing. I wouldn't have to do laundry for a week, and Tyler could have something to wear.

He was awake and sitting up when I returned home. "You sleep? New note." I pointed to the paper on the table.

Tyler nodded and let me know he had found the note.

"I have clothes. They okay clean. Hole in shirt sewed for me." I offered the stack of freshly laundered clothes to Tyler. When he didn't take them, I put them on the edge of the bed.

"You pay for this?" Tyler asked. There was annoyance in his tone.

"Yes, I...." I looked away. I'm not a good liar, "I monies to cloth done."

Tyler's full-body laughter took me by surprise. It was warm and rich, sending tingles of joy to my toes.

"You are a terrible liar, you know that, right?" Tyler said, still laughing.

"I not lie. Idea bad." I laughed at myself.

TYLER

Pip's laughter was like bells ringing in my ears. I couldn't take my eyes off the young man who had feasibly saved my life. He was not a child. He was childlike, certainly. Elvin to the point I wasn't sure Pip was even human. But anyone who worked the streets had lost their childhood innocence long ago.

I knew Pip could have just let me die in the freezing snow. I also knew that someone as waiflike as Jean-Philippe would have had to work hard to drag my big six-four, two-hundred-thirty-pound dead-weight ass into the apartment. Even if it were ten feet, it would have taken a lot of energy and time.

"How long did it take you, Jean-Philippe, to get me into your apartment?" I watched to see if Pip would lie or tell the truth.

Pip said over an hour, and he was just Pip.

Before I could say anything else, Pip moved closer to the bed and looked at the clothes. "I want see side. Yes? Is okay?"

I stretched out on the mattress and uncovered my side. The feeling of Pip's surprisingly long fingers as they touched my skin made my mind go to places I didn't want to go. This kid had done nothing but show me kindness. I didn't think there had been a lot of compassion in Pip's life. Even this hellhole came with some pretty heavy strings, I was sure. Pip considered himself lucky, even if he had to let some asshole fuck him, or god knows what, to keep a roof over his head.

Once Pip announced my wound looked good, I pulled on my briefs and laid back down.

Dinner was roasted chicken, green beans, and rolls. Pip had laid the meal out as if I was a royal guest. Knowing that Pip had probably spent all his money on my clothes and this food, I ate.

I watched as Pip ate a thigh, a spoonful of beans, and half a roll but ensured I ate everything else. I didn't like the idea that Pip didn't eat more, but something told me that Pip hadn't eaten three squares a day in a long time.

While we ate, I asked about the classes that Pip would take. Pip had wanted to take a course for his GED but couldn't, as his reading and writing skills were nonexistent. Someone had put a sign on the bulletin board at work that said, "LEARN TO READ." Pip took it to his boss, Javier, and found out that one of the community colleges had a program to help adults learn to speak, read, and write English. Pip had missed the enrollment but had already put his name on the waiting list for next semester and was saving money. Hopefully, he would get into the classes.

My heart broke. Why would a twenty-one-year-old not know how to read?

I gave my head a sad shake. I knew young kids who came out as gay or trans to their parents were often kicked out without support. Many didn't make it. Pip had, and that said something about his strength.

"You what, hmm, want schools?" Pip asked after cleaning the kitchen and helping me to the toilet.

"Yeah, I actually have a degree," I said without saying that I actually had two degrees or what they were in.

"You need safest life, Tyler. No yourself at bad place. I know this. I help...tell you how safe...." Pip began, but his mouth snapped shut.

"I'm tired," I said, not wanting to even think about what Pip had been through. "Will you lay with me until I fall asleep?"

There was no hesitation in Pip's movements as he stripped down to his briefs. I noticed a tramp stamp at his waistline, and when he turned around, another long line of words between his belly button and the band of his briefs. Over his heart was the pink ribbon associated with Breast Cancer. From elbow to wrist, on his right arm was a string of words. On his left arm, in the exact location, were four rainbows, each with one to three words above. All the words were in French. Except for *important,* I didn't understand any of them.

Pip moved so his shoulder was to my chest, his warm body burning into me. Pip was unaware of the chaos he was causing as he arranged the sheet and blanket before looking up into my eyes. There was trust and hope and something more I couldn't quite understand. I pulled Pip to me and kissed the silky white head under my chin. "Thanks for taking care of me, Jean-Philippe."

There was no response, but just as I drifted to sleep, I heard the beautiful voice of my Elvin angel say, "I little mouse, *la petite souris.* No more, someone make same to me. Maybe."

****

For two days, I was tended to by Pip. When we talked, it was never about anything too personal. I knew that Pip was 152 centimeters tall, which I would have to calculate when I got to my phone. He had no siblings and no aunts and uncles that he knew of.

I shared that I had no siblings but many cousins and worked for the city.

Pip was concerned I would get fired for not calling in and apologized for not having minutes on his phone. I assured him everything was alright and I wouldn't lose my job.

He fed me three small meals each day. I watched as Pip pretended to eat, but he had only eaten the evening meals and not much of them.

Pip let me know he had to work the following morning. He only worked the lunch shift but should be finished at about three. Pip might be able to bring food home from the restaurant, hopefully enough that we both could have something if I was still here. I let him know I would leave when he left in the morning. I had to get back to my life.

It was almost dinner time on the third day when someone pounded on the door. Pip looked over at me, his eyes wide. I was sitting up on the bed against the wall. "What you hears, you no come out. I know who. Please, Tyler. Please."

I hated the fear on Pip's face but promised I would do as he asked.

Pip stepped out and closed the door.

"Hey," A man's smarmy-sounding voice said from the other side. I was surprised that the sound traveled into the room until I noticed a slightly opened transom over the door. "How's my favorite little whore tonight?"

I bristled with anger at the man's words.

"Good, Bernard." Pip's voice was cheery and bright.

"Glad to hear that. I need to collect some rent." I heard the smirk in the man's voice.

"Um, Bernard. Friend here. I do tomorrow? Yes?"

There was the sound of a slap. "No, I want to fuck you now." The sound of scuffling and a small cry of pain from Pip sent me almost out the door.

"Tell friend I go. I follow you at corner. How you liked."

"Okay, I'll meet you there, but don't make me come and get you. I've had a fucked-up day." Bernard's warning echoed through the window.

I hurried away from the door and sat on the corner of the mattress.

Pip opened the door and put a smile on his face. He couldn't hide the tears or the red mark. He didn't try. "Hmm, Tyler. I go for things. I back, hmm, twenty-five minute. I make food. Okay."

I nodded, but it took everything I had to keep Pip from going out the door.

I waited three minutes before stepping into the hallway. It didn't take long for the noise to guide me in the direction I needed to go. Years of undercover work allowed me to watch without being seen, and what I saw made me want to kill Bernard.

Pip's tiny body had been stripped and bound. He was tied, so his ass was in the air, and his head was waist-high. Bernard had a riding crop and smacked Pip's back as Bernard mouth-fucked him. After a moment, Bernard moved behind Pip, pulled on a condom, and, without any prep, slammed his hard dick into Pip.

The cry of pain was followed by Bernard calling Pip every filthy name while pounding him. "You like that, don't you slut? You like it when I hurt you? You better come for me this time whore! I give you a nice place, and you let someone stay without asking."

Bernard screamed as he shot his load. He pulled out of Pip, threw the soiled condom into Pip's face, and untied him.

"You have two minutes to come for me, or you'll be sorry. Do you hear me whore?"

I watched as Pip wrapped his hand around his flaccid dick and worked to make himself hard. Bernard yelled and cursed, slapping Pip in the face. When his two minutes were up, and nothing had happened, Bernard dragged Pip off the table and threw him on the floor.

With a kick to his side, Bernard reached down, took Pip by his long white hair, and pulled him to his feet before leaning down and whispering something in Pip's ear.

Pip shook his head and begged; for what I didn't know. I turned, but not before seeing Bernard slap Pip once more.

Bernard was going to pay!

When Pip silently entered the room, I was in bed, covered up, feigning sleep. Through my thick lashes, I watched as Pip stripped. Even from across the room I could see the red welts on Pip's body, the bruise turning on his face as he stepped into the shower, pulling the curtain around.

Under the sound of the water running, I thought I heard Pip repeating words like a mantra. Several times, there was the sound of sobbing. My heart was breaking, but there was nothing I could do today.

Tomorrow, that would change.

I watched as Pip gingerly pulled on pajamas. Bernard had done some damage to Pip as his movements were slow and cautious. Once Pip was dressed and it seemed he had pulled himself together, I yawned and stretched.

"*Bon. Tu es réveillé*. Sorry, Good. You awaked," Pip smiled at me and told me he would make dinner. He apologized that it would only be eggs and toast but promised he made great scrambled eggs.

I watched Pip take the last five eggs out of the fridge and what looked like the last of the bread and butter over to the Franklin stove. Pip took his time but, within a few minutes, put a plate with almost all the eggs and three pieces of buttered toast in front of me with the last of the milk.

"You need to eat more," I chastised Pip. I refused to say anything about Pip's black eye and swollen lip.

"Tomorrow I get food for work." Pip pushed his half egg around his plate. Despite my strong objection, Pip added what was left on his plate to mine when I was done. "I no need. You, you giant. Need many of food to help you no fall. Same like big tree."

The warmth and humor in Pip's voice and on his face were almost too much for me to take, knowing what Pip had just been through only an hour ago. How did he do it?

Perhaps Jean-Philippe *was* filled with Elven High Magic after all.

After Pip cleaned up the meager dinner, I asked about the guitar. "You play?"

Pip nodded, looking pleased that I had asked.

"Will you play something for me? It's okay if you don't want to." I added the last when Pip looked surprised when I asked.

"*Oui*. Yes." Pip pulled the instrument off the wall and tenderly swung it around his thin body. He explained the guitar was a classical and not an acoustic guitar, letting me know the strings made the difference.

I leaned against the wall and waited as Pip closed his eyes, taking a minute to retune.

"This named *Waltz' from Opus 59*."

I grew up attending the theatre, orchestra, and even ballet. Pip's playing had that type of quality. I felt my mouth drop open, and I gawked at the Elvin angel as the most beautiful sound I had ever heard from a guitar filled the small place.

Beautiful. Breathtaking and mesmerizing.

The music lasted only for a few minutes. Pip didn't say a word after the music ended. He simply got up, hung the guitar on the wall, and walked out the door.

JEAN-PHILIPPE

It was dark when I woke. I glanced over at the clock. It was still early in the morning. I wasn't sure what had awakened me until I heard the moans of a dream coming from Tyler. Tyler had wrapped himself around me. My head rested on Tyler's bicep while Tyler's other arm held me tight against his warm body.

Tyler was rubbing his hard cock against my ass, and the other hand had moved to wrap around my now rock-hard erection.

"You smell so fucking good," Tyler's voice tickled my ear as kisses were planted on my neck.

I didn't move. I wasn't even sure if Tyler was awake. After another minute, Tyler's fingers moved from my cock to my stomach, and a gentle snore came from overhead.

I relaxed.

I wondered who Tyler had been dreaming about. Whoever it was, they were one lucky woman.

The alarm woke me with a start.

"Morning." Tyler's breath warmed my face with the words.

"*Bonjour, mon beau géant*! Good mornings," I amended in English. Again, as almost every morning, I had curled up against Tyler's massive body. Tyler's leg was thrown over mine, and our morning wood rubbed against each other's. I could have kissed the tattooed chest this morning and brushed my tongue over a nipple.

"Fuck. Sorry, man." Tyler blushed and moved his hips back so we were no longer touching. "I'm a snuggler if you couldn't already tell. I never meant to make you uncomfortable."

I tilted my head up, looking at Tyler's chin. He hadn't shaved in the three days he had been in the apartment, and the dark brown beard hadn't filled in. I wanted to kiss the stubble but instead admitted it was nice having my own personal giant to keep me warm at night.

I reluctantly pulled myself away from Tyler's warm body and moved to the toilet. Once done, I offered Tyler the bathroom.

While Tyler showered, I laid out my clothes for the day and took out my wallet from the loose brick behind the stove. There was a five-dollar bill, some change, and my Metro pass inside. I added my ID as today was payday, and I would need it to cash my check at the bank across the street from the restaurant.

I kept my back to Tyler as the giant got out of the shower and dried off before pulling on the semi-clean clothes he had been in for more than two days. Once I was sure Tyler was done, I turned to face him.

"You needs go somewheres safe. See no get fires. I no food, no coffee. I money. Buy you breakfast. We use Metro Pass for to ride at my work. I get kitchen manager, Javier, you use phone. Javier nice. He good for me." I watched the expression change on Tyler's face from joy to frustration. It didn't seem directed at me; I was experienced at reading people.

When Tyler didn't say anything but nod, I stripped, walked around Tyler to the shower, and stepped in. I knew it was ill-mannered, but I wanted Tyler to see I wasn't a child but a man. Even if I never saw him again, which I expected, I didn't want Tyler to remember me as a kid.

Tyler was sitting on a made bed as I dried off. His eyes followed me as I towel-dried my long hair and then, after brushing it smooth, braided it and secured it with a scrunchie. Then, holding Tyler's gaze, I walked to the coffee table and began to dress without saying a word.

I added a stocking cap, pulling it down to cover my pointed ears, although I knew my hair covered them. Then I put on my dark sunglasses.

As we locked up, I told Tyler it was a fifteen-minute walk to the first bus stop, and if at any time he needed to stop, all he had to do was tell me. Tyler didn't say a word but walked next to me. Once we got to the street, I ducked into a bodega and returned with two cups of coffee and a breakfast sandwich, which I insisted Tyler take.

"No, you need this. You hardly ate anything yesterday," Tyler refused. Still, after I reminded him I would eat at work, Tyler reluctantly took the sandwich and coffee.

When the bus pulled up to the stop ten minutes later, I stepped on with Tyler behind me. "Hey, Mary. How you today? I pay for two transfer fare." I smiled and handed Mary, the driver, the other cup of coffee.

"Hey, my elf baby, you need another dollar for that. Sorry." Mary said, reaching to stop me from passing.

"*D'accord*. Sure, I have here." I pulled the change in my pocket and counted a dollar in nickels and dimes.

My face was red when I finally sat next to Tyler.

There was silence before Tyler asked if I had spent all my money on him.

"Yes, today pay. Good. I want get you, so you no lose your job. Maybe you go doctor for checking." I hated that my English was terrible. If only Tyler could speak French.

Oh, right, I would never see him again.

Tyler promised he would go get checked out, but there was no way he was losing his job.

I wanted to believe him.

We changed buses twice before arriving outside the restaurant. We moved down the alleyway and around to the back before ringing a bell near the back door.

"Hey, Jean-Philippe." An older Hispanic man in his early sixties opened the door with a smile and relief, saying, "I've been worried about you. Haven't seen you since your last workday. Didn't even come and get some food. You okay?" Javier touched my face tenderly, inspecting the injuries, then glared at Tyler.

"No, sorry, Javier. I good. It cold." I smiled at my boss and watched Javier's eyes move from me to Tyler again.

"Who is this?" Javier moved me away from Tyler and closer to him with his hand on my arm.

"Javier, this Tyler. He my friend. He lost phone. Need for call. He used phone? I pay. Yes, please."

Javier looked Tyler up and down, and I couldn't hide the smile.

"Sure, come on in."

A coworker, Don, was just inside the door, and I pulled my hat down lower on my head, "There he is. I'm going to need you to suck my dick on break. What do you say, froggy boy?"

I worriedly glanced up at Tyler as Javier warned Don about his language. "You can't talk to another employee like that, Don. We've had this conversation, and you're about to use up your last chances."

"Damn, Javier. You know I'm just kidding Snow White here. I don't mean no harm!" Don tried to worm his way out of the spot he got into.

Javier didn't see it, but I did. I had to ensure I didn't get caught somewhere where Don could get at me. A blowjob was more than Don was after, and I was still hurting from yesterday and Bernard.

"I go for my work," I said, facing Tyler.

Tyler looked around and, finding a chair nearby, sat down and pulled me to him so we were face-to-face. I watched Javier, who seemed unsure of what to do. Tyler leaned in and spoke softly.

"Jean-Philippe. Thank you for everything you did for me. I'll never forget it." Tyler's words were soft. "If you ever need anything, any-thing at all, you just have to ask. I'll try to come by this afternoon to check on you and let you know how I'm doing."

I closed my eyes, but Tyler's strong fingers lifted my chin, so my blue eyes looked into Tyler's hazel gaze when I opened them.

"You no promise thing you no means." I breathed the words out.

Tyler ignored me, "I put my phone number on the table. Use it. Oh, please don't cry."

I didn't want to, but my emotions were bare. I would never see Tyler again, and I knew that. I knew when I worked to pull Tyler into the safety of my apartment that it wouldn't be a friendship. It didn't matter. It had been the right thing to do.

Tyler pulled me into a hug and held me for a minute.

I found my voice, "Tyler. I no child. I man."

Tyler smiled and touched his lips to my forehead. "I know that very well, Jean-Philippe. But even men need a hug now and then. Don't forget to call me, please." Tyler turned to Javier. "I'll give you my number, and if this man ever needs anything, anything at all, I want you to call me. Would you do that for me, sir?"

I moved out of Tyler's arms and towards my workstation, putting my coat on a hook and wrapping a waterproof apron around me.

"Did you do that to his face? Who are you to him, anyway?" I heard Javier's angry voice ask. "Jean-Philippe has had too much shit in his life. If you're using him, I know people. He's a good kid, and dammit, he needs a break."

I didn't hear Tyler's answer as I watched the two men, one I saw almost every day and another I would never see again, head to the back of the house office.

I was able to avoid Don during my shift. We had been busy, and Don, a prep cook, hadn't had time to move more than two feet from his station the entire shift. Javier had checked on me several times during the shift but left me to do my job.

I was strong, not as strong as some of the other dishwashers. I made up in energy and speed what I didn't have in strength. It took me twice as many trips to put clean dishes in their spaces, but the kitchen never ran out of clean dishes, utensils, or cookware when I was working.

After cleaning my station, I clocked out at two, then went to the office to pick up my paycheck and the money from the tip share for the previous week. After making sure Don was nowhere to be seen, I headed down the alleyway and across the street to the bank.

Within a few minutes, I had cashed my check. Then, I went to the bathroom and hid all the money in my shoes and other areas on my body. Next was the booth to add funds to my MBTA card and get more minutes on my cell phone.

Halfway to the apartment, I realized not only didn't I eat lunch, but I didn't have anything in the place to eat. There was a soda or two. It would have to work. It wasn't the first time I went to bed hungry, and it wouldn't be the last.

I was working a double tomorrow. That would be a late lunch or early dinner. Because it was two shifts, I could get a bigger meal and have some to take home. I wasn't hungry anyway.

The room seemed too quiet and too empty.

I stoked the fire before pulling out my wallet, gathering all the money, and putting everything in the hiding place. My ID, updated French and American Passports, birth certificate, and a single photo of my mother were kept secure inside the wall.

Once that was done, I removed my clothes, carefully hanging or folding them. I would wear them tomorrow as they hadn't gotten too dirty.

My pajamas and socks were warm until the stove heated the room.

I passed the time between reading and playing on the tiny tablet I had bought at the thrift shop. There was no Wi-Fi, but the tablet had some games, which was enough. When I was ready, I pulled the guitar off the wall. I practiced the chords, rhythms, and warmups my music teacher gave me for Tuesday and Thursday's classes.

At five, there was a knock on the door. I walked to the door with the guitar, trying not to get too excited.

Tyler had promised.

The smile on my face slid off the moment the door was opened.

"I told you I would bring a few friends over without asking your permission. Seems fair, doesn't it? No matter how hard you try, Pip, you're just a whore. You'll never be more; the sooner you understand, the better my life will be. Your life is a waste. You are nothing and will never be more than trash," Bernard's smile was anything but pleasant as he motioned to the three men standing just outside the door. Bernard snatched the guitar from my hand and smashed it against the door jam.

"Fuck, Bernard, he does look like an elf!" One man said. "He's so fucking tiny!"

Another reached in and moved my hair off my ears, "Pointed ears and all. What the fuck?"

"I told you," Bernard stepped in, the three men following. "Okay. Here's the thing. He's just a whore. Do whatever you want to him. He's paid for. Also, remember, I want this place trashed. All his clothes, books, whatever can go into the stove, throw them in."

"No," I heard myself cry out. It wasn't the last cry I would make, but I was sure it might be the last day I would make any sounds at all.

TYLER

"Tyler Braxton, where the fuck have you been?" The captain, Joseph Mikulenka, yelled through the line in Javier's office. "We've had half the force looking for your ass!"

"Captain Mikulenka, I'll explain everything, but send a car to this address." I read the address on the paper Javier had slid over. "I need to swing by the station, shower, then I'll head your way. Can you call the team? I think I have something that's going to make everyone shit themselves. Oh, also, I may need to go to the hospital."

Mikulenka yelled for a solid minute before letting me know he expected me in his office in less than two hours.

When I hung up the line, Javier was looking at me. "You a cop?"

I nodded.

"That boy is clean. Not working the streets or that horrible agency anymore." There was a fierce protectiveness in the man's attitude.

"I know."

"He's a good kid."

"Not really a kid, though, is he Javier?"

Javier smiled and shook his head, "No. Not really. It's hard to remember that sometimes. He's a good man, Tyler. I'll call you if I need to. But if you're just going to ghost him, you can forget it. I won't let you do that to him."

I promised Javier I wouldn't abandon Jean-Philippe.

I didn't wait long for the squad car to pick me up and take me to the station. Once inside, I blew off everyone's questions and headed to the locker room, where I had fresh clothes and stuff for a shower. When I was clean and in clean clothes, I gathered my wallet, cell phone, and keys and headed to my captain's office.

It took several hours to explain what had happened. Ted Collins was supposed to be a minor player, but I had discovered he had shit on everyone, hence the meeting. The entire operations could go down if they could pull Collins in and get him to flip.

All involved agreed to pull Collins in and let him sweat. Mikulenka promised the reprimand and suspension I faced would disappear if things worked out as they all hoped. Still, if I ever pulled another stunt like the one I had four days ago, I would get my ass canned.

Another car drove me to the hospital to be checked, and to my chagrin, I was admitted.

There were no broken ribs. My nose was messed up, but that was fixable. Pip's stitching had been praised as fine work, but the doctors removed those, disinfected and cleaned the wound, and used *Dermabond* to close the wounds again. When all the doctors, nurses, and their tests had been completed, and I was in a room, I fished out my cell and called my cousin.

Steven Hawthorne Grady was a beat cop, and his beat covered the areas between mine and Pip's place. My cousin had already heard what had happened and was glad I was safe but pissed I had been such an ass.

Get in line, I said to myself.

"Steve, I need a favor," I told my cousin a little about Jean-Philippe. Basically, the kid saved my life. But he also spent all his money ensuring I had eaten and had clean clothes. "Can you and Olan go by and check on him and give him a hundred? I'll get it back to you when you visit tonight or tomorrow."

Olan Rodgers was Steve's partner, and I knew he wouldn't have a problem with what I asked.

"Yeah, man. We can do that, but it won't be until four or five. Is that going to be a problem?" I assured him it wouldn't. I felt that he was in for the night once Pip was in.

We chatted for a few more minutes before disconnecting.

The following morning, I was discharged.

I wanted to head home, but my presence was required at the station house. Collins had been brought in, and yours truly was the element of surprise to get him to turn tails. It took three hours, but it worked.

Collins spilled his guts, and it was messy enough to do precisely what we had hoped.

It was almost two before I was able to check my phone. A message from Javier chilled my blood. "Tyler, it's Javier Gutierrez from Jean-

Philippe's work. He didn't show up today, and that's never happened. You said you would keep an eye on him. I need you to go and see what happened to him, please."

As much as I wanted to go home, I got into my truck and headed to Pip's. I talked myself into believing Pip had fallen asleep or was sick the entire way there. I didn't think that would happen, and even if Pip was ill, odds were, he would still have shown up to work.

It took almost forty minutes before I pulled up next to the door out of the basement near Pip's apartment. It was open, which didn't seem right.

I drew my service revolver before standing at the side of the door. After checking if anyone was there, I stepped in and made my way down the small hallway to the apartment. Its entrance, like the door to the outside, was open. Police tape was stretched across the door. Fragments of Pip's guitar lay like a broken corpse in and around the door.

My heart sank.

The room was trashed.

What little had been in the small pantry or the fridge was on the floor or in the tub. A shirt sleeve stuck out the half-opened door of the Franklin stove, and a burnt cover of one of Pip's children's books was resting on the cement floor.

Pip's mattress was bloodied and cut to ribbons.

The coffee table was also covered in blood. It didn't seem like it was so much that Pip wouldn't have survived, but it scared the shit out of me.

Pulling the phone out of my pocket, I called Steve.

Steve picked up after the second ring, "What the hell happened!" I bellowed.

"Fuck, man. I tried to call you. I've left messages all over the place for you. I'm telling you, Tyler, that kid was as good as dead if we hadn't shown up when we did." Even through his panic and rage, I could hear the horror in my cousin's voice.

"Steve, where is he?" I thought I might be sick. Was this my fault? Did I bring this on?

"Tyler, listen. He was taken to Southwest County General." There was a pause, "So you know, Olan was able to call for backup when we saw what was happening. All four of the fuckers were caught. One couldn't keep his mouth shut, and another cried like a baby and spilled his guts. They recorded everything. Every fucking thing they were doing. What idiots! Those assholes are as good as gone. If you want to know, my precinct has the report. Greenwood has the file, as he'll be investigating. However, it won't be much of an investigation with the videos and the confessions."

I was bent in half, trying to catch my breath. "Hey Tyler, you there?" Steve's worried voice sounded from my cell.

"Yeah! Yeah! Steve, thanks. I'm headed now to see the report and then to the hospital. Do you know what name they have him under?" I stood to clear my head.

"CSI found his wallet, passports, and a few other items in a hidey-hole behind the stove. It's all at the station house. Jean-Philippe Roche is his full name, and that's how he's listed. Hey, Tyler, call me if you need me. Okay, man?" Steve made a few more comments before disconnecting after I promised to call.

The report of what Bernard Miller and his friends did to Jean-Philippe made me throw up. It wasn't just the rape each man had participated in, but the beating. Bernard could be seen on the video telling his friends that the whore wasn't worth the air it breathed, and if they wanted to kill him, more power to them.

One of the men actually strangled Jean-Philippe as he raped him.

Not only was the rape and beating on the video, but the trashing of Pip's apartment and the burning of his belongings were as well. Finally, the slamming of the back of Pip's head on the table. The forensic and medical reports indicated that had been the cause of most of the blood in the apartment.

After reading the police and the attached hospital reports of Jean-Philippe's assault and injuries, it took an hour for me to pull myself together before heading to the hospital. Once there, I flashed my badge at the information desk and was given the floor and room number to Jean-Philippe.

Before taking the elevator up to Jean-Philippe's room, I called Gutier-rez and told him what had happened. The older man quietly sobbed at the news and then, after a minute, told me to make sure Jean-Philippe knew his job was waiting. Also, Javier gave me the information for the insurance, just in case. Jean-Philippe had medical insurance, and Javier wanted to ensure the hospital knew.

I promised to deliver the information and update Javier on Jean-Philippe's progress.

I stood just inside the door. Pip's beautiful hair held a garish pink color. The snow-white skin, usually almost translucent, was pasty and unhealthy. His left arm was in a soft cast, keeping the arm immobile. An I.V. fed medicine and saline into Jean-Philippe's system into his right.

"He's going to be okay," the gentle tones of a nurse assured me. "He's a tough little guy. He's taken a lot of abuse. I mean, man. I hope the coming year is better than the ones he's had prior. His birthday is Saturday, in two weeks. You working the case, hon?" I followed the woman's eyes to my badge and gun.

I cleared my throat and shook my head. "He's a friend. Tough little fucker, that one. He saved my life not long ago. I'd do anything for him. Anything."

"If that's the case, go in and hold his hand. Talk to him. He's been coming in and out of consciousness. The doctor thinks that maybe the kid doesn't think he has anything to live for, and he's stopped trying. Go bring him back." The nurse reached up and patted my cheek before returning to her station.

Pulling up a chair and taking Jean-Philippe's hand was more challenging than I had imagined. It shouldn't have been difficult at all. But doing this, taking Jean-Philippe's small, long-fingered hand in mine, was something I had avoided the three days I was with him.

With the hand disappearing into mine, I stood and leaned in to kiss Jean-Philippe on the forehead. "Hello, my beautiful friend. I need you to come back to me. I'm sorry this happened to you. But I promise I'll never let anyone hurt you again. Do you hear me, Jean-Philippe Roche?"

There was a twitching of Jean-Philippe's fingers in mine. For now, that was enough of an answer. I pulled the chair next to the bed, lowered the railing, laid my head on the bed against Jean-Philippe's side, and fell asleep.

A shrill scream woke me and sent me to my feet. Looking around, I realized the sound was coming from Jean-Philippe. Nurses were moving into the room and telling me to step back.

The nurse who had spoken to me when I arrived was now talking to the screaming Jean-Philippe. "Mr. Roche. I'm Kaitlyn. You're at Southwest County General, and you are safe. See," she pointed in my direction. "Your friend is here. We're not going to let anything happen to you. Can you calm down for me, sweetheart?"

I watched as the panic gradually faded. Jean-Philippe seemed to be searching for me, and once his eyes settled on me, his body relaxed.

"Wonderful. Thank you, Jean-Philippe. I'm going to check you over for a minute, then I'll let your friend come back and sit next to you. Is that alright?" Kaitlyn asked.

Pip nodded, and his eyes spilled over with tears. Before she started to leave, Nurse Kaitlyn asked Jean-Philippe if he wanted me to stay or to go.

"*Rester*," was barely audible.

"French is his first language. Right now, maybe it's all he can think in." I offered.

The nurse asked for someone named Paul, and another nurse came in a moment later. Paul listened to Kaitlyn for a few seconds, then moved to the edge of the bed, taking Jean-Philippe's hand.

"*Chérie. Je suis Paul. Sais tu où tu es?*" Paul spoke to Jean-Philippe, looked at me, and stated he had said, '*I am Paul. Do you know where you are?*'

"*Oui! Oui. Je suis à l'hôpital.*" Jean-Philippe's voice was a bit louder. Paul let them know the patient knew where he was. Paul nodded and asked one more question, "*As-tu besoin de quelque chose? Etes-vous souffrant?*"

Jean-Philippe looked around, "*Pas de douleur. Où est Tyler? J'ai besoin de lui? Dites-lui, je suis désolé. S'est-il fait virer?*"

The French-speaking nurse cleared his throat and said, "Mr. Roche is not in any pain. He is looking for a Tyler and wants me to tell him he is sorry and worried he got fired. Are you Tyler?"

I nodded, and Paul stepped away, telling Kaitlyn he was on until eight and would help if needed.

"Hey, Pip," I said after repositioning my chair and taking Jean-Philippe's hand. "I didn't get fired. Everything is alright as long as you are."

"I thinked you he." Jean-Philippe's words were jumbled as always, but I understood.

"I'm sorry. I was in the hospital. They wanted to make sure I was fine. The doctors like your sewing, by the way. I sent my cousin to check on you. Sweetheart, I'm so sorry." I was surprised to feel tears on my face when Jean-Philippe's hand stroked my hair. I leaned into the touch.

While Jean-Philippe slept, I called Mikulenka and told him I wanted to take some vacation days.

The news of what happened to the young man who saved Sergeant Tyler Braxton had made its way to Mikulenka, the captain I was directly under. I was told to take as much time off as needed since I had accumulated a tremendous amount of vacation time.

I thanked Mikulenka, who reminded me I needed to go to the HR office to fill out the forms.

Nurse Kaitlyn came in one more time before she got off shift to check on Jean-Philippe. She also handed me a toothbrush, toothpaste, and a facecloth to freshen up if I wanted.

Jean-Philippe drifted in and out. Around nine, the night nurse administered a sedative and told me Jean-Philippe would sleep the night away. I took the time to go home, stopping to get something to eat on the way.

My apartment was on the sixth floor of the high-end mid-rise. The three-bedroom, four-bath, and corner unit had been a graduation gift from my folks after graduating with my Master's in Criminal Psychology. My trust funds kept the lights on, let me get a new truck every two years, and never worry about how to make ends meet.

I stood in the living room of the thirty-two hundred square foot apartment and looked around. The largest of the three bedrooms, my bedroom, was at the opposite end of the apartment from the other two. One was a smaller version of my master suite, and the other was a flex space set up as an office with a day bed and treadmill.

One of the reasons I had put so much into my work was that the beautiful apartment was hollow. I seemed to always be alone, except when I hooked up, and those hookups were few and far between lately. Even my fuckbuddies, and I had several, had commented about it. Nothing sat well with me anymore. At thirty, I was tired of playing around and wanted more.

I stripped as I walked into the bathroom to shower. I knew what I was going to do. It might backfire, but I didn't care. Sometimes, you just had to put yourself out there and hope it went like you dreamed.

JEAN-PHILIPPE

When I opened my eyes, they fell on Tyler's sleeping body. He was relaxed, his mouth slightly ajar and soft snoring sounds filling the room.

I looked around, surprised to find myself in a single room. My eyes followed a bloody tube from under the sheets. I lifted the sheets to discover I was hooked up to a catheter. The blood worried me, but I would have to wait to know the damage. No sense in worrying if there was nothing to worry about.

There was an I.V. in my arm with several bags of liquid funneled through the tube. A soft cast was on my left arm. I hoped it wasn't broken, with work....

The memory of what Bernard and his 'friends' had done hit me, and I gasped for air. With no place to live, there was no address. Without an address, I wasn't sure I could continue to work at the restaurant or go to school. The idea of turning tricks made me want to die.

I looked around the room to see what to use to end my life. Once, I had heard that a syringe of air directly in the veins would stop the heart.

That wouldn't work; I was in a hospital. I started to cry and lay back on the pillows.

The press of lips on my forehead had me opening my eyes. Tyler's face was inches from mine, and his hand captured mine and squeezed gently.

I asked Tyler to sit on the bed, ensuring Tyler knew about the catheter. Once Tyler was settled, I carefully wrapped my arms around the giant man and let all the tension flood out of my body.

"I want to hold you back, Jean-Philippe, but I'm afraid I will hurt you." Tyler's voice was gentle in my ear.

"Never, *mon beau géant*!" I believed that with all my heart. Oh, Tyler would hurt me, but not like everyone had done before. A broken body or spirit was survivable, more so than a broken heart.

Tyler helped me back down against the bed and told me he had spoken to Javier, and my job was waiting for me when I was ready to return. I didn't mention that a job might be hard to keep without a place to live.

When the nurse came in for her morning rounds, Tyler left to get breakfast. I asked about the blood in my urine. My kidneys had been badly bruised, but the urologist said there should be no permanent damage. The blood would take a few days, maybe a week to dissipate. My arm was fractured but was not broken. The hairline fracture would heal relatively quickly. Everything else was basically trauma to the body from the beating.

The bruises would fade. The doctor, who would be in to see me around ten, wanted to keep me in for a few more days.

Tyler was back in the room sitting next to me when a handsome black man with a badge on his hip entered the room with a knock on the door frame.

"Mr. Roche. I'm Detective Greenwood. Do you feel up to talking to me?" When the detective noticed Tyler, he paused, "Sergeant Braxton, are you on this case?"

Tyler stood and shook the detective's hand, letting him know I was a friend. Tyler's cousin had been on the team that caught the men responsible for sending me to the hospital.

"I see," Greenwood looked around, then back at me. "Some of these questions are extremely personal, Mr. Roche." The detective warned.

My attention shifted to Tyler with a glare, "You police?" I didn't hide the shock and disdain in my voice.

"Undercover mostly," Tyler admitted.

Fine, I didn't care if he heard every dirty detail. So much for trust.

"He stay. What you question?" I turned my attention to the man at the foot of the bed.

The questions *were* personal.

When had I started turning tricks?

Fourteen.

Why?

Stepfather kicked me out of the house for being gay. I had to eat, have money, and find people to let me sleep in a dry place. I paid for all with my body.

Where were my parents?

My mother died from breast cancer when I was four. I never knew my birth father and had been raised by my mother's husband, who didn't want me.

When I turned tricks, did I work on the street or for an agency?

First, the streets, and then an agency.

What was my HIV status?

Negative, as of my last test two months ago. I wasn't sure about now with what had happened one or two days ago.

Greenwood confirmed all four men had worn condoms, but I would need to follow my regular testing schedule, as I knew.

How had I been supporting myself since I left the agency?

I gave Greenwood the name of the restaurant where I worked and Javier's full name.

Where had I been living?

Bernard Miller's warehouse. Greenwood knew the address, and Bernard had already let it be known he fucked me in place of rent money.

"I have arrested?" I asked, looking over at Tyler, who looked like he was about to punch someone or something.

"No," Greenwood shook his head. "Everyone's pleading out, so there isn't going to be a trial. I might need to ask you a few more questions at another time, but I'll have to wait and see."

Greenwood offered his goodbye and a nod to Tyler before leaving.

"You're mad at me," Tyler said after Greenwood left the room.

"Yes. You think I no have care of you if I know. Me let you die?" I accused.

"No. I wanted what I was doing not to come back on you. If you knew I was a cop, someone might have tried to get information out of you. I couldn't risk it." Tyler scooted his chair close to the bed again.

I looked at him, seeing Tyler in a different light. At some point, Tyler had gone somewhere to change. The clothes he wore were nice. There was a hint of money in his shoes and leather jacket draped over the chair. "Why you here? You, you no owing no things."

It was Tyler's turn to look at me, and it was intense. A look of anger, desperation, hurt, and maybe even affection quickly flickered on his handsome face. His gaze made me squirm.

I watched as Tyler stood up and leaned over me. "It has nothing to do with what I owe you or you owe me. It's more. It's who I am. You mean something to me, Jean-Philippe, and maybe you think you have no one other than Javier. Well, I find that I seem to have no one as well. Not like I want. So, be mad at me. I don't care." Tyler leaned in, brushed his lips over my cheek, and traced his thumb over the corner of my mouth.

"I have some things to do, but I'll be back later."

I stared wide-eyed as Tyler Braxton, a police officer and my own personal giant, left the room.

Que diables?

The doctor arrived sometime later in an efficient, businesslike manner to explain my injuries. I had a concussion, but there would be no lasting effects. There were seven stitches on the back of my head. Most of the trauma from the beating was from my neck down, but there were handprints on my neck as one of the attackers choked me. They had spared my face for some reason, except for the bruise under my left eye.

The rapes had caused some tearing, but nothing that wouldn't heal itself. My kidneys were severely bruised but not damaged. There was some concern about internal bleeding from my stomach and intestines. The staff would monitor that for the next two or three days. The doctor thought the catheter would come out in a day or two. Since the fracture had been about a half-inch long and not very deep, two weeks in the soft cast should provide enough stability for it to heal. After that, I would just need to take it easy.

The hospital ran a battery of tests to check for STDs, and they all returned negative. Still, I should be retested in a month or two, then follow my regular testing schedule.

The doctor asked if I had any questions before leaving without a goodbye.

Javier and Lola, his wife, showed up after lunch. Javier teared up, and even though his voice broke, he assured me things would be there for me when I was ready. If I needed anything, I was to let Javier know.

Javier, the doctor, and the nurses on my floor weren't the only ones who stopped by. The whispers echoing in the hallways were that a real live Elf was in room 1403 had started to circulate. My hair was long and a bit wild, but there was no denying the color, the hair, and the prominent ears.

Middle Earth was written all over my face and body.

Medical staff walked in, apologizing that they were in the wrong room, and turned to leave. All that stopped when Tyler walked back into the room just before six.

"You finish done you need?" My voice wasn't its normal friendly tone. I was still a little mad at Tyler.

"Almost. One more day, and it should be all done." Tyler took his place next to the bed.

"You no worked?"

Tyler turned his hazel eyes to me and shook his head. "Taking some well-deserved vacation time. Was told if I didn't take it, I would lose it. So, I understand your birthday's in two weeks," Tyler smiled as he pulled a large envelope out of his jacket.

"How you knows?"

Tyler pulled a passport out of the beige envelope and waved it in the air. "The CSI team found these. Greenwood had them and gave them to me this afternoon. Do you want to make sure they found everything? If not, I can go look tomorrow."

The envelope was placed in my lap. Inside was my wallet and all the money from my paycheck and tip share. Both passports, my ID, my birth certificate, and the photo of my mother. "It all here."

"Is that your mother?" Tyler asked.

I handed the photo to Tyler. It was my most prized possession.

The image was of a striking woman in her twenties. I looked like her, the delicate Fae features of her face and the creamy complexion.

Four-year-old me was standing next to her, with my hand holding hers. There was no way not to recognize me. In the seventeen years since that picture, I had changed little.

"She's beautiful. I can see where you got your looks." Tyler smiled as he handed back the photo.

I stared at my mother's picture. "It only thing I for take with me I throwed out for fourteen for *ma mére*. No clothes, no food, nothing, this."

Tyler's face turned red, and he growled, "Where is the son of a bitch?"

"Dead. Two-year pass he kicked me out."

"You mean two years after he kicked you out?" Tyler asked for clarification.

I nodded.

"How?"

"He hit bridge. He drunk. Only him killed." I answered.

"So, you have no one? Not even him. Jean-Philippe, I'm sorry." The sadness in Tyler's voice almost undid me, but I smiled.

"*D'accord*," I said.

"It's not okay, Jean-Philippe, but don't you worry. I've got you. Now, what are we watching tonight?"

Tyler watched the television, and I watched Tyler.

The next four days were the same, except Detective Greenwood never returned.

TYLER

Nothing was left to move from the basement apartment to my place. Almost. There had been three old *Dick and Jane* books shoved under the torn mattress. There were no clothes I could use to match sizes and go to the store to replace those that had been burned.

After lunch, the hospital was releasing Jean-Philippe, but I wasn't ready. The apartment was, I wasn't. This could go bad, but there was no way I would let Jean-Philippe roam the streets looking for a place to stay. Not when I had plenty of room.

"You're a big, strong police officer, Braxton. Suck it up and grow some balls. When were you ever afraid of a man, of anybody?" I said out loud, but the answer was just as loud even though it was inside my head, *'Because he matters to you!'*

Before leaving the apartment, I checked my pocket for the extra set of keys I had made. I wasn't sure if Pip had a driver's license, but if he did, there was a compact in the second space allotted to the apartment. I didn't go out and buy a second vehicle. I liked the car and didn't use it as a trade-in when I leased the truck.

Pip was not in the room when I arrived.

Kaitlyn looked up from her desk and smiled, "He went down to pediatrics. Some of the kids wanted to meet the elf, and Jean-Philippe was happy to go. Fifth floor, if you want to go down and see."

I thanked Kaitlyn and took the elevator down. I found Pip dressed in scrubs, a scarf around his neck, in the family room surrounded by fifteen kids and their parents. His white hair had returned to its perfect snowy glow. Pip had pulled it on top of his head so his ears stuck out for the kids and the grownups to spy. I listened as Pip, in French with Paul translating, told a tale of how he had helped Legolas fight off a band of Orcs.

The children were enthralled as Pip ended the tale with a happy ending. There was a round of applause and thanks. Pip bowed and blew kisses to the kids, thanked Paul, then spotted me. The smile he gave me melted my heart and caused many of the adults to look around for the receiver of the smile.

"They loved you," I told Pip as we returned to his room.

"*Oui.*" He commented with a half-smile.

The paperwork was waiting for Jean-Philippe to sign once we arrived back to his room, and within half an hour, he was being wheeled out of the hospital.

Jean-Philippe was quiet as I loaded him into the truck and got on the freeway. "Where do you takes me," he asked.

I turned and offered Jean-Philippe what I hoped was as bright a smile as he had given. "You'll see."

Twenty-five minutes later, we pulled into the underground parking of my building. Jean-Philippe hadn't spoken a word yet but seemed to take everything in.

I took his elbow and led him to the elevator and the sixth floor. I took out the keys when we reached the end of the hall, unlocked the door, and ushered Jean-Philippe inside.

"Why these places?" I was asked, Pip's eyes wide.

"It's my place. Your place until you can get back on your feet, but I would like it if you made this your home." I took the extra keys out of my pocket and held them out for Jean-Philippe.

"You apartment? Those big truck yours? Yes? You haved money, I know. Yes?" The sudden coldness in Pip's voice confused me.

"Yeah, the condo was a gift from my parents when I graduated with my master's degree. The truck and the Honda we parked next to downstairs are mine. I'm not wealthy," that wasn't true, "but I'm not hurting for money."

"*D'accord,*" Jean-Philippe turned his attention to me, looking up with an unreadable expression.

Before I knew what was happening, Jean-Philippe had deftly unbuttoned my jeans and reached inside my briefs, his fingers wrapping around my dick.

"Hey. No!" I grabbed Jean-Philippe's arms, careful of the cast, and pulled them up, holding them in the air between us.

"*Alors,*" Jean-Philippe spoke coldly, "rent same for Bernard. Fucked me? Beats me?" Jean-Philippe stepped into me, grinding his crotch against my leg.

"Fuck!" My angry roar froze Jean-Philippe, and he flinched back from me. I lifted Jean-Philippe off the floor with one arm and carried him to the dining room. I pulled out a chair with one hand and sat down heavily, placing Jean-Philippe between my legs as if he were an ill-behaved child. "You will listen to me, and listen to me good, Jean-Philippe. I am not going to have sex with you. I have more room than I need and want you to share it with me. I expect nothing from you. I want…I want you to be safe and happy and have a place to go to school and work. That's it."

Jean-Philippe looked up and blinked back the tears. I placed my forehead on his and sighed. "I'm tired of being alone, Jean-Philippe. Will you please stay?"

Jean-Philippe lifted his hands, which were now free, and took my face. "I gay. No for whores. Is why father he kicked me out. I like you, Tyler. Of I stay, hurt my heart for you lovers here I am. You know meanings I say? I know you no gay. I attract at you, here," Jean-Philippe moved his hand around the space between our bodies, "hurt more for I want."

I leaned forward and brushed my lips across Jean-Philippe. "Actually, Jean-Philippe, I'm Bi, and I promise not to do that to you."

"I wants you." Jean-Philippe looked me straight in the eyes, leaning in so his center touched mine again.

"I want you too, but not now. Not yet. If and when I take you to my bed, it will be because you want to, Jean-Philippe, not as payment for something. If it happens, it will be because you give yourself freely to me with no strings and nothing more. Do you understand? Let me show you your room."

JEAN-PHILIPPE

It was two-thirty in the morning, and I was standing in the living room. I had gone to bed and had been asleep by eight the night before.

After our 'argument,' Tyler gave me a tour of the apartment, starting with his bedroom. The closet was as big as the basement room, and the bathroom was perfect. The master suite had its own deep balcony.

The room to be mine was a smaller version of Tyler's. The five shower heads in the glass shower and the large soaking tub were incredible. I hadn't had an actual bath since moving out of the agency's apartment.

The kitchen was modern and open, with a long granite island providing room for five to sit and eat. The pantry was again as big as some places I had lived in. Tyler had produced a new French Press coffee maker so I could have my coffee each morning.

The living room was set up so most of the seating faced the glass wall. On the other side of the wall was an eight-by-twenty-foot balcony. Centered on the glass wall was a cabinet with a television that rose up when it was on. Blinds provided shade and were set to rise and fall at the push of a button.

After the tour, Tyler loaded me back into the truck. At our first stop, a thrift shop, I bought four pairs of jeans, tennis shoes, a pair of brown ankle boots, pajamas, and enough shirts to last a week between washings. When I started picking out underwear, Tyler bulked. No way was Tyler letting me wear used underwear.

I paid for the clothes, and then Tyler headed for a department store.

Sunglasses, socks, underwear, and stocking caps were added to the cart. It was all I could afford. There hadn't been enough money for a winter coat or gloves. I would need them, but they could wait.

Yet they didn't.

With an argument and an agreement, I could pay Tyler back for the purchases in cash; Tyler bought the coat, gloves, and a prepaid cell phone. Once the parcels had been loaded into the truck, Tyler handed the receipts to me as agreed.

I was exhausted when we returned to the apartment and started the washer with my new clothes. Tyler encouraged me to take a nap.

When I woke, I found the clothes neatly folded on the dresser. I didn't understand what was behind Tyler's behavior. I was sure it was nothing but gratitude, but at this moment, I was grateful for the security, even if it wouldn't last.

I found Tyler watching TV.

"How was your nap?" He asked as I curled up on the opposite end of the long sofa.

"Great. I requires. What time?" The microwave was the only clock in the house, outside the bedrooms. However, it was low, tucked into the side of the island, and invisible unless you were standing there.

"Six. I was just about to come and wake you. I'm hungry, and I'm sure you are too. I thought I would order spaghetti and meatballs. There is a great place around the corner that delivers. How does that sound?"

I smiled. I said it was a great idea while thinking it sounded expensive.

I watched Tyler set the island with plates, water, and wine glasses. The fussiness of the place setting was at odds with the man's size. Everything Tyler did spoke of culture, education, sophistication, and money. Yet Tyler Braxton looked like a knee breaker for the local mafia.

He was tall and large. There was nothing narrow about his build, from his shoulders to hips. One of his arms was almost as long as both of mine. Yet, this tattooed giant of a man was setting the table for takeaway in a manner that would have put a smile on Martha Stewart's face.

Tyler had even poured two glasses of red wine, a full for himself and half a glass for me, in crystal wine glasses.

The takeaway containers in front of the plates held enough spaghetti, salad, and garlic bread to last me a week. I quickly dished up my portion under Tyler's critical eyes. I kept Tyler quiet with a promise to eat what was on my plate, and if I was still hungry, which I wouldn't be, I'd have more.

When we started eating, Tyler said, "I want to tell you what my schedule will be like this and next week. Today's Thursday, so tomorrow, Monday, Wednesday, and next Friday, I'm usually at the gym by seven. Go ahead and have your breakfast; don't wait for me. Every day I'm not at the gym, I run about ten miles on the treadmill in the office. I have to keep in shape for work. Oh, also, I've applied for a detective spot. They've been after me, so it's pretty much a shoo-in."

I didn't know what a 'shoo-in' was and asked.

"Is job thing you wants?" I questioned before scooping spaghetti into my mouth.

"Actually, it is. I've been thinking about it. Changing, you know. Everything that happened over the last few weeks made me realize now's the time to make a change." Tyler commented with a nod.

"Good!"

We talked about my job.

I would call and speak with Javier tomorrow. Javier wouldn't let me return to work without a doctor's note releasing me for duty. But I wanted to let Javier know I needed to keep the job. I also needed to call my guitar teacher and tell him it would be another week before I could resume my lessons. And that depended on if I could find a cheap guitar to replace the one Bernard destroyed.

Tyler said he would leave the house phone number by the laptop in the office and also the password for the Wi-Fi if I wanted to get online.

There was companionable silence, but Tyler watched me eat. Tyler finally asked when I last had three meals a day. Damn! Tyler wouldn't like the answer, and I told him so. But he insisted.

"Before *ma mère,* she dies."

I thought Tyler was going to have a stroke. "Tell me!" he growled.

Once my mother died, my father stopped cooking. I might get to eat if there was food in the house; otherwise, I ate at school.

"What about the summer?"

"No foods," I shrugged.

Tyler leaned over and pulled me to him, hugging me for several minutes before letting me continue eating.

There was silence for the balance of the meal. I didn't have seconds, but I helped put the leftovers away and loaded the dishes into the machine to clean them.

"Come," I said, pulling Tyler out of the kitchen.

Taking Tyler's hand, I placed our palms together, base to base. My fingertips rested just above the first joint from the palm of Tyler's hand. "Big hand. *Ohhh*, what size you shoe?" I glared down at Tyler's feet, then up at Tyler's face, with a wicked smile and a wink.

Tyler burst into laughter.

That made me feel better.

Next, I moved so we were chest to chest, although it wasn't my chest that rested against the base of Tyler's ribcage but my forehead.

"I too small to you." I put a smile on my face, but it didn't reach my voice. I had hoped there was a chance to be with Tyler, but I knew it wouldn't happen after seeing the difference in our size.

I turned away, but Tyler turned me around, lifted me by my waist, and brought his mouth to mine. The kiss was more than friends but less than lovers.

"I'd say you are the perfect size, Jean-Philippe."

I nodded, taking Tyler's hand once Tyler had placed me back on the floor. "Thanks for today. I make money for give for clothes and phone. I no want you thinked I to take advantage for you. Is good I go my room? I tired. Day too long."

Tyler wrapped me in his arms and pulled a dining room chair over so he could sit. Again! "Pip." Tyler took my chin in his hand and tilted it up. "This is your home. I am not your boss. If you need to go to your room, go. I am going to make sure you eat, but you are free to do as you please."

Tyler lightly brushed his lips to my forehead, then to my neck, pausing to kiss my mouth. "Oh, one more question, then take a nice bath and go to bed. Do you have a driver's license?"

I couldn't help myself. I laughed at the question. "Where I to learn? Bus good for me."

"Would you let me help you get your license? We can practice in the Honda, and I'll sign you up for the online class."

I could not deny this to Tyler. The idea of helping me learn to drive had him happy, and I wanted to make and keep Tyler happy.

"D'accord. You have time. We do this. Good nights, *mon beau géant!"* I let my hand rest on Tyler's cheek before turning and walking to the room.

I replayed the day over again as I moved to the glass wall and looked out over the sleeping city. With a sigh, I returned to the room. This wouldn't last, but I wasn't going to worry overmuch about it for now.

******

I crawled out of the most comfortable bed I had ever slept in at seven-thirty and went to the bathroom. I stood naked after washing my hands and looked at my body. It was an amazing body, tight and robust. It was a man's body, even if it was the stature of a boy's.

It was who I was, and I had learned to live with it, like my albinism, a long time ago.

I thought about Tyler and remembered what he looked like naked and was instantly hard. That was easy enough to take care of, then it would be time for some coffee. So, with Tyler on my mind, I returned to bed and worked a fantasy until I got off.

Returning to the bathroom to clean up my come-covered body and brush my teeth, I pulled on low-slung pajama bottoms and headed into the kitchen.

I pulled out the coffee from the pantry and the electric tea kettle from under the range. I was filling the French Press with coffee when there was a knock on the door.

Maybe Tyler forgot his key.

It wasn't Tyler, but a copy of Tyler in thirty years. The man filling the door, dressed in an expensive suit, was the same size as Tyler, but the years had taken off some of the rough edges.

"Good morning. You must be Jean-Philippe. I'm Trenton Braxton, Tyler's father. Can I come in?"

"My apology, please." I stepped back so Mr. Braxton could enter before closing the door behind him. "I make coffee. I make you coffee, yes?"

"That would be nice, thank you."

"Sit." I moved towards the kitchen, pulled out a bar stool for Tyler's father, and returned to prepping the press. "Cream? Sugar? Yes?"

"Cream is fine, but I'm sure Tyler just has milk. That'll work."

I was aware that Mr. Braxton was checking me out, not in a sexual way, but not missing anything. I wished I had worn a shirt as the pajama bottoms rode low on my hips. However, what were the chances Braxton senior read French?

When I opened the cabinet to get cups, I moaned. The cups were on the second shelf and out of my reach. I looked over my shoulder, "You get three cup, yes?"

A half-smile was on the man's face as he moved into the kitchen and pulled out two mugs and the cream pitcher.

I went back to the coffee-making with a *"Merci!"*

After placing the senior Braxton's mug and creamer in front of him, I went about making my coffee. I was allowed one sip before Braxton asked, *"Je t'en prie. Est-ce que mon fils sait ce que disent vos tatouages?"*

Fuck! Trenton Braxton did speak French. He thanked me for the coffee and asked if Tyler knew what my tattoos said.

This wasn't a friendly visit after all. I could play it as well.

"No, he no understand. Word no for people. I put shirt for you upset you."

"I agree, they aren't for the public, and no, you don't have to put on a shirt. I already know what they say." There was a slightly disgusted undertone to the last statement. "Let me say this first. My wife and I know what you did for our son, and we are grateful. We heard a few stories about you and thought I would come and see for myself." Braxton took another sip of his coffee.

"Quelles histoires?" I matched the senior Braxton's tone and took a sip of coffee.

"There were several. One was that you looked like an exotic fantasy. I would say that one is on point. You must have fetched a high price when you worked for Karnes and his brothers. They are known for the exotic and beautiful." His tone was not rude; it was just matter-of-fact like he was speaking at a conference.

"Oui. D'accord," I waited to see what was next. I took a breath, "Mr. Braxton. I not here to advantage for your son."

He looked me over again, nodding as if coming to a conclusion. "Veronica and I are willing to set you up in an apartment near your job. We will pay your rent and utilities for two years, but you would have to stay away from Tyler. We've worked too hard to get him where he's at to be dragged down by a prostitute. With his new position, he can't be associated with someone like you. It's not personal, Jean-Philippe. We just want what's best for our son, and you are not anywhere near that."

I said nothing but finished my coffee and stood waiting for Braxton to finish.

Once the mugs were in the sink, I moved to the door and opened it, Braxton following and pausing just inside the open door. "Monsieur Braxton. I thinking on what you say. I no whore. You offering no improved as one. Know you insults me. You no know me. I worked for a years to wash dishes. I hold good job!"

"You are a whore even if you aren't fucking for money! What do you think you are doing with our son? Fucking him for a place to live is still prostitution. It would really be in your best interest to take my offer." The warning tone was not difficult for me to miss.

With a smirk to match Bernard's, I looked up into the hazel eyes of Trenton Braxton. "*D'accord.* Monsieur Braxton, only if you murdering me, there nothing, nothing, you do for me not before now happen. *Comprenez vous!* Nothing!" The shock and horror on his face were worth everything as I closed the door.

Before I was a step away from the door, I heard Tyler's voice. "What the fuck did you say to him, Dad?"

I moved away from the door into the kitchen, yet I could still hear the angry voices.

As the door flew open, I could see that Tyler was livid, and his wild eyes flew across the open space until they landed on me.

Because his anger terrified me, I ran from the kitchen toward my bedroom.

TYLER

I had taken the stairs instead of the elevator. It was my way of cooling off after a workout. As the stairs were at the other end of the hallway, there was no way anyone would have heard me. So, I was shocked when the door to the condo opened, and the bulky figure of my father filled the doorway.

"Monsieur Braxton. I thinking on what you say. I no whore. You offering no improved as one. Know you insult me. You no know me. I worked for a years to wash dishes. I hold good job!" Jean-Philippe's voice was strained but level.

"You are a whore even if you aren't fucking for money! What are you doing with our son? Fucking him for a place to live is still prostitution. It would really be in your best interest to take my offer." I heard the warning in my father's voice.

"*D'accord.* Monsieur Braxton, only if you murdering me, there nothing, nothing, you do for me not before now happen. *Comprenez vous!* Nothing!" Jean-Philippe's words painted such a vivid picture that they made me feel sick.

I waited until the door was closed before shouting, "What the fuck did you say to him, Dad?"

The deer-in-the-headlights expression on my father's face would have been funny if not for the words I had heard coming out of his mouth.

He squared his shoulders and looked directly into my face like I was a junior partner, not his son, "We did it for your own good, Tyler. That boy…."

I interrupted, "Man, Dad. Jean-Philippe is a man."

My father waved my comments away as if unimportant, "Whatever. Son, that 'man' is nothing but trouble, and he will drag you down to the gutter with him. Your mother and I offered him an apartment for two years. Rent-free, better than anything any john would offer. All he has to do is keep his whoring little ass away from you!"

I took a deep breath. "I'm my own man, Dad. That man saved my life…."

"You don't owe him anything but your thanks, which you already gave, I'm sure."

It was my turn to ignore what my father had just said. "Not only that, but he is a wonderful person, and I like him. He calms me, Dad."

"Is it just sex, Tyler? If you want to fuck a whore, at least find one with a little more class."

I didn't punch but slapped my father. "Leave. I don't want to see you or Mother."

"I'm your father, Tyler Hawthorne Braxton."

I turned, and in a faint voice my father almost didn't hear, "You were, Dad. You were."

As the door closed behind me and in my father's face, I searched the room for Jean-Philippe and saw him as he started to run from the kitchen towards his bedroom. There was panic on his face, which added to the fire burning in my stomach.

I caught him halfway between the kitchen and the hallway to the bedrooms. Jean-Philippe fought but, after a moment, went limp in my arms.

"I'm sorry," I said as I carried Jean-Philippe to his bedroom and stretched on the bed. I lay over him, keeping my weight on my elbows and knees. "I'm so sorry."

Jean-Philippe's eyes were closed, and his head was turned away from me, and it killed me.

I moved Jean-Philippe's head with my hand to face him. Gently, carefully, I leaned down and took my beautiful Elf's mouth.

At first, there was no response, but soon, Jean-Philippe returned the kiss. I pulled my mouth off and brushed a tear off the porcelain cheek. "He had no right to say any of that to you, Jean-Philippe. Don't let the lies from that old fucker's mouth make you believe anything he said about you. Do you hear me?"

Jean-Philippe nodded, then leaned up and possessed my mouth. I groaned and, without thinking, dropped my center so it rubbed hard against the body under me as Jean-Philippe's legs wrapped around me.

"*Je te veux!*" Jean-Philippe moaned against my mouth.

"What does that mean?"

"I wants you!" Jean-Philippe grounded himself against me.

I froze, pulling my mouth from Jean-Philippe's, and dropped my forehead against the smooth one under me.

"Not after what my father said. I can't, Jean-Philippe. You're too hurt now, and I can't take advantage of you. Please don't be mad at me," It was my turn to let the tears roll out of my eyes and drop onto Jean-Philippe's cheeks.

"You lay here for me? Here for me for time, Tyler?"

I wrapped my tree trunk-sized arms around Jean-Philippe's body, pulling him tight against me. "I'm sorry he hurt you, but what you said, about short of murdering you, there is nothing, absolutely nothing, he could do to you that hasn't already been done. Is that true, Jean-Philippe?"

When Jean-Philippe nodded, hiding his face in my chest, I broke down and cried as if the world had become crueler than I could bear.

We both slept. I woke first and gazed at the sleeping man curled against me. I wanted him, but just not yet. There was still so much crap, and now with my parents adding to it, neither Jean-Philippe nor I could catch a break.

"Hard thing you thinks, yes?" Jean-Philippe's otherworldly voice drifted to my ears.

I nodded but didn't say a word.

"*D'accord*. Sometime world no good place, no?"

I nodded again.

My gaze followed Jean-Philippe's as he turned to look at the clock. It was after two. We had slept for over four hours.

"I go for call Javier. Something you must to do?" Jean-Philippe asked.

"No, just relax. Oh, and start studying for your driving test." That at least made me smile as I heard Jean-Philippe groan.

I watched as Jean-Philippe uncurled his body, got out of bed, and headed to the bathroom. Following his example, I headed to the hall guest bathroom and then the kitchen to get some water.

From the kitchen, I heard Jean-Philippe call his boss. "Yes, I good. Tyler, he takes good care for me, of me. Saturday? Yes. Okay. I there. No, thanks you. Tell Lola hello for mes, I well."

I slid a glass of water to Jean-Philippe when he strolled into the kitchen before I asked about Saturday. A staff meeting for the back of the house started at ten, not tomorrow but the following Saturday.

"Do you need a ride?" I hoped not, as I had plans but would change everything if needed.

"No. I looks at bus table for computer. I think maybe us closer for restaurant here before old place." Jean-Philippe drank some of the water.

"Let's look. I'll go get the laptop."

We spent about an hour reviewing and printing the bus schedules from the apartment to the restaurant. The distance was about the same, but there was only one transfer, unlike from the warehouse, which required three.

Over the weekend, I watched Jean-Philippe relax. We watched TV, which was something new for both of us.

I had a few beers with dinner on Saturday, but Jean-Philippe didn't drink often. Sunday, Steve and I had a few guys came over to watch football and eat hamburgers we grilled on the balcony.

During that time, Jean-Philippe kept to himself. Later Sunday, after all the guys had gone, I got Jean-Philippe to admit that the men were too big and so many were scary. I apologized, but Jean-Philippe assured me it was alright. I should have my friends over; it was my house.

"You knows, many years, I myself only. Weird for me many peoples. Work different, somehow. I no know why. No change this for me. Please no change. I learn." Jean-Philippe nervously told me.

I gave him a hug and went back to clean up the kitchen.

I went to the gym, ran on the treadmill, and checked in with HR daily. Jean-Philippe was often still asleep when I left, so I checked to make sure Philippe was ok. He seemed to just be getting up each morning when I arrived back at the apartment.

I hadn't heard from my parents directly. However, Steve had been the bearer of messages between his mother and mine.

I had made Jean-Philippe promise not to answer the door unless I was there with him. The peephole was too high for Jean-Philippe to reach and check who was there. Better safe than sorry.

While Jean-Philippe kept himself busy, I planned a birthday party. It would be just a few friends, both men and women. There would be pizza, beer, and soda.

I wasn't sure Jean-Philippe would welcome the party, but I felt I had to do something.

JEAN-PHILIPPE

I was up, showered, shaved, and dressed on Saturday morning before seven. It was just a meeting, but doing something outside the house was lovely. I would let Javier know about my doctor's appointment on Monday. Hopefully, I would be released to go back to work.

Also, there would be a paycheck waiting. It was for only four days, but it would give me some cash I hadn't had since leaving the hospital.

Tyler had offered me a ride to the restaurant, although he had something to do after that and couldn't pick me up. But I wanted the normalcy of catching the bus. I was going to miss seeing Mary, the bus driver on my old route, and wanted, at some point, to catch a ride on her bus to let her know I was alright but had just moved.

I was bouncing off the wall when I went to the kitchen to fix my coffee and a piece of toast.

"Wow! You're full of energy today." Tyler's voice came from inside the pantry.

"*Oui!* I excite to move again. I miss around people for work."

"Not Don. Is that douche still there?" Tyler asked.

I turned and looked into the pantry. Tyler was dressed in nothing but his sleeping shorts, and it was all I could do not to drool. I wanted to look closely at Tyler's tattoos but figured I couldn't very well check out Tyler's without revealing mine.

"*J'ai de la valeur! Je suis digne! Je suis important!*" I said while I made my coffee. It had the desired effect I had hoped.

"I've heard you say that before. What's it mean?"

I lifted my right arm and ran a finger along with the words. Without looking at Tyler, I translated the words to English, "I have value! I am worthy! I matter!"

Tyler wrapped his arms around me, pulling me up off the floor and into his chest. "You are more valuable than all the gold. You are worth more than anything I have, and you matter to me more than you can imagine." Tyler breathed the words into my ear and kissed my neck. It was five minutes before Tyler put me back on the floor.

"Thanks you, *Mon beau géant!*"

"It's 'thank you,' and what about the others?" Tyler ran his finger down the rainbows and words on my left arm. "Ah, *We Are All God's Children*! The one on stomach and back, if for another times."

I poured the coffee into a to-go mug, and with a kiss on Tyler's bare chest and a wish for good luck, I was out the door.

The back of the house was crowded. I searched for Don, ensuring I kept away from him, but he wasn't there. Maybe he got his ass fired finally.

The restaurant wouldn't open until noon, and the meeting usually lasted an hour. It was basically the same old, same old. There were a few new bits of information, some at the store level and some from corporate.

As Javier wrapped up the meeting, he welcomed me back and, to my horror, wished me a happy birthday.

There were calls for a song that happened. Some gentle back-slapping from the guys and hugs from the girls. They passed me around until I finally landed in the hands of Don.

"If it isn't Snow White. Been missing you," Don said just loud enough for me to hear. "Why don't you come with me? I've got a present for you."

I stiffened, "I no go for you, Don. I get check. I go home."

Don snickered. "That big thug ain't here to save you, and fucking Javier is busy." Don was big and meaty and held my wrists with one hand as he pulled me out the back door and into the alleyway.

This was not going to happen. Not again and not with Don.

Don pulled off my stocking cap and hooted when he saw the ears. "Oh, fuck! You are truly a weird little mother-fucker. I think I'm gonna pull on those pointed sons-of-bitches while I fuck you. What ya think?"

Don turned me, shoved my face and chest hard against the wall, breaking my sunglasses, and started working on loosening my pants.

"That's it. You're fired, Don," Javier's voice came from next to us, and I turned to see my boss, Javier's boss, and one of the other managers.

Don slowly removed his hands from my waist and stepped away, slapping me on the back of the head so my forehead hit the bricks.

Javier took me into the building while the other two managers dealt with Don.

"You okay, kid?" Javier finally asked once we were in his office with the door closed.

"Yeah! He assholes. Thank for save me. I need my check, so I go home. It too many today."

"Got it. You want me to call Tyler?"

I shook my head and thanked Javier but told him I just wanted to cash my check and head home. Javier wanted to make sure Don had left like he had been told to and was not lurking somewhere to attack.

Nonetheless, I crossed the street with my check in hand and Javier at my side. Finally, with a hug and a promise to call Javier if I needed anything, I got on the bus and headed to Tyler's.

The apartment was full of people, and 'Happy Birthday!' streamers covered the living and dining rooms.

I spotted Tyler, who was on the balcony. Word that I had arrived must have reached his ears because I watched as Tyler made a beeline through the crowd.

Everyone noticed, not only me, the panic on Tyler's face as he crossed the room to sweep me off my feet and hustled me to the bedroom.

"Javier calls. He did, yes?" I said after the bedroom door was closed.

"Are you okay? Did that asshole hurt you?" Tyler's hands roamed over my body, looking for injuries.

It was that that kept me from being mad at Tyler.

The Elf Who Tamed A Giant

"Many peoples there, Tyler." I pointed at the bedroom door with a hint of accusation wrapped with a bit of joy.

"Yeah, I know. I got carried away. Take a few minutes, then come find me. I've something for you." Tyler kissed me lightly before leaving the room and closing the door behind him.

Sneaky! I thought as I pulled myself together. I went to the bathroom, washed my face, brushed my teeth, and ran a brush to smooth out my hair. I wasn't going to wear the hat. If I was going to be in Tyler's life, even temporarily, people needed to see me. I wasn't an elf, not some mythical creature. The ethereal look I had was something to be proud of.

If people wanted to stare, let them stare.

Steve met me in the kitchen. "Happy birthday, Jean-Philippe. Twenty-two, huh? Want a beer?" Steve snickered and handed me a soda, which I handed back and said I wanted some wine. Pointing to a shelf above my head, I indicated a red and had Steve get it down. Once the bottle was opened, I topped off a tall wine glass. The drink would last me most of the afternoon.

I was stopped and had people introduce themselves. For the first time in a long time, I introduced myself by my name, not Pip. People seemed to be a bit afraid or in awe. Most people didn't know what to think of me. Some were surprised, and a few thought I was an actor not yet out of makeup.

Tyler called everyone together and disappeared into his bedroom, only to reappear with a new guitar with a bow around the neck. "Happy Birthday." He smiled as he passed me the expensive-looking instrument. "Play something for us."

There was polite applause as many people echoed Tyler's request. I knew most were just being friendly but focused on tuning the strings while thinking of something to play.

Closing my eyes, I pictured the music in my mind and began to play *Bach's Toccata on One Guitar*.

The noise of the room disappeared as everyone stilled and stared. When the song was finished, everyone burst into applause. I excused myself and took the new treasure into my room, but not before hugging Tyler and thanking him with a kiss.

Later, I watched as Tyler tracked me throughout the room. As before, I wasn't the only one who noticed. This became obvious when I went into the dark pantry to find crackers.

"What the fuck is up with Tyler?" A woman's voice asked just outside the pantry door as it closed.

"Hell if I know. But he's got it bad," a man's voice answered.

"He can't keep his eyes off the fairy in the room," she said.

That made the man guffaw, "Honey, there is more than one fairy in that room. But yeah, I know. Hey, has he called you for a hookup?"

The woman sounded disappointed when she answered, "No. Not in a while. How about you?"

The man or woman leaned against the pantry door, making sure I had no choice but to listen. "Three or four weeks ago, just before Halloween. I don't know what was up, but damn, he was rough. I like a little S&M like the next guy, but I was black and blue for days." The man commented.

"I miss that. Nobody can fuck like Tyler Braxton. Remember that time we both spent the weekend with him? I couldn't walk for a week."

"You," the guy groaned, "weren't the only one. I miss his dick."

"Me too," the woman agreed, "he's so fucking awesome with that thing."

There was some debate about whether I was actually a human and if I was honestly not a child. "Tyler and Steve both swear he's twenty-two," the man offered. "I don't think it really matters. Tyler is so head over heels, he would break every law on the books to be with that Elvin queen."

The woman laughed, and it wasn't a nice one, "Yeah, twenty-two, in the body of an eleven-year-old with the pee-pee of an eight-year-old. Poor little thing. If Tyler gets ahold of that, he'll tear him apart! Do you think either of us has a chance to get laid today?"

"Not here, that's for fucking sure."

The woman lowered her voice, "Let's tell our increasingly bizarre host we have to skip out and go somewhere else."

I waited five minutes before opening the door. No one was in the kitchen, and I reappeared just as five people headed out the door. While in the closet, I laughed at that thought, almost everyone had left.

Tyler and Steve were sitting on the balcony, each with a beer. "This ship is sinking, cousin," Steve yelled in mock horror at Tyler.

"More of everything for us." Tyler smiled over at me, and I lifted my wine glass.

By four, no one was left but Steve, and he begged out soon after, wanting to get home before the early darkness of November.

"I don't throw a very good party, it looks like," Tyler commented as he gathered empty cans for the recycling.

"It wonderful. Thanks you for your gift for me." I teased as I helped with the cleanup.

There was silence as we worked together.

When the house was put back to rights, Tyler turned to me. "I added you to my car insurance so you can drive when you pass your test. Oh, one more little gift." Tyler didn't look at me when he said it.

I drained my glass and poured myself a few swallows more.

"What?" I prompted.

"I got the detective job. That's for me, but I won't be doing undercover work. Maybe that's a little for you."

I nodded. I was happy, although I remember Tyler's father telling me he already had the job.

Interesting.

I didn't say anything about it but looked at Tyler and emptied the wine glass. This would blow up in my face or be the best birthday ever.

"We watch TV, yes. You come, sit."

Tyler didn't raise an eyebrow at the tone in my voice but did what he was told.

Once Tyler was seated, I pushed Tyler's thighs open with my knees and stepped in to put my hands on Tyler's chest. "Many beers do you have?" As much as I wanted to do what I hoped, I wouldn't take advantage of an impaired Tyler.

"Three over four hours, why?" Tyler looked confused.

"Good!" I said, removed my shirt, and crawled into Tyler's lap.

TYLER

I caught my breath as Jean-Philippe straddled my hips and took my face between his small hands. The kiss shook me down to my soul. It had been tender, exploring before it became demanding.

I matched Jean-Philippe's kiss heat for heat. While Jean-Philippe's tongue and lips fried my brain, Jean-Philippe's fingers worked their magic. They had me out of my shirt before I knew Jean-Philippe had worked the buttons.

Jean-Philippe moved to my neck and asked breathlessly, "You wants knows my tattoos say?"

I thought I said yes but couldn't be sure until Jean-Philippe's hands rested on my cheeks again and pulled my attention to the heat of his ice-blue eyes. I watched as Jean-Philippe's hands moved down to his own jeans. Jean-Philippe slowly unclasped and unzipped them before pulling them down to ride below his heavy cock.

"This say," Jean-Philippe took my hand and moved it, so my thick fingers traced the words and the length of Jean-Philippe's erection underneath. I caught my breath, "This say," he stated again and leaned into me, "Fuck you!"

Jean-Philippe growled the words an inch away from my lip while grinding his erection into mine.

"This," Jean-Philippe said, getting up and slowly stepping out of his jeans and briefs, then taking my hand and rubbing a shaking finger over the sentence on his back, "say, Fuck me!"

Jean-Philippe then sat down on my lap.

I was shocked at the animal-like growl that erupted from my chest. I grabbed Jean-Philippe and carried him into my bedroom, tossing him onto the bed.

This time, I only supported my weight on my elbows as I ground myself into Jean-Philippe.

"You are so fucking sexy, Jean-Philippe." I paused each word just long enough to claim Jean-Philippe's mouth. "I want you."

"Have me, Tyler. I wants you."

But as I lowered my body over Jean-Philippe's, Jean-Philippe lifted a hand. "Are you to stop this? I no wants you stop. I need know you wants me, no stop out. Sleep for me, Tyler?"

I interpreted Jean-Philippe's jumbled English. "Not only am I going to sleep with you, Jean-Philippe, but I'm also going to have fantastic sex with you," I growled again, lowering my massive body onto Jean-Philippe.

"*D'accord*," Jean-Philippe lifted his hand to my chest. "Get up, off cloth for me."

My cock twitched at Jean-Philippe's tone, and I couldn't get off the bed fast enough. A minute later, I was naked.

When I tried to take my place back, Jean-Philippe shook his head and, with more power than I thought Jean-Philippe possessed, shoved me onto my back and climbed up my body like a tree that he was desperate to reach the top.

Jean-Philippe hovered over my body, running his tongue up my Happy Trail until his mouth sucked in my bottom lip.

"What? What tattoo you wants?"

I sucked in my breath at the question. I mainly always topped, but seeing Jean-Philippe over me made me want to have him inside me.

"Fuck me, Jean-Philippe."

"*D'accord*. I control." Jean-Philippe demanded, and I complied.

Somehow, I had told Jean-Philippe where to find the condoms and lube.

I had sex, a lot of sex, but what Jean-Philippe did to me was beyond my scope of experience. I had never been rimmed nor finger fucked, until I begged for more.

"Please!" I pleaded as Jean-Philippe's sweet torture blew my mind and wrecked my body.

"Please, *quel, mon beau géant*? Speak me what you wants."

"You, inside me. Please," I whimpered.

"*D'accord*," Jean-Philippe withdrew his fingers and slowly filled me.

"Oh my God," I chanted as my elf pounded my prostate, slowed to long, languid strokes, then pounded me again.

"I wants to kiss you," I thought I heard Jean-Philippe's voice. I tried to focus my eyes on Jean-Philippe.

Here, the difference in our size was apparent. There was no way for Jean-Philippe to continue to fuck me and kiss me at the same time.

"I'll kiss you for a week, Jean-Philippe. I'll do anything you want. I just need to come, please."

"*D'accord*," and with almost a religious zealousness, Jean-Philippe worked me to the edge and back until I was in tears. "Ready, beautiful giant."

"Please!"

With each stroke, Jean-Philippe almost pulled out and slammed back into me. Each thrust sent shock waves through my body. When I didn't think there could be more stimulation, Jean-Philippe took my cock in his hand and stroked me to match his movement.

"Come for me, *mon amour*. I there. I wants come with you. You ready? Ready?" Jean-Philippe was almost in tears as the heat of his orgasm seemed to rock him. "À présent!" Jean-Philippe screamed, and I shot my load to my chin before I momentarily blacked out.

I heard Jean-Philippe cry out and felt his body shutter. It was the most intense experience of my life. When I could finally think again, I reached between my legs, pinched the base of Jean-Philippe's cock to secure the condom, and lifted the catatonic man onto my chest with one arm.

I laughed as I watched one eyelid twitch. "I owe you some kisses."

I rolled over and hovered over Jean-Philippe. My knees bent alongside Jean-Philippe's hips, my cock brushing his, and my lips taking my little lovers.

"*Je suis mort la petite mort, je ne peux pas encore parler!*" Jean-Philippe whispered between kisses.

"What, my love? I want to feel you under me, just for a minute, can I?" I asked.

Jean-Philippe nodded, then repeated the words in English, "I die little death, I no able speak!"

With tender care, I lowered my massive frame so I was face-to-face with Jean-Philippe and took his mouth, this time with such affectionate care that it shattered me.

"I loved you on me." Jean-Philippe wrapped his arms around my neck and legs around my lower back. "Thanks you to let me love you, my beautiful giant." Jean-Philippe's words worked their way into my heart. "I sleep now. Love me tomorrow, yes!" As if someone had turned off a switch, Jean-Philippe relaxed under my body and was asleep.

I moved off my tiny man and marveled at what I saw. I didn't know sex could be like that. Why had I not known? I leaned down and kissed the sleeping mouth before heading to the bathroom to dispose of the condom and get a warm cloth to clean Jean-Philippe up after caring for my body.

With both of us clean, I lifted Jean-Philippe up and held him, pulling down the sheets before placing Jean-Philippe in the center. I took a few minutes to turn off the lights before returning to the bedroom and crawling under the bedclothes with Jean-Philippe.

The lights had scarcely gone off when Jean-Philippe snuggled up to me and, slowly and unexpectedly, wrapped himself around my body and heart.

I had woken to find myself wrapped around Jean-Philippe, who was sleeping on his back. My hand rested on Jean-Philippe's stomach, with Jean-Philippe's hands holding it in place. I knew my eyes automatically searched for him. Yet, I had never allowed myself to study him like I was doing now.

I splayed my fingers, marveling at how much skin they covered on Jean-Philippe's stomach. It was also the first time I paid attention to the hair on his body. Jean-Philippe was hairy, his chest, abdomen, and legs covered in soft, thick curls.

I wanted to laugh but didn't want to wake him. It bothered me that only animals came to mind at the soft fur texture under my hand and against my legs. Jean-Philippe felt like the softest of chinchilla, rabbit, or maybe even a poodle. Still, nothing else I could think of compared to the feeling.

Jean-Philippe had been a fantastic lover. Despite the petite size of Jean-Philippe's body, his uncircumcised dick was not small. I had had bigger and even smaller, but the girth had helped drive me so far over the edge my body still tingled just remembering.

I was a bit above average, both in length and girth. My equipment didn't have porn star dimensions, but enough to excite and please any lover I had ever had.

My eyes moved up the milky white skin of Jean-Philippe's torso, pausing at the colorless nipples and then at Jean-Philippe's face. His diminutive size belied Jean-Philippe's square and ruggedly shaped face. It should be on the cover of a magazine, with its high cheekbones, long slender nose, and full kissable lips. Jean-Philippe was handsome, but more than that, he had an ethereal beauty that everyone who saw him could barely comprehend.

Jean-Philippe's eyes were wideset, and their ice-blue color was so intense they sometimes made me feel both uncomfortable and dazzled at the same time.

I moved closer, only inches from the sleeping man. I was amazed at the beard on Jean-Philippe's face. Although Jean-Philippe had mentioned he had shaved yesterday before he left the house for his meeting, it was filled in. I liked my own face clean-shaven, and although I was built like a lumberjack or a Viking, I was not hairy. But I liked the feel of a man's beard on my face and other parts when I had sex.

Jean-Philippe would sport a beautiful full beard without shaving in only a few days. I hadn't expected that. I noticed only the thick eyelashes on Jean-Philippe's cheeks had color, a dusting of ash. I felt as if I were to breathe across them the hue would simply blow away.

"You look for me maybe I you next food, *mon beau géant*!"

At the sound of Jean-Philippe's voice, I shifted my eyes down, focusing my attention on the man smiling up.

"Perhaps I could use a pre-breakfast appetizer."

"*Ohh, la la*! Sound promise. First, I must go," Jean-Philippe pointed to the bathroom and started to move away.

I pressed my hand down on Jean-Philippe's stomach, holding him in place. "Can I ask you not to shave?"

Jean-Philippe turned his face into my chest and rubbed the scruff against the skin, causing me to growl.

"*Bon*! Keep that thinking. I back for ten minute," Jean-Philippe crawled out of bed and dragged his fingers over the tattoo on his back, giving me a wicked smile over his shoulder before disappearing out of the bedroom.

'*Ohh, la la, was right!*' I thought as I hurried to the bathroom.

JEAN-PHILIPPE

I stood before the mirror and regarded my reflection after emptying my bladder and taking time for some pre-sex prepping. If I went back into that bedroom, I would be lost to Tyler. I already knew this, but the more we connected, the harder it would be to walk away from him or have Tyler walk away from me.

"He will leave you or keep you; be man enough to take the chance," I told my reflection in French.

I didn't think what was going on was just for sex. It wasn't on my part, and something about how Tyler had touched and whispered words to me made me cautiously confident it wasn't on Tyler's part either.

"You can do it!" I nodded and turned to return to Tyler's bedroom.

I pulled up to a dead stop at the bedroom threshold. Tyler was propped up on the bed, back against the padded headboard, his engorged cock covered with a condom and glistening with lube. A sly, self-assured grin spread across his face.

I watched as Tyler patted his thighs on each side of his shaft, "Jean-Philippe, come here and have a seat. I have something for you."

My body shook with anticipation as I crawled up the mattress between Tyler's legs. My tongue moved up a leg and then Tyler's balls.

I leveraged myself up and paused with the tip of Tyler's cock brushing my tight hole. "You wants me sit here?" I lowered my body just a fraction.

Tyler's Adam's apple bobbed, and he nodded.

With deliberate slowness, I lowered myself onto Tyler.

"Oh! My! God!" Tyler sighed.

Tyler aggressively reached behind my head and brought my mouth to his. The kiss was hard, dirty, and demanding. The need to let Tyler devour me was overwhelming. But the words of the two people speaking about Tyler while I had been in the pantry returned, *'…but damn, he was rough. I like a little S&M like the next guy, but I was black and blue for days.'*

I inclined back, placing my hands on Tyler's chest. I looked into the dilated hazel eyes and leaned in towards Tyler. "I not break, please, *mon beau géant,* please no hurt me. I tired people always hurt me, please, not you."

Tyler reached for me and pulled me against his chest. "My beautiful angel. I will never hurt you. It would kill me. I might get carried away, so I expect you to tell me if I do. Promise me you will." Tyler said the words over my head and then eased me away so we were eye-to-eye again. "Promise?"

When I agreed, the wicked smile returned, and Tyler began to rock.

Tyler's hips were wide, so I moved up and down with difficulty. Tyler groaned, moved his hands to each hip, lifted me up, and thrust me back down. The motion brushed my prostate each time Tyler's cock slid out almost to the tip and grounded out.

"You feel so good, fuck. Where have you been all my life?" Tyler moaned.

"*Je suis ton cowboy*! I your cowboy, me rided you," There was a joke in the words somewhere, but I was lost in the feeling.

Between Tyler's strong hands helping me thrust up and down, it was a few minutes before I watched Tyler's eyes grow dark. He threw his head back and roared, "Oh, fuck, Jean-Philippe. I'm gonna come."

The sound was wild, animal-like as Tyler's body quaked under me. Tyler's hands kept me in place as he chanted, *'Don't move. Don't move! Don't move!'*

I leaned my forehead on Tyler's chest but gasped as Tyler wrapped his long fingers around my vibrating cock and began to stroke. His movements were as slow and deliberate as mine had been when I had mounted him. Tyler increased his pace as my breath became ragged, and whimpers escaped my lips. My body actually vibrated. I felt Tyler's semisoft cock become hard again with the vibrations.

"Look at me!" Tyler pleaded. "I'm going to come again. Oh, Christ, I can't think!"

The build of a powerful orgasm spread throughout my entire body. "I close. Wait!" Gasps became whimpers and then sobs as I threw my head back as the climax wrecked me.

I collapsed onto Tyler's chest, resting my head under Tyler's chin.

"You shatter me!"

Tyler's laughter rumbled through his chest, "I don't even have a word for what you did to me…twice in less than fifteen minutes. I don't think there's a word for that."

Tyler leaned up and wrapped his arms around me. Holding me as our bodies returned to normal, kissing the top of my head, and pulling me up so Tyler could kiss my mouth.

"I want take you for breakfast. You need you energy fill," I informed Tyler thirty minutes later while we were still in bed, intertwined around each other. "I have pay…money. I get discounted. We eat my job."

Tyler was quiet a beat too long, so I laughed, "You no want peoples seen me and you, I know…I understanded." I tried to make the words sound like a joke, but even to my ears, the joke fell flat.

"I'll go have brunch. I am starving, but only if you shower with me." Tyler said, kissing my neck.

"I afraids shower with you make *more* sex," I warned.

"Good, I was hoping you would say that," Tyler cheered as he pulled me out of bed, threw me over his shoulder, and carried me into the glass-enclosed shower.

TYLER

Jean-Philippe was correct. A shower with me did mean more sex.

How had that even been possible?

Twenty minutes later, still in the shower, I had to shoo Jean-Philippe out of my bathroom so I could finish getting ready for breakfast.

I didn't need to shave, so after brushing my teeth and hair, I opted for the lumberjack look as the bedroom windows showed it was snowing.

I pulled mine and Jean-Philippe's winter gear out of the hall closet and threw them over a bar stool. I was happy I had just had the all-weather tires put on the truck and would be making an appointment to install a new set on the Honda.

I looked around for Jean-Philippe's sunglasses. I had noticed he never left the house without them and asked. Jean-Philippe had said part of albinism was light sensitivity. It was one of the reasons he even wore them when he worked; he had provided a doctor's note. He had had Lasix surgery, so he didn't need glasses to see, but over time, he would. Because of this, there were sunglasses all over the apartment.

I heard Jean-Philippe coming down the hall and turned. Jean-Philippe was dressed in a well-fitting Henley tucked into the waistband of a pair of jeans. His shoes were the pair of boots he had purchased. I could tell Jean-Philippe had tidied up his beard and mustache, and it looked fucking sexy.

But there was something different. I couldn't place it, but after a moment of admiring the hot bod inside the clothes, I got it. Actually, there were two.

Jean-Philippe always, always had a hat on his head when he went out. This morning, he didn't. His hair was pulled away from his face, and the tip of his left ear stuck out. I was sure he would add a hat before we left the apartment.

The other was his eyebrows.

"What did you do to your eyebrows?" I moved over and looked down at Jean-Philippe.

"I have eyebrow color. Same for lash. Calling 'Ashen' grey. It help people see expression at my face. It is bad?" Jean-Philippe's hand moved to touch an eyebrow.

I leaned down and kissed Jean-Philippe's mouth, "No, Babe. It's good. I've just never seen it before on your eyebrows. You don't have to do it for me, but I appreciate it. Are you ready?"

We sat inside the truck after pulling into the restaurant's parking lot. I had held Jean-Philippe's hand most of the drive but noticed him tensing up as we neared our destination. Maybe it was because Jean-Philippe had left the house without his ears covered. Just in case, I had put the stocking cap in my jacket pocket.

"Babe, you alright? Oh, do you mind my pet name? I can change it, or I can just use Jean-Philippe. You need to tell me. Also, I have your hat if that makes you feel better." I seemed to have picked up on Jean-Philippe's nervousness.

Jean-Philippe turned his attention to me and smiled. "I love you call me Babe, *mon beau géant.* I never go at like person, like to eats. Never for all year. I brave and no take hat. Just know people stare. They, how you say, glared. I look like, and I walk in with most handsomes man *dans le monde,* for my side. You must prepared, yes. Many peoples work front part not knows me. Maybe knows for me, elf for kitchen. This different."

That was a lot to deal with. "I'm here, and I won't let go of your hand. Can I hold your hand, Philippe?" The smile on Jean-Philippe's face was all the reassurance I needed. "Ready?"

"*Oui.*"

The expression on the hostess's face was priceless. I looked good, but Jean-Philippe looked model-hot!

"Don't you work in the back?" The hostess had asked.

"Yes, I feed my boyfriend. I wants eat him here. I means, have him eats here."

I wasn't sure if Jean-Philippe had had a slip of the tongue or had meant to fluster the hostess. Whatever the reason, it was sexy as hell with his French accent, and it was fun to watch the hostess's mouth drop open and her face turn scarlet.

Jean-Philippe had been correct. There was pointing and gawking. I heard several children as they loudly informed their parents that an elf was in the restaurant.

"See. I tells you this." Jean-Philippe commented as we were seated in one of the small two-top booths.

The manager on duty showed up before the waiter appeared to take our drink order.

Jean-Philippe was about to introduce me to the manager when I stood. I shook the man's hand and introduced myself as Jean-Philippe's boyfriend.

The manager failed to keep the shock off his face as he looked up at me.

He shook off his shock and addressed Philippe, "Jean-Philippe. I heard what had happened from Mr. Gutierrez. We are sorry, both about the attack and Don." The man honestly looked shamefaced. "Nice to meet you, Mr. Braxton. Thanks for taking good care," the manager's eyes scanned me from head to toe, then cleared his throat, "of Jean-Philippe."

Jean-Philippe thanked the manager and told him he had a doctor's appointment tomorrow and would hopefully be released to work.

With an 'enjoy your meal,' the manager fled the table.

"That fun!" Jean-Philippe laughed as the waiter appeared.

We each ordered a Bloody Mary to go with our Eggs Benedict, and I noticed Philippe drank only half of his.

I offered to take Philippe to his doctor's appointment as we ate, which he accepted.

I thought I would hear from HR and the captain, whose squad room I hoped to be assigned to. It helped that I had a Master's in Criminal Psychology. I wasn't sure what the hours would be but was looking forward to it.

We talked more about Jean-Philippe's class, including a French class he wanted to take. I asked why the hell he would take a French class as he was French.

"You no like it, but I tells you." Jean-Philippe took a swig of his drink. "My father…"

I growled in a whisper, "That motherfucker doesn't deserve to be called your father, your dad, nothing. He doesn't deserve it. Call him a sleazy bastard or an…." I struggled to think of a word, "…asshat. Anything but father."

I watched as Jean-Philippe smiled and continued, "The asshat, I liked word, he no make positive I go in school. We live far to city. Easy for him. Someone say thing, we moved. I miss many schools."

A lot of meals too, I thought. Jean-Philippe was correct. I didn't like it.

"So, I have good language, but I no reading or writing nice. French, I speaked good, but," Jean-Philippe shrugged his shoulders, "English no. It why I wash the dish. Javier help things to read and write for work."

As Philippe spoke of his struggles, there was no hesitation, no humiliation in his voice. That Jean-Philippe had made it to where he was in his life, despite everything, astonished me.

"You are the most wonderful, fearless man I've ever known, Jean-Philippe. I am in awe of you." I leaned in to kiss him.

"I knows," Jean-Philippe winked, "is why you having more sex to me soon."

I almost choked at Jean-Philippe's words. "No, Babe. Not sex. I'm going to make love to you every chance I get," I whispered, kissing Jean-Philippe's neck.

Our breakfast was punctuated with visits from children, with their embarrassed parents behind them, who wanted to meet the elf. Jean-Philippe was gracious and told such a short tale that their parent's discomfort vanished even as the children laughed.

When it was time to pay the bill, we were informed that the meal had been comped. Jean-Philippe refused to let me take care of the tip or contribute to the bar bill.

We spent the rest of Sunday lounging on the sofa or in the bedroom, studying for Jean-Philippe's driving exam. I knew when Jean-Philippe called to set up his appointment, he could request the test to be read aloud. Jean-Philippe wasn't aware of this, and the tension eased from his body with the knowledge.

Monday, I drove Jean-Philippe to the doctor's office and waited as he had his checkup. Philippe only needed to wear the soft brace when working for four weeks just as support. A quick stop was made to give Javier the return to work note, and Philippe was back on the schedule starting the following Saturday and Sunday for the lunch shift.

I heard from HR on Tuesday and was to start working that Thursday. Jean-Philippe asked what that meant for my working hours, and I admitted I wasn't sure and wouldn't be until after the first few days.

Over the next week, using the online course, Jean-Philippe was able to study and take, with my help, practice tests for his upcoming written exam.

Because the city kept the roads ice and snow-free, Jean-Philippe practiced his driving skills with me at his side. By the following week, even with our work schedules, Jean-Philippe had scheduled his driving test and had passed. He was still nervous about driving to work in the snow, but we drove around the city each day when I could.

I worked hard to make sure Jean-Philippe wouldn't need to ride the bus to and from work and school longer than necessary.

TYLER - THREE WEEKS LATER

Tyler Hawthorne Braxton, you are the luckiest son-of-a-bitch in the world, I thought as I looked out the plane's window.

Eight weeks ago, I was beaten, bleeding from a stab wound, and left to freeze to death. That had been the luckiest day of my life. Jean-Philippe had found me.

I had worked to get Philippe into my house and then into my bed. Actually, Philippe had been the one to get me to let him into my bed.

Lucky dog!

We had clicked not only in the bedroom, which was mind-blowingly fantastic but as friends and more. We talked about everything. The best, almost as good as the hot sex, was when I started calling Philippe my boyfriend, and Philippe hadn't freaked. I already knew I was in love with him. Just waiting for Jean-Philippe Roche to catch up.

I had heard from my mother and father a week after slapping my father in the face. I apologized but warned my parents not to interfere in my life. There was nothing I didn't know about Philippe, and despite what my father had said, Philippe wasn't fucking me in place of rent. Both my mother and father agreed to try to be more respectful.

It wasn't much, but it was a start.

Philippe returned to work the same week as I started my new job.

There were seven in all on the Force, and I had been paired up with a senior detective who would be a good mentor while learning my job. The hours were awful, but no matter when I crawled into bed, Philippe was there waiting.

I was surprised when my boss told me he wanted me to attend a workshop on the newest techniques for interviewing suspects. Captain Clayton explained that the three-day seminar would benefit me the most because of my education. Also, he expected me to share the information with the rest of the squad.

The workshop was held in a city, a one-and-a-half-hour flight from Boston. Another precinct in the department had sent a detective as well. I didn't know Scott McPherson, but we would share a room.

The hotel was a fifteen-minute drive from the airport. Tonight was a *Meet and Greet,* with *hors d'oeuvers* and an open bar. Breakfast, then workshops followed by a bagged lunch, and more workshops would end on Friday with everyone on their own for dinner. Saturday was another breakfast, a day's worth of workshops ending with a sit-down dinner and presentations. Sunday, there was a two-hour seminar and wrap-up session before the detectives were free to return to their hometowns.

I had been uneasy about leaving Philippe alone, especially after my father's unexpected visit.

I added a camera to my security system because Philippe couldn't reach the peephole in the door. If someone was at the door, Philippe or I could see who it was on the monitor attached to the wall.

Philippe assured me he would be alright and would call if there was an issue.

I had texted Philippe before putting the phone on plane mode. I was never sure if Philippe ever got any of the texts. His damn cheap phone was always hit-and-miss. Texts floated around the cloud for days before appearing on the screen, if they appeared at all. Phone calls were better, marginally, yet with Philippe's work schedule and guitar lessons, it would sometimes be hours before any message was received.

It had taken most of two weeks of constant nagging and begging, but I thought I had worn down Philippe's proud, stubborn streak. Enough so that Philippe wouldn't balk when I added him to my cell plan with a new smartphone.

---

[1] Love Behind the Lies – O'Connor Sister Trilogy

McPherson was already in the room when I entered. He sat on the bed, the TV on, but stood as I closed the door.

"Scott McPherson," he offered his hand, "Nice to meet you. You just get in?"

I shook the man's hand, "Yeah. Tyler Braxton. How about you?"

We made small talk as I unpacked the duffle bag, and McPherson moved to sit back on the queen closest to the windows.

Scott McPherson worked homicide. He was a short, five–nine or ten, stocky man in his late thirties. I noticed a gold band on his left hand, which McPherson twirled around his finger with nervous energy. "You worked undercover for four years, I heard."

I moved across the room to plug in my phone and check if Philippe had texted me. "Yeah, but I gotta tell you, I don't miss it. I know some guys who do it their entire careers. Four years was enough for me. I wanted a life."

McPherson agreed. He spent more time at home with his wife and three kids now than when he was a beat cop. The hours were weird, especially when they caught a case, but better.

By agreement, we pulled out our paperwork for the upcoming workshops. We had been paired up as we were coming from the same city police department. There would be two more as part of our group of four. Everyone would meet up at the reception to-night. From what I had understood, there were about a hundred detectives for the weekend. That meant the other two members of our group could be from anywhere.

The schedule of events clearly posted that all events were casu-al. Most police departments had some sort of dress code for their detectives, so being able to dress down would be a nice change. I opted for pressed jeans, an Oxford shirt, and new boots.

I checked my reflection in the mirror and gave myself a grin. Even in a three-thousand-dollar suit, I had four in my closet, and with my clean-shaven face, I looked like a mountain man who wres-tled bears for fun.

"I heard you were big, but damn!" McPherson laughed as I walked out of the bathroom.

"Yeah, believe it or not, I'm the runt of the family." That was not precisely true, as I had no siblings. Still, almost all of my cousins, including the women, were tall.

The banquet hall was set up with twenty-five tall tables. Each ta-ble held a numbered sign in the center, and as we checked in to pick up our credentials, each person was assigned a number. McPher-son and I were in group eighteen.

After getting a drink at the bar and a plate of *hors d'oeuvers,* we began searching for table eighteen.

A tall, slender woman was already at the table. She was perhaps in her late fifties with a tight cap of salt and pepper hair. Not as tall as me, she was taller than McPherson. She introduced herself as Pearl Hullinburg -Grossmeyer from the Palm Springs PD.

As soon as the round of introductions was over, we started again. Jess Bush from Kansas City arrived with a beer and a plate of food. I knew this group would bond and work well together when the Meet and Greet was over.

Scott, Pearl, Jess, and I sat together at breakfast, discussing the upcoming workshops and why we had been sent to attend this particular seminar, at least in our opinion. Both Pearl and Jess were senior detectives in their units. Scott was his team's 'nerd.' I admitted I was the nerd on my squad and the newbie with a Master's in Criminal Psychology.

The workshop could have been boring as hell, but I found it fascinating. Not only were the experts doing the instructions knowledgeable, but the packets of information provided would be instrumental in sharing the data with my squad. The first workshop was over before I realized it, and I was stunned when I noticed almost two hours had passed.

There was a thirty-minute break before the next seminar. I checked my phone and was thrilled to see a message. "Hello, *mon cher*. Gotted you text. I worked all day Friday be home before nine. Maybe work Saturday on Sunday. Not know, maybe. You not home, so… Yes, I remember eat. No you worry. Have fun. Learn many things. I misses you, *je t'aime*."

Philippe's messages were always short, to the point, and in awful English, and they always made me smile.

"That's a happy smile," Pearl's Kathleen Turner voice said. "Girlfriend? Wife?"

I looked up from the phone and gave a lopsided grin, "Boyfriend, and hopefully husband soon!"

Pearl blinked, a slow smile spreading across her face, "Didn't see that one coming." She laughed.

I admitted that most people didn't, which worked perfectly with my job.

"Got a picture?"

Here was the tricky part. Although I didn't like it, not one bit, I had learned the need to 'preface' any photo before showing anyone a picture.

"Yeah, I do. But let me say something first. Jean-Philippe is tiny, like five feet…."

Pearl whistled and looked me up and down, shaking her head. "That's a huge difference. What are you, six-three, six-four?"

I cocked my head to the side and raised an eyebrow. "Six-four."

"My mom used to say it all evens out when you're lying down," Pearl gave a cocky grin.

I choked on a laugh and, after a thought, agreed completely.

"Also, Jean-Philippe's unquestionably beautiful, and most people are surprised. Are you ready?"

When Pearl nodded, I opened my photo file on the cell and searched for a recent one of the two of us dressed to the nines for a cousin's pre-Thanksgiving party. I was in one of those three-thousand-dollar suits, and Philippe was in an equally tailored suit he had rented. I had badgered Philippe into letting me buy one for him, but he had refused.

"Oh wow! I see what you mean. Umm, he looks like an elf," Pearl said, slapping her hand over her mouth as if she couldn't believe she had said that.

"It's okay. Really. He does. Even has pointed ears," I laughed, "Philippe's been asked to go around the pediatric ward at the local hospital in a few weeks to deliver holiday presents to the kids. He's excited. I want to go, but I'd have to go as the abominable snowman!"

Pearl said that was sweet and thought I, as a Yeti, would perfectly complement Philippe's elf.

Before walking in, I asked Pearl not to say anything about Philippe and was touched when she crossed her heart, leaned on her toes, and kissed my cheek. "I have a gay stepdaughter. I get it. No worries, dear!"

Lunch was a box affair with a hoagie, chips, a drink, and a cookie. Team eighteen sat in the lounge area, eating and discussing the two seminars that had just been completed.

There were two more workshops. One at one and one at three-fifteen. Afterward, we agreed to go to dinner and return to the hotel for drinks.

When I rechecked the phone at eight that evening, Philippe had left a message letting me know he was headed home to take a bath and go to bed. Working a nine-hour shift, standing on his feet, had wiped him out.

I laughed because Philippe used the word 'wipeded.' In person, I was allowed to correct Philippe.

When I asked about his English, Philippe explained that he spoke no English when he was brought back to the States. The 'asshat,' as we now called Philippe's stepfather, had kicked him out a few months after their return and two months after Philippe's fourteenth birthday.

Philippe had learned his English from the rent boys and girls who shared the blocks he worked on for the first two years. The johns never cared if he spoke English or not. Philippe confessed that some of the words he had been taught didn't mean what he thought, and on occasion, he had to learn the meaning of the words the hard way.

These tiny confessions always threw me for a loop, emotionally and sometimes literally knocking me on my ass. How Philippe became the caring, warm man he was was beyond my comprehension.

Saturday went by as quickly as Friday. Before we knew it, it was time to go to the banquet hall for the sit-down dinner and presentation. Over dessert, Pearl and I swapped contact information. Pearl invited Philippe and me to come and visit.

Throughout the evening, I continued to check my phone. Philippe had said he might work on Saturday, so perhaps he was pulling a double again. When there was no response on Philippe's cell, I called the house phone and left messages there.

Sunday morning, I was back in the hotel room at eleven and packing. Scott had left before the end of the morning wrap-up, leaving me to myself.

I tried both Philippe's cell and the house phone. I knew calling Philippe at work at this time could get him into trouble. It was the lunch hour on a Sunday, and I could wait until I got home.

Don't worry about something that's not there, I admonished myself.

At three in the afternoon, I walked into an empty apartment. Panic hit immediately, and I rushed to the shared closet to ensure his things were still there. They were, but I couldn't find Philippe's backpack, wallet, phone, or even his favorite sunglasses.

Looking at the old answering machine on the phone stand, I counted the times I had called the house in my head. There was one more than that number, and I stilled myself and hit play.

JEAN-PHILIPPE - THREE WEEKS LATER

I worked a week before the meeting with the literacy program's counselor. I was excited about the upcoming classes and happy that I had gotten a meeting. I turned down Tyler's offer of a ride when I went to the scheduled appointment with the counselor.

The woman smiled warmly as I knocked on her door. "I, Jean-Philippe Roche," I introduced myself before entering the cubical.

After a moment's hesitation, as she schooled her face from the surprise of seeing me, she introduced herself and asked me to sit down. I watched as she pulled up something on her computer and reached for a file on her desk.

"How are you today, Mr. Roche?"

"Good, thanks you."

"Hmmm, well. As you know, we are part of the Community College system here in our fine city. We've reviewed your application and are happy to offer you a spot in our program starting in January. Are you interested?"

I puffed up like a peacock and told the woman I was most definitely interested. She told me I would need to come in next week with a one-hundred-and-fifty-dollar deposit on the class. The balance was required to be paid a week before the classes start, which would be the fifteenth of January.

The classes were Monday through Friday from eight to ten. The small classes focused on speaking and reading and would teach essential writing skills. If I had any questions, I could contact her anytime. The counselor gave me her card.

I left the counselor's office feeling as tall as Tyler Braxton.

There was another appointment that I hadn't told Tyler about.

When I was fifteen, I started taking guitar lessons.

On the street where I worked, a music store offered classes. I had saved enough money and bought a guitar at the pawnshop. After almost two years, my teacher told me he couldn't teach me anymore. At first, I thought the man had learned I was a prostitute and was turning me away.

That hadn't been the case. I, according to the teacher, was a bit of a prodigy. I knew I was doing more than picking at the strings. It always sounded good to me, but a prodigy? Instead, the teacher gave me a card and told me to contact the man on the card.

Dr. Federico Greco was an accomplished classical guitarist and the conductor of one of the city's award-winning symphony orchestras. Since I had placed that call, except for the two weeks I had been in the hospital and recovering, I worked with Greco.

Greco had asked me to come by as he needed to discuss something. I was afraid my beloved teacher would tell me he could no longer take the time to work with me.

That was not what happened.

Two of the three scores of music I had been working on for the past seven months had been the guitar part for Rodrigo's Concierto de Aranjuez and Messa Flamenca. Federico Greco had asked me to be the guest guitarist for an upcoming benefit concert. Greco assured me I was up to the task, would play beautifully, and to trust my teacher.

I accepted the offer. There would be two weeks of rehearsals with the city orchestra. By the time it was performance time, Greco had assured me I would be fine. And I was expected to continue coming to my bi-weekly classes.

I left Greco's office with the complete orchestration for both scores tucked inside my jacket. I had felt as tall and big as Tyler after leaving the counselor's office; now, I was walking on air.

When I arrived back at the apartment, Tyler wasn't there. It was not a surprise as Tyler had started his job and, most days, left the house at six and was home by six in the evening. I couldn't believe my life now. My beautiful giant had opened his home, then his heart, and most definitely his bed.

---

[1] Love Behind the Lies – O'Connor Sister Trilogy

The Sunday after my birthday, Tyler had insisted I move all of my things, the few things I had, into his room. Every night, I shared Tyler's king-sized bed. We had taken our time to learn about each other's bodies and what we liked and didn't like.

I told Tyler what I had heard the day of my birthday. Tyler blushed, looked ashamed, and confessed that particular 'friend' liked rough sex. Tyler admitted he did as well, but not all the time. Tyler also acknowledged seeing what Bernard had done to me and why he hadn't stopped it. For that, not stopping, Tyler would go to his grave, hating himself for letting anyone hurt me.

I had crawled into his lap and held him, letting Tyler know it was alright and I was not mad.

After moving into Tyler's bed, he started calling me his boy-friend. I had started using the French for 'my dear,' which was the same as telling Tyler I loved him.

It was now two weeks since I got my driver's license. It had taken me another week to feel comfortable driving, but the route to and from work was almost a straight shot. Tyler liked that I wasn't tak-ing the bus. I had to admit to enjoying the security of not having to wait for the bus, especially when I worked nights.

Thursday afternoon, Tyler had left for a work conference. He had been excited, feeling his boss had shown confidence by sending him. Since Tyler was gone, I agreed to work late on Friday.

Before I moved in with Tyler, I worked many long shifts. I needed the money, and even though I tried to save some cash, I was always living paycheck to paycheck. Javier made sure I would get out early enough to catch the buses.

Living with Tyler had changed some of that. I helped out when I could. I bought groceries, and even though Tyler had a housekeep-er show up every other week, I did my best to keep the house clean. I wouldn't accept money for gas and even tried to get Tyler to take payment for the car insurance, which he refused.

So, I cooked, cleaned, and did what I could, but I was mostly there for Tyler when he got home.

"You better get going!" The evening back-of-the-house manager called out that Friday night.

It was almost eight, and I was exhausted. It had been a while since I had worked a shift like today. Javier didn't let me do it often, but he had allowed it because Tyler was out of town.

"Oui. I leaved now!" I lifted a hand to wave on my way to clock out. The line cook had offered me something to take home for din-ner, but I just wanted to get home, take a hot bath, and sleep.

The manager walked me to the car, waited until I got in, and locked the doors before leaving. Don had threatened payback for getting fired, and the management just wanted to keep me safe. I appreciated the extra effort they put into that.

Before starting the car and pulling out, I emptied my pocket. I spilled the contents, wallet, and phone into the console between the seats and called Tyler. "Hello, mon cher. Gotted you text. I work all day now but in car for home. Maybe work tomorrow, Saturday on Sunday. Not know, maybe. You not home, so… Yes, I remember to eat. You no worry. Have fun. Learn many things. I miss you, je t'aime."

I wasn't going to work either day, but if Tyler thought I was, he wouldn't worry about me being alone. Tyler worried too much.

Putting the phone back in the console, I headed home. Five miles from the apartment, red and blue lights flashed in the rearview mirror. I looked to make sure the lights were on, but they came on automatically when it became dark. I wasn't speeding, and as it was a straight shot until I was almost to the apartment, I knew I hadn't made an illegal turn or even run a red light.

It didn't matter. Maybe there was a taillight out.

I pulled over and rolled down the window, letting the cold air fill the warm cab. Tyler had told me to keep my hands on the steering wheel if I ever got pulled over. I would, but I took a second to put my wallet in one hand and the registration and insurance cards in the other and waited.

When the light from a flashlight filled the car, I squinted and looked out the window. "Quoi?" escaped my lips at the sight of a gun pointing at my head.

"Get out of the car," The officer ordered.

I didn't move fast enough for the man. The door was wrenched open before I could put down the wallet and insurance card, and I was hauled out of the car. I started to speak but was thrown face down into the dirty snow at the side of the road and had a knee placed on the small of my back. I turned my head, spitting the dirty snow out of my mouth, and asked, "Quoi? What?"

"Don't play dumb with me," the officer said while he cuffed me and then yanked me to my feet. "Fuck, you aren't even old enough to drive. Gonna throw you under the jail by the time they're done with you."

"What I do?"

The officer shook me like a rag doll and shoved me hard against the car. "First, you're driving a stolen vehicle. Secondly, you're in possession of a fake driver's license. I bet your visa has expired, and you're here illegally, so yeah, you're fucked."

"No, I, my friend, his car. I drive. I no stealed. I have driver's licenses for wallet, you look, yes. I twenty-two. I America."

"Sure you are," the man snarled as he opened the door and threw me into the back of his cruiser.

I watched from the back seat as the officer turned off my car, pulled my backpack out, secured the car, and pocketed the keys. The officer returned to his car. I listened as he called for a tow truck to take the vehicle to impound, confirming that the perpetrator who stole the car was in custody.

"I no steal," I tried again.

"I'd shut your fucking little mouth if I were you," He warned.

We waited until the tow truck arrived and hitched the car before driving off.

I was scared. I had never been arrested. Not in all the time I worked on the streets or at the agency. My hands were cuffed behind my back, so I couldn't even wipe the cold dirt off my face.

Once at the station, I was dragged to a window, where all my possessions were taken and placed into a clear bag. Then, from there, I had photos taken and fingerprints scanned. Everyone talked around me, and no one would answer my questions.

"Are you sure he's over eighteen? Don't want to throw a kid in with that crowd." Another officer commented.

"Sure, don't let his fucking weird looks fool you. Twenty-two and breaking a shitload of laws." The officer who had pulled me over thrust me at the other man.

"Okay, if you say so. Come on, Casper. Got a nice warm place for you."

I, still in handcuffs, was led down a series of halls before being uncuffed and shoved into a cell with five huge and very drunk men.

Panicked, I reached for the officer's sleeve, "Phone call?"

"I'd let go of me unless you want to add assaulting an officer to the counts you already have. And yeah, you get a phone call in the morning if you're lucky."

I was not lucky.

Two men thought it would be fun to fuck around with an elf and roughed me up for several hours before someone checked. From there, I was taken to the station's first aid room to be cleaned up before being put in a different cell, this time with two men who bragged they had robbed a liquor store.

They didn't hurt me, but one of the men pulled me to the cot and covered me with his body until he fell asleep. When the man rolled off, I crawled to the floor and got under the cot.

Saturday, I thought it was Saturday, I had been put into a room and was questioned about stealing the car, having a fake driver's license, and resisting arrest. All I could do was shake my head in denial. If that hadn't been bad enough, the USCIS or U.S. Citizenship and Immigration Services showed up later and threatened me with deportation. All the while, I repeatedly told them I was born in Buffalo, New York, and was an American citizen.

Not once had I been offered food or water. I had been allowed twice to use the restroom with a fat officer glaring at me through a doorless bathroom stall.

At four in the afternoon, I had been arraigned on four counts: illegally being in the country, car theft, resisting arrest, and driving with a counterfeit driver's license. I tried to explain to the judge that the car wasn't stolen and I had just passed my driver's test, but the public defender assigned to me told me to keep my mouth shut.

After the arraignment, I was led to a room, ordered to strip, and given prison attire. They had nothing to fit me, and the smallest pair of clothes was four times too big. I was told to roll the cuffs of the pants and the shirt sleeves. An officer, one I hadn't seen before, looked at me, and I begged again. "I call my friend. He help."

The officer shook his head but told me to write down the phone number and the friend's name, and he would call for me during his break.

Grateful for any help, I wrote Tyler's name and the house phone number on the sticky note the officer handed me with a thank you.

This time, the cell was jam-packed. Twenty men were waiting for transportation to the county jail.

"Damn," one man leered, "look what we have here. Come over here, and I'll keep you safe," He offered as he grabbed his crotch.

"Not today," the guard warned, pulled me out of the cell, dragged me to a bench on the outside of the lockup, and handcuffed me to a bar.

I closed my eyes and ignored the man who had moved to the corner to share with me everything he would do when he had the chance.

For some reason, I wasn't moved when the men, except for one old man, were led out late that evening. I stayed handcuffed to the outside of the cell and tried to sleep. When the station house became quieter and fewer officers were around, I was escorted to the restroom and then back to the bench.

"I'm hungry," I told the officer.

"Yeah, well, should have thought about that before you stole the car. What the fuck were you thinking, kid?"

I let the tears roll down my face and ignored the grumbling of my stomach.

When I opened my eyes, the station was busy again, and sunlight filled the space from the high-placed window. I was taken to the bathroom. When I returned, I was placed in the lock-up, which was packed again.

There was no offer of food or water.

I was starting to feel weak and sick. So, I curled up into a ball in the corner of the cell and wished I had died when Bernard and his friend tried to teach me to think I was better than I was.

One of the men, the old man left behind earlier, moved to sit beside me. "Having a tough time, hey kid?"

I didn't say anything.

"That's okay. You just get some rest. I'll sit here and keep everyone away from you. You look lost and exhausted." The man patted my arm and sighed, "I've been watching. They've treated you pretty badly. Someone's pissed at you. Sorry. Sleep! I've got your back."

I closed my eyes and welcomed oblivion.

TYLER

"Tyler, my name is William Towns. I'm an officer at the fourth precinct. We got an albino kid here who asked me to call you. He was arrested Friday night for illegally being in the country, car theft, resisting arrest, and driving on a counterfeit license. He said you would help if I called, and since I... Look," Towns dropped his voice to a whisper, "I don't think he's had food or water or even a phone call. I told him I'd call. If he's your friend, he's in a heap of trouble and needs some help."

I listened twice to the message before placing two calls.

I stood outside the station and waited for Robert Waldron, my attorney, and my cousin, Ashton Braxton, the Assistant Deputy Chief of Police. Waldron and Braxton had warned me to wait for them outside and not enter the building until they were there.

I knew it was good advice as I felt like tearing someone's head off. I just didn't know whose. I was relieved when Waldron showed up, and my cousin arrived in full police uniform a minute later. When I raised an eyebrow, Assistant Deputy Police Chief Braxton informed me it was his way of shaking the tree.

Together, we walked into the station house. Indeed, I could feel the anxiety spread through the place when we were noticed. The officer at the front desk almost knocked his chair to the floor when he stood up, "Assistant Deputy Braxton, how can I help you?"

"It seems," Even I tensed up at the tone of my cousin's words, "you have falsely arrested someone currently in your custody. Who's on duty?"

The officer squeaked out a name and offered to call back, to which Braxton declined the offer and headed to the back with Waldron and me in his wake. There was dead silence as we entered the back. The commanding officer of the hour practically ran to meet us.

"Good afternoon." Braxton's attitude implied nothing was good about it, "You have a Jean-Philippe Roche in custody, and I need him now!"

"Yes, sir. I, umm, I think he's in holding."

I barked out, "He's fucking where?"

My cousin put a hand up to try and stop me, but I headed to the back where the holding cell was. Pretty much all of the precinct stations were designed the same way. I knew where to go. Once I was by the holding cell desk, the officer on his feet looking worried, I bellowed, "Jean-Philippe!"

An old man stood from a corner, "That the kid with no color?"

"Where is he?" My voice dropped dangerously low.

"He's right here, son. I've been watching him since they threw him in last night, and I mean threw!" The old man glared at the guard and then back over his shoulder.

Braxton calmly told the guard to open the cell door. Once it was unlocked, I pushed into the cramped space and scooped Philippe into my arms.

"Let me look at him," the lawyer and my cousin said.

"He's beaten up," I shouted.

"He ain't been fed or given water since they brought him in Friday night. I've been here. I've seen it." the old man said.

"What you in for, old-timer," Braxton asked.

"Possession." The man smiled an almost toothless grin. "I do love my buzz!"

"Tyler, you here, maybe I dreamed," a thread of Philippe's voice drifted to my ears.

"Yes, sweetheart. I'm here." I kissed my lover's lips, not caring who saw me.

With Philippe in my arms, the commanding officers, Waldron, and I headed to a conference room. They all took seats at the table except me, who sat on the ratty sofa cradling Philippe.

"I want to know," Braxton started, "who reported the car stolen? Additionally, I want to see the dash and body cams of the arresting officer and the precinct CCTV. Thirdly, I want to know when it became a policy to deny a person in our care safety, food, water, and due process. I can assure you, Lieutenant, there will be heads rolling when this is done. Get me the files. Now!"

Philippe woke while the police spoke. "You come."

"As fast as I could." I wanted to say more, but Waldron asked Philippe to tell him what happened and to not forget any details.

With each word, I became more livid. My cousin looked as if steam would pour out of his ears as he read the report and shared the information with Waldron, including the visit from **USCIS**.

The caller reported a stolen vehicle down to the VIN number and provided the description of the person who stole it. The call was from a number both Ashton and I recognized. "I want you to file charges on that bastard." I jumped up and paced around the room.

"Look, Tyler. This will be investigated; I promise you that. I will back him if Mr. Roche wants to file charges against the department. If it can be proven that your father or mother placed that call, they will be dealt with."

"*Cher*, I sorry. This trouble of me." Philippe went silent, and I gathered him in my arms and walked out of the station.

Ashton showed up at the apartment several hours later with Philippe's belongings. "Where is he?" He asked, setting the backpack and a bag with Jean-Philippe's belongings on the table.

"Sleeping. I got him into the bath. He's pretty banged up. Then I got him to eat a little before he collapsed.

"I gotta ask. Not as your commanding officer but as a cousin. What is he to you?"

"I love him. I want to go to bed every night and wake up every morning with him. I want to love and make love to him every chance I get, and I want to spend my life with him." I stood tall and looked my cousin directly in his eyes.

"Okay. I get it. I'm sorry to tell you that your mother made the call. You have to decide what you want to do, and I will go along with your decision. Choose carefully, little cousin."

The wind was knocked out of me, and I slumped to the floor. "Mother?"

My cousin nodded.

"They wants best." Philippe's exhausted voice drifted into the room. He walked to stand before me, lifting my chin up to face him. "I no goods for you. Look happened. Bernard tell me I live better I deserve. He true, perhaps. You give me too much, I no worth. You no lose you family for me. You hate me for happen. You should."

Each word broke my heart, and I wept.

"Don't believe that, Jean-Philippe," I heard my cousin say. "You have been the best thing to happen to this man, ever. Don't you know that? Don't let anyone tell you differently. Tyler's mother can be a cold woman. But you are not a cold man. Look what your words did. This man loves you with all his heart. I know you heard him. I saw you standing there. Don't be afraid to let yourself love him back."

My long arms shot out and encircled Philippe, bringing him to me so I could rest my face on Philippe's chest and breathe in his scent. I felt Philippe kiss my head, then rest his cheek on my hair. "My love, I love you. Buts you think your future be with me. You lose your apartment, car, your money. They pull all if I stay. Think, *mon cher*, think."

That is when I started to laugh. Philippe tried to move away, but I didn't loosen my grip. "No, it's okay. Do you want to tell him, or should I," I asked Ashton?

Ashton sounded shocked when he admonished me, "You haven't told him? Why? That's an asshole move, considering what I heard your dad already pulled."

This time, Philippe did manage to get away and took several steps back from me.

"Jean-Philippe. The condo, the cars, the house in Hawaii, and all the money are mine. They can't touch it. That's what pisses them off. They have nothing to hold over my head. There is no threat of me losing anything. Okay. None!"

Philippe looked from me to Ashton and back, "You haved house on Hawaii?"

"Yeah, I was saving that information for our honeymoon." I reached out and took Philippe's hand.

"Honeymoons?"

"I'm leaving now. You need to let me know what you want to do. I think you should let me bring her up with charges. She won't get time, but it will embarrass her. And she'll have to pay a hefty fine. I'll give you two days." Ashton nodded, then pulled the door closed behind him.

Three hours later, I woke with Philippe in my arms and bed. Philippe was awake and looking up at me.

"Are you in too much pain," I asked, kissing Philippe's brow.

"I have badder. They no hurt me." I didn't like how Philippe accepted that it was okay for anyone to hurt him.

"You?" Philippe moved over to put his head on my chest. "What you do? She you mother."

I shrugged. I really didn't have a clue. Part of me wanted to hang her out to dry, another portion wanted to scream and yell in her face, and still, a tiny part just wanted to cry and ask her why.

From what my father had said, I knew what they thought of Jean-Philippe. Trying to buy him off was one thing. Having him falsely arrested and threatened with deportation was on a completely different level. A level I didn't know if I could forgive.

"Ashton said he'd give me a few days. I'll need to think about it. Right now, I'm just so fucking pissed. I want her in jail."

That made Philippe laugh, which made me laugh.

The laughter was good!

It was almost nine, and we were in the kitchen grazing when there was a knock on the door. I got up, looked at the monitor, and growled, "You've got to be fucking kidding me!"

"What?" Philippe moved to my side, taking my hand. "*Vous devez vous moquer de moi!*" Philippe repeated my words in French.

Not only was my father on the other side of the door, but my mother, Ashton, and another person I couldn't quite make out.

"I know you're standing right there, Tyler. Open the door." My father's base voice passed through the door.

"What do?" Philippe asked.

"Fuck, I don't know." I answered as my mother said, "We can hear you talking."

I watched Ashton disappear down the hallway. Then the cellphone charging on the island rang, and I walked over and glanced down. It was Ashton. Ashton had done me a solid. The least I could do was answer the phone.

"Please tell me this wasn't your idea, cousin."

The laughter on the other line was forced with no humor whatsoever. "No. The other man with us is their attorney. It's going to get ugly. I've already called Waldron. He's on his way."

I felt sick. What I had told Philippe was correct. The money and all my possessions were untouchable. In fact, the trust funds set up by my grandparents, my mother's parents, were ironclad. So, if they couldn't go after me, their only course would be to go after Philippe.

"What do I do, Ashton?"

Ashton advised me to let them in and invite them to sit. Do not talk to them or the attorney until Waldron was there. That went double for Philippe. I agreed, saying I would unlock the door, and Philippe and I would go to the bedroom. Ashton was to escort them in and send Waldron to the bedroom when he arrived.

I turned to Philippe, who looked stricken. "What happens?"

"It's 'What is happening,' and I don't know, but Ashton told us to go to the bedroom and wait. Go, and I'll be there in a minute." I waited until Philippe was in the bedroom, and the door closed before I unlocked the front door. I hurried to the bedroom, locking that door behind me.

"You safe, no?" Philippe asked when he dragged me to the bed and curled around me.

"*We* are safe. I just don't know what they're playing at. Listen. I love you. I want to spend my life with you. Nothing they can say or do will change that. Do you understand? Tell me you understand and believe that, Philippe. I need to hear you tell me."

"Tyler Braxton, I believed you. I trusts you. I loves you. I want you know I fight too. I fights all my lives. They no scared me. Scared me only for you!" Philippe climbed into my lap. "Tell me, you believe. I no child. I man. I fight *avec* you. You no fights alone."

I answered with a kiss that I hoped would tell Philippe everything he needed to know.

We took a quick shower and dressed in clean jeans and comfortable shirts. I had learned to braid Philippe's hair, so I took a few minutes to help with that. There was no way to hide the bruises on Philippe's face, and Philippe assured me he wanted my parents to see what had been done.

Waldron knocked on the door, and I let him into the bedroom. He wanted to see what they had up their sleeves first. "I looked over everything last week like you had asked. Your grandparent's legal team was one of the best in this part of the country. As you thought, it's untouchable. So, they're going to come at you from a different angle. Just keep your calm, okay, Tyler. You too, Philippe."

Once we agreed, the three of us left the bedroom with Waldron telling us to go out, sit, and not say a word.

Ashton leaned against the television cabinet with his legs crossed at the ankles. He was still in his uniform and looked as exhausted as I felt. Sitting on the sofa, my parents looked pissed that they had been forced to wait.

Philippe and I settled ourselves on the loveseat across from my parents. Philippe's legs weren't long enough to bend at the knee if he sat against the back of any recliner or couch. I watched as he curled up, sitting Akimbo. I smiled at this. I looked at my man, took his hand, kissed the small knuckles, and rested both on Philippe's thigh. Then I turned my gaze to my parents.

My father started to speak, but Ashton cleared his throat, straightened up, and moved an equal distance between the two parties. "I want to get this out first, and since everyone has their lawyers present..." he let the last hang for a second before continuing. "As of now, seven officers, including the Captain for Precinct 4, have been suspended until further notice."

I watched as my mother's eyes widened.

Ashton went on. "I'm confident that when the investigation is over, at least four, including the captain, will be terminated and lose their pension. Also, the public defender in the courtroom with you, Jean-Philippe, has been suspended. Mr. Pullman, the old man in the holding cell that kept people off Mr. Roche, is, in fact, the grandfather of the mayor's personal secretary. This incident has already hit the mayor's ears. Let me tell you, he is royally pissed."

"Because of that, the Mayor is insisting on a full investigation. Uncle Trenton. Aunt Veronica. There will be an investigation, and you will be called in for questioning. It is beyond me to stop at this point. If it is found, Aunt Veronica, you indeed did call in a false report of car theft, you will be fined at the very least. Additionally, as no officer followed regulations regarding Mr. Roche's arrest and processing, it is believed that someone pulled in a favor. It appears that the favor was to treat Mr. Roche in the worst possible way. Twice, this behavior put his life in danger."

My mom's mouth was opening and closing like a fish gasping for air. I could almost hear the words *'recalculating'* in her head as her eyes shifted around, trying to figure out how to weasel out of the mess she had created.

"My advice is to turn yourself in tomorrow morning. It will go easier on you if you do." Ashton finished.

"This is preposterous!" Trenton, my father, yelled and started to stand, but his attorney placed his hand on my father's shoulder and pressed him back down.

I watched as my mother looked over at my father and the attorney at his back before clearing her throat. "I might have done this the wrong way, Tyler. I never meant to get anyone fired. I'm sorry."

I almost believed what she said.

"You're apologizing to the wrong person, Mother."

She didn't like that. "Well. I am sorry."

Sorry, you didn't get rid of Philippe, I thought. Veronica Braxton was not about to apologize to Philippe, and I knew it.

"We're worried about your mental health, sweetheart."

Oh, no, she didn't!

Ashton, who had kept a neutral distance, moved to stand beside Waldron, who was standing behind Philippe and me.

"I assure you, Mrs. Braxton," Ashton's voice was as cold as I had ever heard him, "the department had Tyler evaluated completely before he could return to work. As required, he met the department's psychiatrist for ten visits before Dr. Westheimer signed off. He has a clean slate and does not have any emotional, mental, or physical issues. If needed, the entire Boston Police Department will stand behind this fact and him. I would try another tack."

When my mother started to speak again, my dad put a hand on her knee. "I'm sorry this was done, but again, we are concerned for you. This," my father's eyes drifted to my hand in Philippe's, "is just so out of character for you."

I laughed. It startled my parents, who looked at each other as if their worst fears were realized.

"Robert, let me know when I need to shut up, okay."

Robert Waldron leaned down and muttered he would slap the back of my head if the need arose.

"Mom. Dad. I've been fucking both women and men since I was fifteen. I've been in two serious relationships before Philippe. One was with Amanda Pollack. You remember her. Nice girl. The other was with Carlton Weems' grandson, Dean." That brought gasps from my mother and a horrified look from my father. "That doesn't include the three 'fuckbuddies' I've had for the last four years. Two women and a man, and sometimes, Mom, I fucked them all at the same time."

"I don't have to listen to this," my father stood.

"Sit the fuck down, Dad. You will listen because of what you've done. I want you to understand you don't know a goddamned thing about me."

"But you're so big. So manly," Mom hissed.

"Yeah, and girlfriends and boyfriends find that hot! You two need to decide what you want. I don't need anything from you. If I must choose between Jean-Philippe and you, you've made that choice easy."

"*Cher. Non.*" Philippe's soft voice caressed my ear.

I turned to Philippe, "Yes, love. Why would I want to have people in my life who behave with so little regard for others? At least seven, eight people will lose their jobs because of what she did. Those people have families, and soon they'll be unemployed. She knew enough about you to sic the **USCIS** on you. She knew you were a petite man, yet she had you thrown in the holding cell with twenty men, all twice your size. I can only imagine she hoped one of them would kill you."

There was a cry from my mother and cursing from my father at my words. "How can you think that, Tyler?"

I was calm when I looked at my mother. "Because everything you did was to get Philippe out of my life."

Philippe stood then and laid his hand on my cheek. "I haved thing for say."

Waldron nodded his go-ahead, and Philippe turned to my parents. "You no know me. I say this before at you, Mr. Braxton. I had two months of fourteen, my stepfather throwed me out. I in pajama. It January and snow. He told me wait to door. He bringed me sock, shoe, coat, glove, and hat. Only passports, paper for birth and photo in," Philippe turned to me and asked what the thing was on his jeans. I told him the word, "pocket."

"He shove all at me. He push me outside. I have two month of fourteen. My birthday November. I fourteen for only two month, on street. I have no money, nothing. I walk and walk. A man he see me. He spoke to me, but I no have English. I no know what he say, but he smile.

He take me to hotel. I think he say to the man, I his son. It nice hotel."

I retook Philippe's hand and squeezed it, "I'm here, Babe."

"I not have sex. I thirteen. That night, he have sex in me three time. He try be soft, it hurt. He hold me, I cry." Philippe didn't try to stop the tears or his voice's choked sound as he spoke. "Morning, I wake, my clothes nice fold on table, and hundred dollar wait to me."

"I teenage prostitute for fourteen to seventeen. I work sex agency. I had food. I have health. Yes, I beat, and yes, I go hurt. No one take care for me. I a boy. A scare boy! I took care for myself. I stop at twenty. I work. I wash dish because I no read or write. I go to school soon and learn, and I play guitar. I no trash! Tyler know this. He see me. I do nothing to take from him thing he not have. No, not, hmm, I not want hims things, only him. I hold job."

I was proud of Philippe as he puffed out his chest and lifted his chin, "You thinks me garbage, I good person. I save you son. It right thing do. I know he nevers comes back to me. I know he forgots me. I save him. It right thing do. I good person. You show you son, you not! I done." Philippe sat back down, hiding his face between my shoulder and the back of the couch.

There was silence in the room. I couldn't tell if what Philippe had said had touched either of my parents, but the attorney looked angry and sad at what he had heard.

I carefully moved Philippe to the side of the loveseat and stood, "Unless there is something else, I would appreciate it if the two of you would leave. If any communication is required, please contact Mr. Waldron; he can forward them to me." As I talked, I walked to the door and pulled it open, standing back just enough so no one could touch me.

Ashton and Waldron stayed after my parents and attorney left for a few more minutes.

"If you need anything other than what we discussed last week, Tyler, let me know," Waldron said on his way out.

"I can get you covered for tomorrow if you need to take the day off. Today was fucked eight ways to Sunday. I might need to take the day off myself." Ashton slapped me on the back as he neared the door.

"Nah, I'm good. Going to bed as soon as I lock up. Thanks again, cousin. Sorry, this all has become such a clusterfuck."

"Family sometimes sucks," Ashton agreed as he waved goodbye.

JEAN-PHILIPPE

I watched Tyler as he stood with his back to the living room and his head resting on the closed door.

"Tyler, *cher*, we go to bed." I moved to stand behind him, resting my hand on Tyler's waist.

Tyler turned and looked down at me with tears in his eyes, "I love you, Philippe. I am so sorry. So sorry."

I stepped into Tyler, speaking slowly. I wanted to get the words right, "What I do?"

I was lifted up, and Tyler pressed me to the wall. His mouth was rough on mine, and I returned the hurt hunger Tyler was giving.

"I need you, Babe, so bad. Please."

I understood the need behind the demand. I needed to be with Tyler as well. We both required to have something magnificent, bright, and sound.

"What do you want?"

I was carried to the bedroom and, with gentleness, laid on the bed. Tyler removed his clothes and then worked his magic until I was naked. Tyler was hard as he thrust his cock against mine.

"I want you in me," Tyler said before taking my hardness into his mouth. He sucked for a moment before getting off, moving to the nightstand to toss condoms and lube on the bed. "Now!"

Tyler got down on all fours and looked over his shoulder at me.

"Don't take your time, Babe. I can't wait."

I did as asked, taking only a moment to put on the condom and apply some lube to Tyler's tight hole before adding some over the condom. Without any warning, I slowly sank into Tyler.

I pulled out and slammed back in again and again. Leaning to my left just a little allowed me to reach around Tyler's wide hips and wrap my musician's fingers around Tyler's shaft.

As Tyler got louder, I slammed harder and stroked faster.

"Oh, fuck, Babe. I'm…I'm…ahhh!" Tyler roared as he came, and I shot my load an instant later.

Resting my cheek on Tyler's lower back to catch my breath, it dawned on me that Tyler was sobbing.

Pinching the base of my cock to keep the condom from coming off, I pulled out, tied and tossed the condom on the floor, and heaved Tyler onto his back. Carefully, I crawled onto Tyler's chest and laid my head against Tyler's.

"My love?" I kissed Tyler's face.

"I hurt, Philippe. They hurt me!"

"I know. I here!"

Tyler's arms wrapped around me and tightened. It was uncomfortable, but I didn't say a word.

"Don't leave me, Jean-Philippe. I know this is hard for you, but please. I think I would die. You ground me. You are what I didn't know I was missing." The confession shook my soul.

"*Jamais. Tu es mon coeur. Tu es mon esprit. Tu me donnes la force de vivre. Je vous aime! Toujours!*" I said, then translated it so Tyler knew precisely how I felt. "Never. You, my heart. You, my spirit. You give me strength live. I love you! Always!"

We didn't get out of bed to clean up. Tyler moved just enough for me to settle over him, not letting his arms fall away. "We'll get through this, I promise," Tyler whispered into my neck as we drifted to sleep.

I wanted to smash the clock when it went off at six the following day. Tyler didn't seem much happier with it going off as I was.

We both crawled out of bed. I picked up the tied-off and discarded condom and headed to the bathroom. We took turns using the toilet, shared the shower without messing around, and went about getting ready for our days.

Tyler took the time to strip the bed and toss the soiled sheets into the laundry hamper. He said something about remaking the bed later and then finished getting dressed. Tyler was going to skip his usual Monday morning workout, so we had coffee and croissants before he kissed me and wished me a good day.

I didn't have to be at work until ten today. I spent the time with the laundry and working on the concert pieces Greco had given me and another I had been working on. It was already into the first weeks of December, and rehearsals started the following Monday. Greco had given me the schedule, and today, I would have to work with Javier to set that up. I was excited to share that with Javier and get him and his wife tickets.

With everything that had happened, I had forgotten to tell Tyler. I would check when Tyler thought he would be home later today and fix a nice meal. It would be an excellent way to end the day and share the news.

Javier wasn't around when I walked into the back of the restaurant. I was about to remove my coat and hang it on the hook when Mr. Mitchell, the general manager, called out my name. "Can you come to my office?" He asked and turned around for me to follow.

I had a sinking feeling in my stomach as I stepped into the small office, and Mitchell closed the door. "Have a seat," he said, still not looking at me.

Mitchell sat at the desk, clasped his hands in front of him, and finally looked up. "Saturday, the police and **USCIS** showed up. They asked a lot of questions and shared a lot of disturbing information. You've been arrested for stealing a car, and there is some uncertainty regarding your immigration status. We try to hire only people legally able to work in this country, and at this moment, it seems you might not be."

I closed my eyes and listened. When it seemed Mitchell was done, I tried to explain.

Mitchell nodded and made appropriate noises, but I knew it was a lost cause.

"HR is unhappy with the attention this brought and has recommended we let you go. I know you've worked hard for us. You're a good employee, Jean-Philippe, but it's out of my hands. We will mail you your last check and the monies from tip share to your address on file. Sorry about this."

Mitchell stood, opened the door, and escorted me out of the back door into the alley.

I sat in the Honda for a few minutes. I was mad. Of course, I was. But I had money saved, a little over seven hundred dollars. I could wait until after the New Year to look for another job. This maybe wasn't a bad thing.

Well, it was a bad thing, but it would work out. It always did.

I stopped at the market for something nice for dinner and then headed home.

The Elf Who Tamed A Giant

TYLER

Clayton was waiting by my desk when I entered the space that held the squad. "Braxton, I need to speak to you for a minute. Come into my office. Close the door behind you."

Hearing your boss say those words was never good first thing in the morning. I did what I was asked and stood in front of Clayton's desk until I was told to have a seat.

"Word is you had one hell of a day yesterday." Clayton looked pointedly at me.

I didn't say anything but nodded, wanting Clayton to speak first.

Sensing this, Clayton nodded, saying, "It's a big fucking mess over at the 4th. I'm thinking a head or ten will roll before this is all done. I want to know what this is all about. I've heard bits and pieces, none I like, I can tell you. So, I'm coming straight to the horse."

I started with the most basic, "I'm not sure you are aware, sir, but I'm Bi and in a serious relationship with a man."

"I know this already."

Okay, I wasn't sure, but I continued.

"My boyfriend worked as a prostitute from the time he was fourteen until he was twenty. Got kicked out of his home for being gay two months after his fourteenth birthday."

Clayton was impassive, keeping a blank face as I spoke.

"Anyway, Philippe got out of the business. He's been working as a dishwasher for the last two years."

Clayton interrupted, "Didn't he recently get gang rap...beaten up by a john and his pals a few months ago."

I took a deep breath before explaining Philippe had been staying in a converted one-room maintenance space. The owner of the building, one of the men who had gang-raped, I used the word Clayton hadn't, was letting him stay there for service.

"So, still a prostitute!" Clayton was shaking his head in disgust. I wasn't sure I liked what was happening here.

I cleared my throat, "Anyway, my folks have freaked out. They didn't want to acknowledge I am Bi and thought that Philippe was trying to take advantage of me."

Again, Clayton interrupted, "Are you sure he isn't? Once a whore, always a whore."

That stopped me. I leaned back in the chair and looked at Clayton. I was good at my job, and now, now that I was paying attention, there was something off. The friendly tone was gone when I spoke again, "Excuse me, Sir. I am a thirty-year-old, educated officer with eight years under my belt. Four as an undercover officer. I'm good at reading people, Sir."

"Men often think more with their pricks than their brains sometimes, Braxton. We just want to make sure that isn't the case with you." Clayton's friendly banter evaporated, and I wondered who the fuck 'we' were.

"Where is this coming from, Sir?"

Clayton didn't answer for a beat, then looked down at his desk before looking at me. "I think until this mess is over, you need to stay clear of working any cases. We are going to suspend you with pay until this has been cleared. That should take less than a week. My suggestion to you, Braxton, is to go home and clean up the mess of your life. You need to get your head on straight. I'll have HR call you when it's clear for you to return to duty. Have a good day," And with that, I was dismissed.

I didn't go home, not right away. I needed to think, but not about my relationship with Jean-Philippe. That was currently the only thing that was solid in my life. I called to see if Steve was on duty. He wasn't, and we agreed to meet for an early lunch and a few beers.

Over Mexican food, I told Steve what my commanding officer had said.

"That is totally fucked up in so many ways. How did your folks get to Clayton?" Steve mused.

I confessed I had no idea, but this had my parent's fingerprints all over it.

"Resign!" Steve said over the rim of his beer mug.

"What?"

"Quit. Listen, you and I know we don't need to work a day in our life. Grandpa and Grandma set us up good. I work because I get bored. Same for you. If and when I find someone I want to settle down with, I might give it up, find something to do that's not dangerous, or live the country club life. God, that would suck. Scratch the country club. Shit, Tyler. You don't need all this bullshit. Uncle Trenton and Aunt Veronica have lost their fucking minds. How they think this isn't coming back on them is beyond my imagination."

I didn't say anything.

Steve was right. I didn't need the job. I could teach or go back to school. I had minored in history and English. I felt I could teach both. Hell, I could do anything I wanted. I could go off to Hawaii for months just to lie in the sun and think about it.

"Got ya thinking, didn't I?" Steve's voice filled the silence.

I nodded. This was an option I hadn't really thought about. I wanted to speak to Philippe but didn't want to scare him. Steve made me pay for our lunch and promised to come by in a few days and check up on Philippe and me. I told him to let me know, and we would grill some burgers or something.

It was two when I unlocked the door, Philippe's pale blue eyes going wide as he looked up at the clock he had hung on the kitchen wall.

"What are you doing home?" We asked over each other.

I walked over and kissed him. "Whatever you're making smells good."

"Beef Bourguignon. It a surprise." Philippe hopped onto the island and wrapped his arms and legs around me.

"I'm surprised. What you do home?"

Philippe kissed me hard, asking me to keep my temper, and told me he had been fired because of Friday.

I lifted my head and yelled, causing Philippe to flinch away. "Sorry. I've basically been fired too. It's stunk of Mom and Dad."

"Sorry, *cher.* What we do?" I didn't like the look of worried panic on Philippe's face.

"First, tell me what all this sheet music is doing. That's a lot of notes." I lifted Philippe off the island and, in one arm, took him to settle on the sofa.

I couldn't believe my ears, and I was so fucking proud. "Oh, my god, Babe. That's incredible. I am so proud of you. We need to get you a tux. You don't want a rented one. Not with your size and build.

We need a week or so to have it altered. We'll do that tomorrow."

Philippe was shaking his head. "I no have money for that. Rent one good."

It was time for me to have the same discussion I had with Steve.

"Okay, listen…" and then I told Philippe everything.

"So," Philippe said after listening, "you worked as police why you bore. You wealth and no need work ever."

I nodded, trying to read my lover's expression.

"If quit, what you did?"

That was an easy answer. "We would talk about it, but I was thinking about going and getting my teaching certificate. I'd like to teach, maybe. I think, anyway. There's a Magnet School not far from here." I took a minute to explain what a Magnet School was before continuing. "It's an LGBTQIA+ campus called The Harvey Milk Academy. A safe place for those kids to go. They even have a program for homeless kids, and I think it might fit me. Do you think that's stupid?"

"Who much money you talk for…about? I no want. I snoop." Philippe's wicked smile was turned on me.

"First, it's 'How much money are you talking about.' Okay, what if I tell you I could make love to you on every continent and most countries in Europe and Asia and still have enough to never work." I leaned over and pulled Philippe into my lap, nuzzling his neck before whispering a dollar figure that almost made Philippe fall off my lap.

"Now I sees you parent for crazy. I no want you money, Tyler. I want only you." The playfulness on Philippe's face had disappeared, and the earnest man I loved was there.

"I know, Babe. And that's why I'm going to marry you. Waldron already drew up a prenuptial. Don't want people to automatically assume you married me for my money. That way, you can always tell people that if you want and don't want to tell them to fuck off, you signed a crazy prenup. Actually, it's not that crazy, but that's between you and me."

"You want married me?"

I kissed him, "Marry you, and yes, this week. Unless you want something fancy, and that's fine too. I just want to know I'm yours."

Philippe laughed. "Tyler, *cher*. I your with no marriage. What prenup?"

Dinner was delicious. The hours' worth of dessert was fabulous!

The following day, Philippe was fitted for a tux. The tailor was almost drooling as he measured and marked the garment. "This is going to be so hot on you," the tailor had been one of my old boyfriends. It was nothing serious, but we had remained friends. "With his looks," Boone had looked over at me, "he is going to melt every pair of panties and jockey shorts for miles. Damn, Tyler, you did well!"

Boone promised he would have the Tux ready for a Friday fitting.

There had been a day's worth of discussion about last names. I wasn't sure if I wanted to hyphenate our last name, pick one name over the other, or decide on a new title altogether.

"Is Roche the asshat's last name?" I had asked.

"*Non*, my mother's. Asshat name Burgeon. He no wants me to have name. I good for that."

I thought about that. How would I feel if I took Philippe's last name? It was a beautiful name, and Tyler Hawthorne Roche had a nice ring. My parents would explode, which was on the plus side, but in reality, that had nothing to do with my decision.

"If I took the last name Roche, would you like that?"

Philippe looked at me briefly before answering, "Yes, but what *you* want, Tyler?"

In the end, we decided to go with Roche. It honored Philippe's mother, and my middle name already honored my maternal grandparents.

The name Braxton left a bad taste in my mouth.

I called Waldron to see what would be required for the name change. I was informed that all we needed to do was add the name in the appropriate space when filing the paperwork for the marriage license. Philippe and I went to the courthouse after the phone call and a late lunch. We filed the required documents for our marriage license. I paid an expediting fee to have the paperwork ready for us to pick up on Wednesday afternoon and an additional fee to keep it out of public records for six months.

Wednesday morning, we spent several hours signing the prenup Waldron had worked on the week before.

Thursday, we arrived at the courthouse at nine for our nine-thirty service. We agreed only that Steve, Javier, and Lola were witnesses and none of my family. There was some confusion when the official got a look at Philippe, but we were prepared with passports, driver's licenses, and IDs to prove his age. To my delight, Philippe had grown a full, well-trimmed beard. However, that didn't seem to work well when proving his age.

Jean-Philippe and I were pronounced husbands at nine-forty a.m., with matching platinum bands.

I surprised Philippe when we arrived at the Ritz-Carlton Hotel instead of going home.

JEAN-PHILIPPE

I snickered when Tyler lifted me off my feet and carried me across the threshold of the honeymoon suite. The bellhop placed the one small overnight bag on the bed and asked if there was anything else the newly married couple needed.

Tyler shifted his hold with practiced ease, so I was held with one massive arm as he handed the waiting man a fifty. "Thanks. I've got it from here."

I thought I heard the bellhop say, "I bet you do," under his breath, but I wasn't sure.

"So, Mr. Roche, would you like to have lunch, consummate our marriage, light snack, more consummating, a hot bath in the super-sized tub, dinner then still more consummating, or just get to the consummating?" Tyler asked, swinging me around to be in both of his arms.

"I think," I exaggerated my accent, "we consummate same like *lapins*...rabbit."

Tyler tossed me into the air with a whoop, "I like how you think."

He threw me onto the bed, went to double-check the lock, and slid the bar on the door. On his way back to the bed, Tyler stripped.

I started to pull off my shirt, but Tyler shook his head, "That's my job, husband."

I couldn't resist and said, "So, you haved job now? Nice."

I thought it would be frenzied, sex like starved men. I was wrong.

Tyler started kissing my stomach, running a trail from my navel to my mouth. He worked his way around my neck up to my ear. "Can I kiss you there," Tyler asked? He had never done that before. I thought he was afraid to do so as once, not long ago, I had been sold for just that.

"I am you, husband. Where you desire."

That was all the permission Tyler seemed to need. He ravished me. Kissing, licking, and nibbling until I was burning. My whimpers had become sobs by the time I was begging Tyler to take me.

"Do you want me," Tyler had questioned?

"Oui, mon Dieu, oui!" I cried, and Tyler chuckled.

I may have already been ready to combust, but Tyler was nowhere near done stoking the flame. I writhed as Tyler worried my body with teeth, tongue, and lips. Tyler's mouth pulled away for a moment. I thought I had been asked a question, but I wasn't sure. Tyler arranged my boneless body on the bed and leaned against the headboard before dragging me to his lap.

"Look at me," Tyler demanded.

I lifted my eyes to my husband, and the love in them took my breath away. Tyler's mouth found mine as he lifted me up and sat me slowly down over his waiting condom-covered cock.

I moaned, closing my eyes as Tyler filled me.

"Look at me," Tyler said again, and I lifted my eyes. "I want you to see me when I come and see your beautiful face when I make you come."

It was the last thing that was said as I found my rhythm. Our lovemaking was slow, never increasing in pace, not even when the eruption shook Tyler first, then me.

Like before, Tyler begged me not to move but pulled me against his chest.

After a moment, Tyler said. "For the rest of my life, I want to make sure you see, every day, that I love you. That I want you. And that you want me too."

That was something I could agree to without even thinking.

We showered and changed back into our jeans and winter shirts before going to the restaurant for lunch. Tyler asked over a grilled salmon and a fresh spring salad, as today was Thursday, if I had a lesson with Greco.

I nodded, speaking slowly, "Sorry, I can no not go."

Tyler smiled at me, took my hand, and grinned, "Well then. It's lucky I happened to pack your guitar and music in the truck. Let's go to the mall across the street. There is something I want to get, then I'll take you. Can I sit in?"

I was worried about the shopping trip but excited that Tyler wanted to sit in a lesson.

On Monday, we'd start rehearsals for the benefit concert in just over two weeks. After the show, there was one week until Christmas. It would be the first Christmas since I was four. The thought made me melancholy and happy at the same time.

I would present one of my gifts to Tyler on the evening of the concert. Although the score had been on paper for months, I had worked on that gift in earnest almost since I found Tyler in the freezing cold. Another gift, I had spent virtually all the money I had saved. The third was something dirty and for the bedroom, and I couldn't wait to give it to my husband.

The trip to the mall was for a new smartphone. Tyler had been threatening to get me one, and now he had. "You need a more reliable phone than the one you have." Tyler had insisted at my first objection. "Besides, I want to see your beautifully handsome face when I FaceTime you and your crap phone doesn't have FaceTime."

I held my tongue until we were in the parking garage. "Tyler, I no like you spend money for me."

Tyler stopped dead in his tracks and turned to look down at me. "Okay, I get it. I do. But here's the thing now, husband. Remember the prenup you signed?"

I nodded. The attorney, Mr. Waldron, had a French Language Interpreter read the document to me and even clarified words I hadn't understood.

"You don't have access to the bulk of my money. However, since nine-forty this morning, you are now rich. Maybe not wealthy, but rich is a good word. Tomorrow, we will go to the bank after we pick up your tux, and you will get a debit card issued for the checking accounts. Also, I've already added you to my five credit cards, and you should be getting them in a week or so." Tyler took my hand and continued the walk to the truck as he spoke.

"But I no wants money. I wants only you." I knew I sounded childish. But I didn't want to give Tyler's parents any ammunition to use against me, despite Tyler's promise that the prenup would make the point moot.

Tyler kissed me, opened the door, and waited until he was behind the wheel to carry on, "It's weird for you, Babe, I know. But you have money now, and I know you didn't marry me for it. I'm the only one you should worry about, and you don't have to worry about me."

It would take time, I knew. Already, there was more money in my wallet than I had ever had. Yesterday, I walked across the street from our apartment to Starbucks. I spent ten dollars on a caramel coffee and a pastry. Ten dollars! I'd never done that before. I had been almost drunk with excitement.

"*D'accord*. I understanded. You needs more patient for me. I lean...I will learn. Thank you for phone," I leaned over the console, kissed Tyler, then told him not to make me late for my guitar lesson.

TYLER

Yes, I was a giant of a man. Yes, I had worked undercover, infiltrating some of the most hardcore gangs in the city for four years. And yes, I could kick anyone's ass with one hand tied behind my back. However, it was all I could do right now not to sob at the breathtakingly beautiful music my husband was making.

Jean-Philippe had introduced me to Maestro Federico Greco as Tyler Roche, his husband. Greco had looked between us, six-four me and five-foot Philippe, and back again before bursting into laughter. "You are perfect, oh my god, perfect for each other. I can see that. Like good harmony." His Italian accent was thick with humor.

"You never told me you were married, Jean-Philippe," Greco had commented after he pulled himself together.

"Only today, Maestro. The mornings."

Greco looked up at me with a sly smile and asked, "So you took Jean-Philippe's name. What was it before?"

"Yes, sir. I did. Braxton was my maiden name; I guess you could say it that way. I decided to let my parents keep it." Even as I said the words, I was shocked at the hurt in my voice.

"Ah. Is your mother Veronica? You look like your father. Between you and me," Greco looked at Philippe, who was setting up for his lesson, "and you, Jean-Philippe. Veronica Braxton is a cold bitch! Pardon." There had been no regret on Federico Greco's face.

"You do not know the half of it, sir."

"Well. Congratulations to you, Tyler. *Il nostro angelo dotato*, our gifted angel, is a miracle and one of the most wonderful men I know. You are lucky to have found him and smart to marry him. *Meravigliosa!*"

"*Sono pronto, Maestro!*" Philippe said as he sat with his guitar in perfect Italian.

"So, you are."

There had been about twenty minutes of warm-up, or what I thought was warming up. Greco seemed harsh at times, then almost cooing the next. After that, Philippe played several songs I had never heard before. The first was slow and lyrical, the second so fast I could hardly see Philippe's fingers.

The two hours flew by. Philippe packed up, and I inquired about tickets. I wanted tickets for myself, Steve, Javier, and his wife. Greco assured me he would take care of everything and for me to text him the names so he could make the arrangements. "You will go to the will-call window, and they will have them there for you. Thanks for coming today, and you are always welcome."

Dinner had been provided by room service.

It had taken me some time, but I had been able to get Philippe to eat, well, maybe not full three meals a day, but better. He still ate like a bird, but I realized that was just Philippe and years of not having food or knowing when his next meal would be.

Dessert was carried to the bed by Philippe, who called over his shoulder for me to follow. "I have many thing I to do for strawberry and whipped creams."

I couldn't get to the bed fast enough.

Our lovemaking was not the slow, methodical pace earlier in the day. Philippe was a man on a mission, and I was the objective. Philippe was surprisingly strong at times, and tonight, he manhandled me in a way no one had before.

It was so fucking hot!

His words were French, and even though I didn't understand, I knew they were dirty, which was a turn-on. When Philippe finally filled me, I was in the same state as I had put Philippe in only hours before. I begged, pleaded, and wanted Philippe to end my suffering now. However, my *"le petit elfe"* was on a quest to destroy me with my life's most exquisitely fantastical sex.

Monday, Philippe drove off to the first of the week's rehearsals, and I went to the station. Clayton didn't seem surprised to see me when I stepped into the squad room.

"Morning, Braxton. How was your week? Get your head on straight?" These were Clayton's first words, which didn't bode well for either of us.

"It was actually a terrific week, sir." I poured on the charm. I needed to see how this was going to play out.

"Good. Good. Did you get that issue we discussed solved?"

I knew what Clayton was asking but decided to play it ignorant. "Issue, sir?"

Clayton's eyebrows raised, and the pleasant countenance slid off his face. "Don't play dumb with me, Braxton. You know damn good and well, we gave you the week off to get your shit together. Keeping that little whore in your life will drag you down in the gutter, and I thought you understood he needed to go."

The fact that Clayton had used, almost verbatim, words both my parents had used confirmed that one or both had Clayton doing their dirty work for them.

"I see," I said, taking a deep breath. "As you are referring to my boyfriend," Clayton didn't need to know I had married Philippe, "it seems to me we are at an impasse. I've given this a lot of thought, and," I pulled out my service revolver, removed the bullets, and placed both on Clayton's desk along with my badge, "I resign."

Clayton sputtered, "This is not what we were hoping for. You just can't throw away your career, Braxton. Not for some little whore. Think about what you're doing."

"I'll swing by Human Resources on my way home and complete the appropriate paperwork. Sorry you let my parents pull your strings, Clayton." I talked over Clayton, not really caring what he had to say at this point.

Clayton was shouting as I left the squad room. *'I had better get my ass back in here. I was going to be sorry. I needed to get my shit together.'*

I felt light. As if the weight of the world had been taken off my shoulders. Philippe calmed me and centered me like I had never been centered since I was a child with my maternal grandparents. Philippe made me feel like I didn't need to prove myself to everyone and certainly not to myself. For years, I lived on the edge because, well, what else was there? I knew my parents never approved of me being Bi. I needed to prove I was a man. Joining the police forces and working undercover proved that loving a man didn't make me less of one, regardless of what I had been taught.

Philippe had given me the subtle nudge to fully accept who I was. And that alone was enough to make me love Philippe with everything I had. By the time I had filled out and turned in my resignation paperwork, my phone was going crazy. It was no surprise that both my parents were calling. It took two hours before Waldron's number came up.

"Wow! You know how to cause a shit storm, don't you," Waldron had said when I answered the phone.

"It seems it doesn't take much to do that these days."

Waldron chuckled, "As you can imagine, I've heard from both your parents and, surprisingly, a Captain Clayton. They all tried to convince me that I needed to talk some sense into you. I assume you didn't talk about going back to school. Or the fact that Jean-Philippe is now your husband."

"Nah! No point," I laughed into the phone.

I could hear Waldron sigh, "Okay, kid. How do you want me to handle this?"

I wasn't sure, but it wasn't really my parent's business, and it certainly wasn't Clayton's. I really did want to go and get my teaching credentials. I had already put out feelers with a friend who worked at the Magnet School I had discussed with Philippe.

"I don't know why Clayton is involved, so I wouldn't worry about him," I said after thinking. "As far as my parents, I'm a thirty-year-old man. Damn, Robert, they're treating me like I'm a fucking ten-year-old having a tantrum. I am absolutely stunned, and frankly, I have no idea how to handle them. I've already told them to fuck off. What more can I do?"

I had a point, Waldron said, and suggested sending a text or letter or maybe even calling to let them know I was going back to school. "You don't need to tell them why or what for but give them something."

I said I would think about it, thanked Waldron for his help, and was sorry about the mess with my parents.

"It's what you pay me for, Tyler." And it was.

Philippe was home when I walked through the door.

"The phone, it go *crazy*." After kissing me, these were the first words out of Philippe's mouth.

I pulled a soda out of the fridge and told Philippe exactly why the phone was going crazy. Philippe listened. His face held a shocked and worried expression until the explanation was done.

"Why, boss. He is who? Cousin?"

"No. I just think, somehow, he's wrapped up with my parents. Also, now I'm beginning to think maybe the only reason I got that job was that my folks had something to do with it. That fucking pisses me off, Philippe."

It pissed off Philippe as well. But he led me to the sofa, climbed into my lap, and kissed me. "I thinked maybe it true. The first timed you dad he come to house, he say you have new job. He know before you. Anyways, you go start school on January likes me. Do what you wants, yes. You will more happy for that. I will more happy that you no a police. Too many danger."

I didn't correct Philippe's English; I just pulled him in for a kiss before switching subjects. "Teaching High School might be just as dangerous! How was rehearsal?"

Greco had warned the members of the orchestra about Philippe's looks. He was an albino. He was a small, handsome man with a rugged appearance and pointed ears, like an elf. They either hadn't believed the Maestro or couldn't comprehend what he described. Needless to say, it took almost twenty minutes for everyone to calm down so they could rehearse.

Afterward, Philippe smiled; everyone wanted to speak with him and take their photo.

"Does that bother you?" I worried.

"No, it fun. I thinks they know, hmm, thinked, I no real guitar play, but after today, that no question. I nervous like hell but excite. Maestro Greco said he might have someone who wanted me to work for a band or ensemble. What you thinked? I do, yes?" Philippe vibrated with excitement as he told me.

"I'm not surprised, and I think you should hear them out if that does happen. Babe, this is just so perfect for you." I pulled Philippe to me and hugged him, "Let's go out for dinner."

We went to the small Indian restaurant near the apartment. The staff knew us, and Philippe's appearance was not a surprise. Even some of the guests were regulars and didn't bother to stare.

It was nice.

JEAN-PHILIPPE

After rehearsal on Monday, Greco told me the tickets had been arranged for Tyler and three more with seats together. I thanked the Maestro and started packing up my things. Just as I was about to go out the stage door, Greco asked if I would be interested in meeting with someone about a professional gig. It wouldn't be until after the holiday. Greco wanted to be able to pass it on if I was interested.

Even though I would discuss it with Tyler, I told Greco I would happily meet the person.

I made it home forty minutes before Tyler.

We had rearranged the furniture in the office to make more floor space and had turned the room into my practice space. I usually put my things in there, but I put everything on the kitchen island today. While I cooked, I would work on music for the concert.

After years of living in spaces sometimes the size of the pantry in the kitchen, I was still getting used to all the room. Some days, I just couldn't believe this life was real. I would look at my left hand, see the platinum wedding band, and stop...just come to a complete stop. I never thought I would get out of where I had been.

Sure, I still couldn't read or write well in French and almost nothing in English. Until recently, I had had a job that paid okay, enough to keep me safe, somewhat considering Bernard, and paid for my guitar lessons and even the literacy program. Now I had a driver's license, a car to drive, more money than I could have ever imagined, and a man who loved and married me.

I gazed up to the ceiling and thanked my mother. It had taken her some time. Maybe she had been in purgatory all these years. However, I really didn't believe such things, but wherever she had been, her spirit was watching over me now.

I wiped my tears and went to make some coffee.

Before the coffee was started, the house phone began to ring. We had turned the volume down after Tyler's parent's last visit, so I didn't know who was leaving messages, but they were calling and leaving a lot. By the time Tyler walked into the house, there were fifteen.

I looked over as Tyler closed the door. He looked different, somehow. Taller, if that was possible. There was a lightness to him, one I hadn't seen before. I soon learned how Tyler's day had been. Also, now it was clear who all the calls were from. Tyler was excited to tender his resignation, and I shared my good news with my husband.

Rehearsals were exhilarating for me. To get to play with such talented musicians was unbelievable. Even more incredible was that those same musicians praised my skills. No one could believe I had picked up the guitar less than seven years ago.

On the third day of rehearsals, the schedule was set and shared with the musicians. There was a twelve-year-old concert pianist who would start the performance. After her, I would perform. After me, a nineteen-year-old tenor would take the stage. The orchestra would play three selections for the holiday season between each guest performer and have a brief intermission to reset the stage.

The pianist, the singer, and I would sit among the tux or evening gown-wearing members on the evening of the performance. I just hoped I wouldn't be sick.

"You are so freaking handsome. I'm not sure I should allow you out in public," Tyler's reflection said as he adjusted my bow tie.

I *was* stunning. Boone had tailored the suit perfectly. I had never worn something so expensive and something so perfectly fitted to me. I thought the difference between the black of the tuxedo and the white of my skin would be appalling, but it was exquisite. I had braided into my hair a black ribbon Boone had fashioned out of the same material as the pants and jacket.

At first, I tried to cover my ears but gave up when the tips kept sticking out.

"They just make you look hotter, Babe. Don't worry. People are going to be too mesmerized listening to you to notice your sexy pointed ears." Tyler had assured me with a kiss to my right ear.

I was shaking when we pulled up to the concert hall's rear entrance. Tyler helped me with my guitar and music before leaving me to park the truck and wait at the will-call window for Steve, Javier, and Lola.

An assistant met me just inside the door. She took my guitar, promising it would be on stage and set up when it was time. She showed me the 'green room' and my chair between the violin and cello sections.

Once done, she returned me to the 'green room' and left me with the pianist and the tenor. It was nice to know they were just as nervous and freaked out as I was. We have been working together over the last two weeks.

Maestro Greco came in before curtain time to give us a pep talk. We had been chosen because of our amazing talents. We had nothing to prove, and everyone - the musicians and the maestro - was proud of us. Oh, and 'break a leg!"

TYLER

Our seats were third-row center. I couldn't believe it, nor could the other three who had joined me. I had dressed in a suit, Steve looked uncomfortable in his, and Javier and his wife, Lola, were dressed in their Sunday finest.

"Jean-Philippe said he played the guitar, but he never told me he could *play* the guitar," Javier sounded somewhat hurt and amazed.

"Most people play the guitar. Jean-Philippe makes music. You are not going to believe it, Javier. I still can't."

We had arrived early, and the auditorium was still filling up when my parents stood, looking shocked to see me there.

"Oh, fuck," I said under my breath to Steve.

"I hope this doesn't get ugly." was my cousin's comment.

"I'm surprised to see you here, Tyler." My mother said, a smile plastered on her face and her eyes glancing at the bouquet of flowers in my lap.

"I suppose we are all surprised," I mimicked my mother's smile and tone before looking at my father.

My father looked dejected. I had never seen that expression on his face. Well, once, when my dad's mother passed. My parents acknowledged Steve warmly, and I introduced Javier and Lola Gutierrez.

"This benefit concert, I hear, has some phenomenal guest performers. I can't wait to hear them. Greco wouldn't let just anyone on that stage." My mother's voice pulled my attention back to her.

"When do you start school?" Dad asked.

"January, thanks for asking, Dad." I accepted the white flag. "Where are you sitting?"

My father pointed to one of the box seats on the second level. "We're going out for drinks afterward. You are all invited to join." There was a hint of hope in my father's offer. "Come backstage after the performance and let us know. Your mother is on the board and has to make an appearance."

I nodded.

"Oh, my god! We've got a clear shot of seeing Aunt Veronica's face when Jean-Philippe steps out onto the stage." Steve didn't attempt to keep the glee out of his voice.

Javier asked why, and I had no problem sharing every detail of my mother's evil deeds. Lola shot daggers at my mother in her box seat. Javier said something in Spanish that I didn't understand. I didn't need to know what the words meant to understand Javier was cursing.

By the time the lights went down, the auditorium was packed.

"Break a leg, Jean-Philippe. I love you," I whispered into the ether.

There was a brief introduction by an elegantly dressed emcee. She explained the charity and how grateful they were for the co-operation of Maestro Greco, the symphony orchestra, and the wonderfully talented guest performers, whose names were not mentioned. The printed program listed each guest performer as Pianist, Guitarist, and Tenor. There was applause for the charity and a louder one when Greco was introduced.

He stepped to center stage and bowed. "Ladies and Gentlemen, as you have just heard, we have three amazingly gifted guest performers tonight, along with the talented musicians of the Symphony Orchestra."

"It is my pleasure to introduce our first guest performer, Ms. Elizabeth Grander. Ms. Grander has been playing the piano since the tender age of three. We are indeed lucky that her grandmother had a piano in her home. Welcome to the stage, Ms. Grander." Greco turned to stage left and bowed as the twelve-year-old pianist made her way from the back of the orchestra to the baby grand waiting for her. She bowed to the Maestro, the orchestra, and the audience as the applause echoed in the grand hall.

With the orchestra accompaniment, Ms. Grander performed

Gershwin's _Rhapsody in Blue_, followed by Tchaikovsky's _Valse Caprice op. 4_. The audience was entranced. When the last note was played, they wildly rose in appreciation. Grander was in tears as she bowed again to the conductor, the orchestra, and the audience.

"Ladies and Gentlemen, Ms. Elizabeth Grander." Greco stepped from the podium, hugged the shaken girl, and walked her back to her seat near the percussion instruments.

Once the audience had taken their seats, the orchestra played three pieces from The Nutcracker before the curtain was drawn for a ten-minute intermission.

I felt as if I were going to pass out. I couldn't even begin to imagine how Philippe was feeling. As I glanced up at my parents, I was thankful that Philippe had no idea they were there. I was sure it wouldn't affect his performance, but Philippe didn't need the stress.

The curtain opened, and I held my breath.

"Ladies and Gentlemen, I am excited to introduce our next Guest. This young man has been playing the guitar for only seven years. Fortunately for me, he outgrew his first teacher, who contacted me and begged me to take over his training. Don't tell him, but he out-passed my skills years ago," laughter filled the space behind Greco and the audience.

I could see the affection in Greco's eyes. "It is my personal pleasure, and soon yours as well, to introduce the exceedingly talented Monsieur Jean-Philippe Roche."

I wanted to watch my husband walk across the stage, but my eyes had been on the box since Greco started his introduction. The look of disbelief was shocking. It flickered across my mother's face a second before the rage. My father's eyes drifted to me, giving me a sad smile.

I watched my mother stand, and my father reach up and pull her back to her seat. Priceless! As the commercial said.

Fortunately, Philippe couldn't see who was in the seats or the boxes where my parents sat. I allowed my eyes to go between Philippe and the box seats. As Philippe played, the expression on my mother's face seemed to change. There was begrudging awe underneath the anger.

When Philippe had finished his last piece, he stood and bowed to Greco, the orchestra, and the audience, who were again on their feet, clapping and yelling. I risked a glance at my mother. She looked as if she was crying.

The tenor received the same style of introduction as Grander and Philippe. He was equally as gifted as the previous two. When the tenor, Leroy Kilgore, was done taking his bows, Grander and Philippe returned to the front of the stage.

"It is not in the playbill; however, we have one more treat for you. Tonight will be the world premiere of a new arrangement. Music, lyrics, and orchestration by one of tonight's guest performers. Ladies and Gentlemen, we present Monsieur Jean-Philippe Roche's *A la Lumière de Son Amour*."

Grander took her place on the piano, which was wheeled back on stage. Philippe was placed between the podium and the Steinway and Kilgore between the two of them.

Quickly and intricately, Philippe's guitar started, soon joined by the piano, the strings, and finally, the full complement. For several minutes, the introduction built, and then suddenly, there was a breath's measurement of silence.

Then Kilgore's tenor filled the silence and then intertwined with the music.

The music brought tears to my eyes. It was dark, profound, and complete. Then, an unexpected light, a perfect soul's brightness, weaved its way into the music. The darkness shied away from the light, yet the light shined brighter until the dark was no more. Even without knowing the French lyrics, the music moved with the darkness and the light. It merged beautifully as they became something new. The music's illustration of the two souls was so faultless that the beautiful words were almost redundant.

When I looked up, Philippe's eyes were on me, and like my own face, tears ran down. Was that how Philippe saw me? The light that filled his darkness. How could it be when Philippe had filled the blackness in me?

"*Ceci est pour vous!*" The music had sighed, "This is for you!"

When everything had stopped, the people in the audience couldn't seem to move, as if the spell of the music and words still held them in their places.

Then...it was an eruption.

For ten minutes, the ovation lasted. I watched as Philippe deferred to all the other musicians on the stage, bowing low to each and then hugging them in a show of evident gratitude.

I turned to Javier and Lola. They had the expression of the proudest parents in the world on their tear-soaked faces. Even Steve was roughly clearing his throat and wiping his face with the back of his hand.

"Did you know?" Steve asked, and all I could do was shake my head.

I looked up at the box, and it was empty. *Please, God, don't let them make trouble*, I said.

125

JEAN-PHILIPPE

The reception room was crazy. It was a vast rectangular room usually set up for banquets. Tonight, the room was packed with the orchestra's musicians, well-wishers, and reporters from printed and television news. I stood between Grander and Kilgore, Greco at our backs, talking to reporters.

I tried to deflect some of the attention off myself onto the other two guest performers. Greco seemed to understand what I was attempting to do and maneuvered questions so Grander and Kilgore could have their spot in the limelight.

I could see Tyler, Steve, Javier, and Lola in my peripheral vision. Tyler and Lola had a bouquet of flowers in their arms, and the love on their faces bolstered me.

The *Q&A* lasted about ten minutes. When the reporters broke away to question others in the room, my '*petite entourage*' descended. Tyler picked me up off the floor as was his want and kissed me until my toes curled. I could hear Steve laugh and an 'ah' from Lola before my feet touched the floor.

Steve gave me an awkward one-armed hug, and Javier and Lola kissed and hugged me and told me they could not be prouder of me as if I were their son.

"You are, you know?" Javier's Spanish-flavored accent croaked, "We love you like a son. We are happy to have you in our lives, and we want you to think of us as your adopted parent."

Lola, who had been born in the Bronx and still had her heavy

New York accent, added, taking my hands in hers, "If you could do that, we would be so happy. Javi and I never had kids, but we'd love to have you think of us as yours." She sniffled and wiped her face.

I wrapped my arms around them, telling them I would love to be their family.

After about ten minutes, Lola and Javier excused themselves to go home, making me promise Tyler and I would come over for Christmas dinner.

Steve was chatting up a woman from the woodwind section, and I scanned the room until my eyes fell on Tyler, heading my way with two flutes of champagne.

"You are one sneaky little bastard, my love," Tyler said just before brushing his lips across mine.

"*Oui.*"

Tyler looked for a chair nearby and pulled it over to a side table before sitting down. Tyler did that a lot, especially if we both were standing. Sitting in a chair, Tyler and I were eye-to-eye. "How did you do that, and I not know? With both of us not working and in the house together?"

"I practice four-hour day, *cher*. You hear music, you no how, hmmm, way, hmmm…I am tired. You no know whatever music I play. So, Tyler, it easy." I smiled over my champagne glass and then took a gulp.

"Okay, I'm not doubting you. I am totally fucking amazed. I can't even hum in tune, and you wrote the music and the words, then made it all work with every instrument in that orchestra. How does a mind work like that?" Tyler was obviously impressed, but more than that, he was full of pride.

The sound of a throat being cleared pulled my attention up and into the face of Braxton Senior. He looked from his son to me and back to his son, and Tyler slowly vacated the chair.

I looked at the two men. It was like looking at majestic mountain peaks, one worn and weathered by time, the other sharp and just beginning.

"Dad," Tyler's voice was neutral.

Trenton didn't speak but took Tyler's chair and looked at me. Trenton held out his enormous paw, and I hesitantly took it. Trenton's grip was firm but gentle. He turned his attention to me and spoke, "You are one talented young man, Jean-Philippe. What I heard tonight amazed me. Thank you for sharing your gift with us."

As the man added his other hand, Tyler's father held my slender hand and said, "I am sorry. I cannot tell you how sorry I am. I see how happy Tyler is, and really," Trenton looked up at his son, "that's all that matters. I want to give you a bit of advice, Philippe. I wouldn't blame you for telling me to go jump off a bridge, but I think this is important for you to hear. Don't let Veronica bully you. She's good at it," Trenton chuckled and smiled when Tyler laughed too. "We all have things in our past we aren't always proud of. But the past is the past, right?"

My nod was what Braxton was waiting for.

"Good. Good," Trenton cleared his throat and stood, still with my hand in his. "You're a good man, son."

I watched as the elder Braxton turned to Tyler. "Your mom has a headache, not surprisingly. I've missed you, son." Trenton took Tyler into his arms and kissed his temple. "I've missed you."

I looked around and spied Veronica Braxton near the door, glaring between her husband, me, and then at Tyler and back. When she noticed me watching her, she visibly stiffened her spine and turned her back on us.

"Merry Christmas, you two. I'm not going to see you, I'm sure. Not this year anyway. With any luck, all this crap with be behind us next Christmas," Trenton winked at me and headed to join his wife.

We stayed another two hours.

Two reporters took half that time asking how I knew I could play the guitar. Greco and I had worked over the last few weeks on the best way to answer questions that might pop up. I was ready, even when the questions touched on sensitive subjects.

When asked about my love of the guitar, I had admitted that I thought I remembered my mother, who had passed when I was four, playing the guitar and singing. Although it might be only my imagination, I clung to it as one of my only memories of my mother.

When asked about my life, I told in the most general way that I had been born in Buffalo, New York, but returned to my parent's native France at six weeks old. My stepfather and I returned to the US when I was thirteen. When asked about school, I lied and informed the reporter I had been homeschooled.

Greco had hovered near the reporters and me as they asked their questions. He used his station as a buffer, moving the questions to a specific topic when needed. When the reporters left, Greco congratulated me on giving a great interview and promised more would be in my future.

When we finally arrived home, I stripped off my clothes and curled up naked next to Tyler before passing out.

It was almost eleven the following day when I stumbled into the kitchen. Steve, the woman I remember Steve talking to last night, Javier and Lola sat around the kitchen island. I was glad I had pulled on some pajama bottoms.

"You should woked me," I said as I stood on my toes, and Tyler leaned down to kiss me, then handed me a cup of coffee.

"It's all rather impromptu. Javier and Lola brought over something for lunch. And Steve and, oh, this is Marie, his girlfriend. They just dropped in." Tyler filled me in as I sipped my coffee and tried to wake up.

Everyone chatted around me as I finished my first cup of coffee and poured a second. "What do all your tattoos say," asked Marie.

Tyler looked freaked as I smiled and pointed to my arms. I read the words on my left, then my right. Explained that the pink ribbon was in memory of my mother. The sentences on my lower stomach and the tramp stamp on my back were not for the public. I looked up and winked at Tyler, who turned red with that pronouncement.

"Okay then. There's enough for everyone," Lola announced and told me to go finish getting dressed, and she would get everything ready.

While I was getting dressed after my shower, there was a knock on the door. "Are you decent?" It was Marie's voice.

I walked over and opened the door. "Yes. Only my hair. You in orchestra. You play violin? Did you know I was families?"

"No, not until last night. Steve said you were with his cousin. I'll braid it if you want. I always like doing that." She offered. She brushed out my hair and asked, "Okay, I'm dying to know about the other tattoos."

I had been a bit worried about that. I had seen the look on Marie's face when my eyes had shifted uncomfortably to Javier and Lola.

"Okay. I not say for Lola and Javier no like...Not like it. The front said, "Fuck You! And the back said, Fuck Me!"

Marie burst out laughing. "Oh my god, that's so perfect. Maybe I should get one of those. Well, not as a tramp stamp, but you know." She blushed and then finished braiding.

"When you tell Steve. Do at home. I tell Tyler I say to you the words. He no like it. I think Steve and Tyler is friends, yes. No only cousins, no?"

Marie patted my shoulder, announcing she was done, and turned me around. She was four or five inches taller than me, so I didn't have to strain my neck to look at her face. "I'll wait. And yeah, they are the only two who are the same age. The other cousins are all Braxtons. Also, they are the only grandchildren of Alistair and Beatrice Hawthorne. So, they're pretty tight."

Lunch was enchiladas, refried beans, and rice, which were delicious. I even asked Lola to teach me how to make the food. For most of my life, I had eaten what didn't need to be cooked or could be eaten out of a can. I tried to eat fruit whenever possible and vegetables.

Having the luxury of food was something I wouldn't take for granted any time soon.

JEAN-PHILIPPE

It was four in the morning, and I stood staring at the Christmas tree.

The weekend of the concert, we got the tree. It filled the living room corner up to the ceiling, and Tyler had made sure there were enough decorations and lights to light up the room like Times Square.

This week, the week of Christmas, I tried to control my emotions but failed. I didn't remember having a tree or even celebrating Christmas. My stepfather never had, and once I was on the street, Christmas was just another day to make money and survive. Twice when I lived in the Agency's apartment, the four kids sharing the place swapped simple gifts. There had been no tree or festive meal as we all had work that day.

Today, there would be both.

In addition to the two envelopes I had placed on the tree as Tyler's gifts, there were perhaps thirty more boxes, all shapes and with different colors of wrapping paper, that hadn't been there last night when we went to bed. A closer examination revealed all the boxes were from Santa and were addressed to Tyler, me, or both of us. I didn't remember Tyler getting out of bed, but maybe the two glasses of wine helped me sleep more soundly than usual.

I knew he was there before Tyler's arms wrapped around me. "I waked you?" I asked.

Tyler kissed the top of my head, saying, "No, Babe. I've been awake for a bit. Your excitement's rubbed off on me. Do you want to open a few packages? Not many, just a few." I laughed at the enthusiasm in Tyler's voice.

For my answer, I walked over to the tree. I selected one of the two envelopes from the pine needles and sat on the sofa. "Open this ones."

Tyler walked over to the tree, gazed at three envelopes I hadn't placed on the tree, picked one, and then sat next to me.

We swapped the envelopes, and after a short debate, we agreed to open the gifts simultaneously.

Inside my envelope was a handmade coupon redeemable for a weekend at Javier and Lola's for cooking lessons.

I watched Tyler as he ripped open his envelope and raised an eyebrow at the paper with one word artfully colored in rainbow colors, *souple*. He shook his head and lifted the paper to show me.

"What does it say? Am I going to have to learn French? I am, aren't I."

I crawled onto Tyler's lap. "Learned French be fun, yes. But I tell you word. It meaning best like 'bendy.'"

"Bendy?" The word hung briefly before Tyler's eyes widened, and his mouth formed a perfect O.

"I no tell you. I very, very bendy. I no ready to show. But no, I think you will life...live. You want me show you?" I kissed Tyler's jaw a second before I was gathered into my husband's arms and carted into the bedroom.

As we both were in pajama bottoms, it took only a second before we were naked.

Tyler placed the lube, condoms, and a few towels on the corner of the bed before he lowered his massive body over mine.

"Show me," he begged as he took my mouth.

We took no time at all to get each other incredibly turned on.

"Show me!" This time, it was a demand.

Tyler was ordered on his back. He moved so fast that he almost knocked me off the bed but caught me by the ankle before I tumbled off.

"Just since that. I show you very hard." I growled, but it sounded more like a purr.

"Fuck, ya!"

I took my time getting Tyler ready. Tyler's sweet hole was ravished with lips and tongue. Each time Tyler reached to take his swollen cock into his hands, I slapped them away with a *"Non, c'est le mien!"*

I finally slid into Tyler, stroking long and slow. I adjusted my position so my cock rubbed Tyler's prostate each time I bottomed out.

"You ready for me to show?" I asked.

Tyler merely snarled, his hands clutching the comforter on the bed.

A wicked smile spread across my face, and I relaxed, rounded my back, and took Tyler into my mouth.

"OH! MY! GOD!" Tyler shrieked, and it was the only sound he was able to make for the next several long minutes.

Tyler came so violently that I was afraid he had a heart attack, with me following quickly after. Tyler didn't move, well, other than his twitching cock and a muscle in his right pinky finger for a very long time.

Finally, "I love you. I love you. I love you. Marry me. Oh my god, you are…I am so fucking unworthy. Come here!"

Tyler dragged me up and onto his chest. It was a place I loved to be.

"That is the most beautiful, mind-altering, ball-busting thing I have ever experienced. I just have to find a way to do something like that for you. I can tell you now I'm not bendy, though." Tyler's voice was rough as he spoke.

I was quiet as Tyler rubbed my back with one hand and held my head with the other, applying kisses to my forehead.

"Tyler. You do for me is more. More for sex. More for a world to me. You do nothing never again but hold me same now, it enough. It enough," and tears spilled onto Tyler's chest.

TYLER

I slept until eight on Christmas morning. Philippe was sound asleep, but we had a busy morning, and as much as I dreaded it, I would have to wake my husband up. I carefully rolled out of bed and used the bathroom before heading for the kitchen. Breakfast in bed sounded like the perfect way to begin our Christmas day.

Forty minutes later, I carried a tray with two cloche-covered breakfast plates, coffee, and orange juice and called out Merry Christmas. Philippe must have been in the process of waking up because he sat up with a smile, rubbing his hands over his face.

While Philippe busied himself in the bathroom, I got another tray and set our breakfast up when Philippe emerged and crawled back up on the bed.

"Merry Christmas," I kissed Philippe, then handed him his coffee.

"Merry Christmas. What is breakfast?" Philippe sipped his coffee and looked at the covered plates.

With a flourish, I took the cloches off. Eggs, bacon, hash browns, and buttered toast were neatly arranged. On one of the trays was salt, pepper, and jelly for the bread.

"What times you up?"

I handed Philippe a knife and fork before answering. "About an hour ago. You were sleeping soundly. We have much to do today, so I thought this was the best way to wake you up."

Philippe raised an eyebrow, "You thinked food best way?" Tsking as he took a bite of his bacon.

"Well, maybe not the best, but I'm still wiped out from this morning. I see why you have kept this superpower to yourself until now. I was afraid I wouldn't even be able to get out of bed after that."

I watched as Philippe smiled his wicked little smile but didn't say anything as he dug into his breakfast. I followed suit.

After breakfast, we showered and dressed, then moved to the living room.

There was one envelope in the tree that was for both of us. I pulled it out, and we opened it. It was our last test results. We received a clean health bill, both HIV-free and since we were monogamous, we would no longer be using condoms. It was the perfect gift for us as a couple.

After that, I made two piles of gifts, one for each, and Philippe insisted I open all of my presents first. Most of the gifts from Santa were off Santa's naughty gift list. There were flavored lubes. A small number of toys Santa Tyler had been talked into buying, but actually wasn't sure what a few of them were for.

I received an envelope from Philippe with tickets for two people for five of my alma mater's upcoming home games.

"Oh Philippe, these are great. Thanks Babe," I moved over to thank Philippe with a kiss. "How did you know I liked Basketball?"

Philippe explained he had heard Steve and me talk about the games. Since I had had Steve over at least three times to watch the games, Philippe figured it was a good bet that, as a gift, it would be appreciated. "You know. I no must to go. Take Steve, good for me."

I knew Philippe didn't really understand any of the sports I enjoyed. I might take Philippe to one, but Steve would gladly go.

When it was Philippe's time to open his gifts, I was careful with their presentation order. First was Santa's 'you're nice when you're naughty' gifts. Then, in a specific order, I handed Philippe one present at a time. First were two pairs of short cargo pants, then three shirts. Finally, a wide-brim Panama hat and an economy-sized sunscreen bottle, SPF 80.

Philippe looked at me and pointed out the glass doors, "Cher, outside -2 C and snows. You can see, yes?"

I nodded, told him to wait, and handed him the last gift, an envelope. I held my breath as Philippe slowly opened the gift.

Inside the envelope were two first-class tickets to Oahu, leaving in two days, on the twenty-seventh.

"I've already planned for some late afternoon, early evening excursions. The pool is heated, and there is a covered cabana so you can swim during the day or after dark. We'll be there for ten days. If that's okay. If not, I can change the flights." I waited expectantly for Philippe to say something. He just kept looking from the tickets to me. "We'll be home about a week before our classes start, and you told me about your meeting with Greco and his associate isn't until the twentieth, so...."

"You best husband. I no wait, thank you." Philippe pulled me down for a kiss.

We were warming up to something more than a kiss when there was a knock on the door. I smiled and stood, adjusting myself as I walked to the door. When I saw who was on the other side, I turned and mouthed the word 'Dad' to Philippe.

"Merry Christmas, son," Dad said when I opened the door. My dad took me into his arms for a hard hug.

"Um, come in, Dad." I looked out in the hall, thinking my mother might be there, but she wasn't. I stepped back as Philippe joined me at the door.

Seeing my search, my dad said, "I snuck out. Told her I had forgotten something at the office. I just couldn't not come and see you. Not on Christmas." Dad pulled out two envelopes and handed one each to Philippe and me. "This is from me."

Inside the envelopes were gift certificates for a B&B in Key West, Florida. "They're open, so you can go anytime within the next year. You'll have to call to check for dates, but, umm, I thought you would enjoy that." His eyes shifted to Philippe, and a red tint covered his face. "Oh, maybe a week in the Florida sun isn't a good idea. Sorry, Jean-Philippe, I didn't think."

I watched as Philippe moved over to take my dad's hand in his, "No, Mr. Braxton. It perfects. Thanks you."

"It's Trenton or Dad," he offered as he leaned down and hugged Philippe. "Look, I got to go. I actually need to stop at the office. I purposely forgot one of your mom's gifts there. I've been planning this little clandestine meeting for a few weeks. Don't tell!" He smiled.

"Don't worry, Dad. Won't say a word." I smiled. It was nice that my dad was making an effort.

Just as he stepped out the door, Dad turned around. "I finally found out what one of your mom's problems is. She thinks that since Philippe turned you gay," my dad gave an eye roll at that, "she will never have grandkids. I tried to talk to her. I know Philippe, you didn't turn Tyler gay, and I also know gay couples have children all the time. I tried to tell her that, but you know how your mother is, Tyler. Just give her some time. Okay. Love you both, and Merry Christmas." Trenton Braxton gave a little wave and headed to the elevator.

"That was unexpected," I turned to Philippe, who was adding our gift certificates to the pile on the coffee table.

"You think. I no think is unexpected." Philippe carefully said, "I think you dad…your dad, he embarrassed little. He work change your mom, yes?" Philippe returned to me and wrapped his arms around my waist.

I leaned into the embrace. "I hope so, but I doubt it. But you know what?" I looked down as Philippe looked up and shook his head. "I don't really care, and I am not going to worry about it today, or maybe not even after we get back from our trip. Let's get ready to go to Javier and Lola's."

We had both done the shopping for Javier and Lola's holiday gifts. Philippe admitted he hadn't known much about Javier's personal life other than his marriage to Lola since they were teenagers. Lola had told us to come comfortable as the holiday dinner was about family, not showing off. "We'll be in stretch pants, sweaters, and socks, so come dressed appropriately," she had warned.

Philippe and I drove in the snow to the Gutierrez's home. Standard in the city's old neighborhoods, the small two-story duplex wore bright Christmas decorations next to the blue and white Hanukkah-colored decorations on the other half of the building. The house was a thirty-minute drive in the opposite direction from the restaurant where Philippe had worked.

We located a parking spot two blocks from the house and made our way back as the snow began to come down harder. When we arrived on the covered porch, we, and the packages we carried, were covered in about an inch of snow.

Philippe rang the doorbell. The front door flew open. A stranger pulled Philippe and me into the foyer as another took the packages from our arms. Still, another called out that Philippe and I had arrived. Lola came down the hallway in a dirty apron, leaned down to kiss Philippe and up to kiss me on the cheek, and told us to follow her.

I reached down and took Philippe's hand as we maneuvered through the narrow hallway into the heart of the house. Javier stood beside the stove, an equally messy apron around his waist. "Oh, good. We were worried about you making it in the snow. Don't worry. If it gets too bad, we have room for you to sleep. Hey, everyone, come meet the kids!" Javier had shouted.

I stood greeting Javier and Lola's extended family, knowing I would never remember anyone's name. While the introductions were going, Lola handed everyone, including the kids, name tags with each name printed in black ink. "There, now you'll know who we are." She nodded at a job well done and started speaking Spanish to a woman who looked enough like her to be a twin.

Not including Philippe and I, twenty-one family members were crammed into the house. Not all the people were family, I learned. Seven of the twenty-one were the Goldfarbs from the duplex next store. The Gutierrez and the Goldfarbs had been neighbors for almost thirty years and, although not blood-related, were family, nonetheless.

Everyone seemed to have a task, and the Roches were no exception. Under Goldie Goldfarb's instructions, Philippe, I, and five others were assigned to rearrange the living room. Once furniture had been pushed up against the walls, tables, and chairs were set up and arranged, and another team moved in to set the tables. The arrangement was placed so that one gigantic table took center stage in the living room, enough to seat everyone together.

"This very overwhelmed." Philippe's voice cut through the cacophony of noise.

I smiled at my husband, who looked shell-shocked and pasty despite his milk-white complexion. "Yes, it is a bit overwhelming, Babe."

The smile on my face grew wider as I heard Philippe repeat the words, a bit overwhelming.

God, I loved this man.

JEAN-PHILIPPE

I stood against the living room wall, Tyler's hand in mine, and watched as people I didn't know but who had treated me like family moved about. They had spoken to me as if they had known me all their lives and hadn't seen me in a year or two. Never had I been a part of something like I was experiencing in all my life.

I was honest when I applied for the job and answered Javier's questions. Javier had always treated me more than an employee. He had tucked me under his wing almost the first day I had begun to work washing dishes.

When I admitted to my potential boss that I could not read or write in English, Javier helped me fill out the application. But Javier had also asked why, and I had told him. There had been no scowl of disapproval or disgust on his face. In fact, Javier congratulated me for changing my situation and improving my life.

Javier had promised me that day to help me, and he had.

My arrangement with Bernard was the one thing I had never shared with Javier. That I couldn't do. In the hospital, Javier and Lola had told me I had a place with them. They would have provided me a safe, loving home if I had said something.

Now, I could see what they had offered. I wiped a tear off my face with the back of my hand. Sometimes, the journey was difficult and often painful, like living in the basement of Bernard's building. But had I not been there, I would not have been there to find Tyler. I had always believed things worked the way they did for a reason.

Even the years of selling my body and all the abuse given to me by johns and Bernard were worth the pain, struggle, and sacrifice to have Tyler in my life.

So, there was nothing to regret.

I would have no regrets.

A call to the kitchen had me putting a smile on my face and following the line. As people entered the kitchen, we were handed a bowl, plate, or serving dish and told to set it on the table. When the conga line of food was complete, Javier called everyone to take their place at the table.

Javier sat at the head of the table while Harold Goldfarb sat opposite. Lola had saved the chairs next to her for Tyler and me.

A hush fell on the crowd as Javier stood.

"Every year for over twenty-five years, we have gathered together as a family. Harold and Goldie were newlyweds just starting out, but look at them now. Three beautiful children and now grandchildren. Lola and I watched as they grew, left, and returned. Lila," Javier looked at the woman who was indeed Lola's twin sister, "you and Nolan and your kids have always been near, and for that, we thank the Lord. Jamie, thank you for being such a wonderful brother, and Gabi for putting up with his stupid face."

After the round of laughter quieted, Javier continued. "Today, we welcome two more to our family. As you all know, Jean-Philippe and I worked together for a few years. The first day I met him, I lost my heart. I came home and told Lola about this beautiful angel of a man who showed up at my door."

I couldn't stop the sob that coughed out at Javier's words.

Javier turned his face to me and smiled. "I told Lola I would do what I could to keep you safe. To help you in any way I could. You have been dear to Lola and me from almost the first day. We love you like a son and welcome you and your wonderful husband, Tyler, to our family. You two are never alone again. We are here."

Javier's voice choked as he spoke, and Lola reached over to take her husband's hand. I stood. "I say some word. Not English. French. You no know what mean, but..." I shook my head, cleared my throat, and spoke. *"Les anges se trouvent partout si seulement vous regardez. J'en ai trouvé beaucoup en si peu de temps. Javier et Lola, vous avez été mes anges même quand je ne savais pas que vous étiez là. Tyler, tu es l'ange qui m'a sauvé, m'a comblé d'amour et m'a donné une vie que je n'aurais jamais imaginé pouvoir avoir. Je vous aime tous!"[1]*

Angels are everywhere if only you look. I found so many in such a short time. Javier and Lola, you were my angels even when I didn't know you were there. Tyler, you are the angel who saved me, showered me with love, and gave me a life I never imagine I could have. I love you all!

A round of applause shook the room momentarily before Lola lifted a hand and said a blessing. The Gutierrez/Goldfarb family enjoyed the bounty of family, food, and love.

The seriousness of the beginning gave way to laughter. There were stories, family jokes, and loving teasing. Javier shared stories of things at work, and I added to them. No one seemed to struggle to understand my butchered English. And by design or neglect, my looks never once seemed to phase anyone.

For the first time, except when I was with Tyler, I was not seen as an oddity. That itself was one of the best gifts I received.

It was almost eleven when I snuggled up against Tyler. We hadn't been able to go home. The snow had continued to fall, burying the city in a thick blanket for Christmas. The holiday crowd was split, so half slept in spare rooms, on pallets and sofas at the Goldfarb's, while the rest at the Gutierrez's. Lola's sister and husband had one guest room, while Javier's brother and wife had the other. Grandkids and teenagers were in the finished basement, and Tyler and I were in the den.

"I tire. So much thing today." I kissed Tyler's chin and rested my head on his chest.

"I am tired too, and it was a busy day." Tyler agreed. "The roads should be cleared in the morning, and we'll head home after breakfast. I already promised Javier we would stay. Then I think we should go home, pack and spend the night at a hotel near the airport, so we don't have to worry about fighting traffic. What do you think?"

"It idea, good. Hmm, it good idea." I corrected myself.

"Yes, it is a good idea," Tyler pulled me tight, then pushed me back a few inches. "Look, if you don't want me to correct your English, I won't. It's kinda rude. I'm sorry if I'm upsetting you. I didn't think."

I smiled and shook my head. "No. I need. I say when you too much tell me."

"I'll try to not too much tell you!"

When we woke, Lola had produced new toothbrushes and travel-size tubes of toothpaste for Tyler and me. Then, we waited our turn to use the restroom to clean up after the night.

It was almost two when we stumbled into the apartment. We were full and exhausted. "I thinks maybe we must naps," I said after stepping out of the shower and pulling on sleeping pants.

"I think we need a nap also. Let's do that, then get up and pack." Tyler agreed.

I darkened the room with blackout blinds and crawled under the covers to nuzzle into Tyler. "You missed you family?" I spoke into the dark.

There was a long moment of quiet. I could feel Tyler breathing and knew he wasn't asleep, but I waited. As wonderful as it was, I was sure yesterday had been hard for Tyler. I couldn't be positive, but I didn't think the holidays were often not spent with the Braxton tribe. I hoped there would be more of these types of family events we could share between the Gutierrez and the Braxtons.

Time will tell.

"I do. It's not as crazy and fun as we had at Javier and Lola's, but it's what I've done all my life. I know we could have gone over to my cousins or even my aunt and uncles. However, I wanted you to have this time. Something that is ours." Tyler finally spoke, confirming what I had thought.

"Next years, Tyler, be better."

Tyler's laughter filled the darkness as his lips brushed across mine. "Yes, Next year will be better. Get some rest. We have a big day tomorrow."

I curled around the mountain of a man beside me and fell asleep.

TYLER

I was thankful we had decided to spend the night near the airport. As our plane was scheduled to take off just after seven a.m., we would need to be at the airport and check-in before five-thirty. Philippe and I arrived at the hotel after six the evening before. We checked in, ordered room service, and were in bed asleep by nine.

I had not changed my passport, although I had changed my driver's license. After being reminded by Waldron, I ensured the reservations were under Braxton and Roche. Check-in went quickly because we were flying first class. Once we passed through security, with only a minor delay as security freaked out a little at Philippe's ears, we headed to the first-class lounge to relax.

"What time we at Hawaii?" Philippe asked over his shoulder as he watched the planes take off and land.

"Almost 3 p.m. local time. The flight is over eleven hours, but we can nap if we want. The seats recline. We'll have breakfast and lunch on the plane. There are movies if you get bored. I think you can even set the language to French if you want." I watched Philippe's expression change to wonder at my words.

"Don't you remember your flight when you returned to the US?" I asked.

Philippe moved and sat next to me, wrapping his fingers around the coffee cup the hostess had just returned with.

"No, no really. He gives me sleep medical so I no bother he."

Philippe smiled at me from his cup.

I thought it was good that the asshole was dead, or I would have killed him.

I didn't know what to say and was given a reprieve as our flight was called for first-class boarding.

Watching Philippe explore the first-class cabin was more fun than I could have imagined. As soon as we were in our seats, a flight attendant came by to offer mimosas and drop off the breakfast menus. When Yvette heard Philippe's accent when he asked about the breakfast menu, she answered in French and gained a friend for life.

Each time Yvette stopped by, the two engaged in a lengthy discussion before the flight attendant had to leave to tend to other passengers. After breakfast, she showed Philippe how to change the language for the movies from English to French.

"You says this nice. Tyler, nice no word. Better for nice." Philippe leaned in and kissed me.

"Yes, Philippe, it is better for nice." I kissed my husband back and accepted my and Philippe's second mimosa.

After breakfast was cleaned up, I answered Philippe's question about what we would do for the ten days we'd be in Honolulu. I had made only two actual plans. One was a New Year's Eve Costume party that donated half the ticket price to a Hawaiian LGBTQIA+ youth program. Because of the party, I had asked a friend of a friend of a friend who owned a special effects/makeup/costume company that worked with the television and film industry in Hawaii for costumes to hook us up with outfits. I had agreed to do some publicity stills in place of a fee. I had to explain what that meant, but Philippe seemed to agree without hesitation.

We wouldn't have enough time to go to the house before Philippe and I would be required to be at the company providing our costumes. But I had arranged for Rafi Tiu, who worked for me, to take the bags, including Philippe's guitar, to the house, then come back and pick us up.

The other event was for a Luau on the evening of our seventh day. The rest of the time was open, and once settled, we could search for things we wanted to do or do nothing but relax.

Philippe leaned into my space and whispered, "We have many sex?" And added an eyebrow wiggle for effect.

"Yes, my love, we will have many sex."

We both napped and watched movies between breakfast and lunch. Yvette brought water and offered snacks and other drinks throughout the flight. While I had slept, Yvette and Philippe talked about things to do. She had even written some of her favorite things to do in French and English when she had downtime on the island. Philippe presented the list to me when I woke.

Over lunch, Philippe asked about the house.

The house had been remodeled several times since my grandparents built it in the late 70s. Steve and I had done a renovation six years ago when we inherited the property. My grandparents, and now Steve and I, had been the only owners. It was rented out for most of the year. Still, we had kept the months of January and September free. Often, together or separately, we spent time there.

Rafi Tiu picked us up at the airport. I greeted Rafi with a hug before introducing him to Jean-Philippe. Rafi covered his surprised look with a half-smile, then became the professional chauffeur he wasn't. Once everything was in the trunk, Rafi delivered us to *Na Mea Huna Inc*. He promised to return once everything was delivered to the house. Rafi also let me know that his parents, who ran the household, would be at the place around nine the following day. They wanted to give us time to recoup from the flight.

The offices of *Na Mea Huna Inc.*, or Hidden Things, Inc., were fifteen minutes from the airport in an area near one of the leading production studios. Once the car had pulled away, leaving Philippe and me outside the office, we walked into the building. A long hallway led from the front door to a dead end, a doorbell with a placard saying "Ring Me" over it.

Philippe had excused himself to the restroom near the front door, and I waited near the end of the hallway. When the entrance to the bathroom opened, I pushed the bell.

The door immediately opened, and a forty-something man dressed in a Hawaiian shirt and cargo shorts opened the door. He nodded and looked past my shoulder, watching Philippe coming up the hall. "Hey, kid. The makeup department is two buildings over." The man said to Philippe and then told me the actors got mixed up all the time.

"Umm, he's not an actor. That is my husband, Jean-Philippe, and I am Tyler Roche." I corrected the man and extended my hand.

"What?" The man distractedly pumped my hand and stared at Philippe.

"We're friends of Sean Laurie in Los Angeles. Sean talked to Alan about doing costumes for a New Year's Eve party." I pulled my hand from the man who was still watching Philippe.

"Oh, my lord. You're The Roches?" the man turned to look up at me. "I'm Alan. Sean told me you were big but failed to mention your husband. I'm sorry," Alan said, shaking Philippe's offered hand and stepping back to let us into the space behind the door.

I let Philippe enter before following and waited for Alan to join us. The space we had stepped into looked like a kid's Toyland fantasy. Costumes, props, makeup stations, and things I couldn't even name filled the warehouse-sized area.

Alan motioned us to follow and spoke over his shoulder, "Now I know why Sean told me something from Middle Earth or a Fae fantasy would be perfect for the two of you. My team has done some preliminary sketches and ideas."

Alan stopped at an area set up as a living room, motioned for us to have a seat, and called for Sally. A tall African-American woman stepped around the corner and abruptly stopped. "Whoa!" She gushed before apologizing and asking Alan what he needed.

"This is Tyler and Jean-Philippe Roche. Can you get the team working on the Rainbow Gala costumes to come here with their sketches?" She disappeared for a few minutes before returning with four people behind her. In Sally's wake, the two women and two men had the same expressions on their faces as she had.

"Okay, pull it together people. This is Tyler and Jean-Philippe Roche. We've been working on costumes based on Sean Laurie's suggestions. Now you all can see why. We're gonna need to do some tweaking, but we have several days to pull it together. Zeb, you have the sketches?"

A short, scruffy-looking man stepped forward and handed Alan a sketchbook. Alan turned a few pages before nodding and handing the book back to Zeb.

"This is what we've had in mind." Zeb put the opened book on the coffee table and pointed to the full-color drawing.

I heard Philippe gasp and looked over at him.

Philippe's hand was over his mouth, and his eyes were wide. "Babe?" I leaned over to put my hand on Philippe's thigh.

"*C'est beau, mon amour. C'est beau!*" Philippe's fingers traced the images tenderly. "Is beautiful."

I looked from Philippe to the sketch. The biggest of the characters was dressed as a soldier. Something between Tolkien and Game of Thrones. The look was rugged and almost brutal. However, it was not what drew my eyes to the page.

Next to the sword-wielding giant was a winged Fae. Its double set of wings, looking more like a dragonfly and less like a butterfly, seemed to flutter on the page. The Fae was dressed in delicate garments, a braided crown around its head. A long dagger was held by a belt matching the crown.

"You do this?" The wonder in Philippe's voice was not masked.

"Yeah, we can," Sally answered, her voice matching Philippe's.

There was a moment of silence before one of the others spoke, "I gotta ask, are your ears real?" Despite being almost as tall as me, the man's voice sounded like a kid on Christmas day.

Alan scolded the man, but Philippe laughed. "Yes. My ear. You touch…you wants touched?"

I whispered, 'Do you want to touch,' and Philippe corrected his wording.

After that, it was a Special Effect artist free-for-all. They touched Philippe's ears, running their fingers through his hair to get a better look. I, at first, wanted to protect my man, but Philippe's laughter as he answered questions soon helped me relax. We spent the next three hours being measured, having different color materials placed against our skin. I was olive-complected, but Philippe's ivory-white skin was more challenging to match.

Rue, one of the three women, asked how much skin Philippe was comfortable showing. Philippe agreed he was good with very little as long as his junk wasn't on display. The same questions were asked of me. My answer was the same. Although I did ask about tattoos.

Philippe and I pulled off our shirts and showed the team our tattoos. Zed told us they could cover the tattoos easily with special makeup if there was an issue. The other tats were visible, and Nils, the tech who created moving parts for costumes, gasped and turned bright red.

"*Alors, tu lis le français? Oui*?" Philippe asked, and Nils answered in English that he did read French.

I felt my blush crawl up my neck and onto my face as Nils' eyes moved from me to Philippe and back. I laughed as the man covered his red face and left the room.

"Nils red easiest." Philippe laughed.

Everyone looked at me as I translated, "Nils is easily embarrassed, I see."

It was after seven when Alan walked us out of the building. "You two need to show up about four, no make that three, on the thirty-first. If you can come by one time before that, maybe on the twenty-ninth, for a fitting. It'll give the team time to make any adjustments."

We promised to come by as asked and contact Alan to double-check the time for the first fitting.

I asked Rafi where a good place to pick up takeaway was on our way to the house on Hanapepe Loop. He recommended a food truck that would be on our way. Fifty minutes later, we pulled up to my 6-bedroom, 7-bath, and 6,312-square-foot home. Rafi wished us goodnight and told me the house had been opened, a few lights had been left on, and our luggage had been taken to the master suite.

We didn't stop inside, although I had to pull Philippe by his arm as he gawked at the house's interior as we made our way to the pool cabana. Setting the to-go containers on the table, I got Philippe to sit and eat.

"This room very bigged. Many peoples can lives here." Philippe commented after a few bites of our late dinner.

"Yeah. When my grandparents were alive, it was often full of family. After they were gone, only Steve and I ever came. Steve's brought a girlfriend or two. I've had a few friends come with me, but not many." I watched Philippe as I spoke. His face was still one of awe. "It's rented out most of the year like I said, and its location and size make it very profitable."

I couldn't even imagine how all this felt to Philippe. He had lived on the streets since he was barely fourteen, doing what he did to survive, then working as a dishwasher to scrape by. Now, he had money. Flown first class to spend ten days in a massive home on a cliffside on the Pacific.

It wasn't only the material things. From everything I had learned about Jean-Philippe's upbringing, he'd basically been hungry since he was four years old. I've never been hungry a day in my life. This made me love him more and want to make sure he wanted for nothing. But watching him, his pale blue eyes wide with wonder, I suddenly felt like the person I was, a pampered, wealthy man who had wanted for nothing.

"I love you, Jean-Philippe," I told him.

His eyes traveled from the view of the lush vegetation to my face. The smile on Philippe's face melted my heart.

"*Je t'aime mon mari!*" He said as he reached across the table to take my hand. "I loves you!"

We were done, or at least I was done with my dinner, so I moved to stand before my husband. "Let's go skinny dipping!" I suggested as I pulled off my shirt.

"What skinny dipping?" Philippe asked, and as I explained, a broad smile spread across his face.

When I was completely naked, I moved to the electrical panel and turned off all the lights on the terrace, including the ones in the pool. Once that was done, I ran and hurled myself into the deep end. When I popped out of the water, Philippe, beautifully naked, was sitting on the top step in the shallow end, his skin glowing in the moonlight.

"Come on. It's great," I slowly moved toward Philippe.

"I no swim," he told me, ducking his head so his hair covered his face.

That was okay. There was time enough to learn, but maybe tonight wasn't it. I swam between Philippe's legs, pushing them apart with my shoulders. I raised my head out of the water, smiled, took a deep breath, and slid under the water, and took Philippe's growing cock into my mouth.

When I came up for air, I lifted Philippe onto the pool's edge and continued. He was begging me to finish him when he came. I continued until every last drop he was giving me was gone, then I pulled him so the head of my dick was at his hole and slowly pushed in.

I wasn't gentle. But I made sure I wasn't hurting Philippe either. After I came, and while I was still in him, I pulled Philippe into the water, keeping one arm around his waist, and used the other to put his arms around my neck.

"Pool sexed. I liked," Philippe mumbled into my ear.

"I like any type of sex as long as it's with you," I kissed his cheek and then his lips while moving us around in the pool. "I'll teach you to swim if you want." I offered. After a time, I slid out of him but held on tight.

"You can teached me anythings," Philippe's voice was tired.

I walked us out of the pool and moved into the cabana for towels. I took a few minutes to dry off Philippe and myself before locating a blanket and moving us to one of the double reclining lounges. I tucked Philippe against me, covered us up, and kissed him goodnight.

JEAN-PHILIPPE

It was morning when I woke. We were outside on the surprisingly comfortable chaise under the roofed cabana. I was tucked up against Tyler and enjoyed the feel of him against me as he softly snored. His snoring mixed with the sound of waves as they crashed behind the wall of trees and bushes.

I needed to pee, but I wasn't about to move and wake him. Instead, I looked at where we were.

From the chaise, I could see into the blue of the sky that stretched over the Pacific. Behind us was the house. The walls facing the garden/pool area were made of glass and glass doors. They all seemed to be open to the breeze coming off the ocean. An outdoor kitchen was tucked against the far corner of the house, and I could see the indoor kitchen from where I lay.

"It's a lot." Tyler's sleepy voice rumbled.

"It is most beauty. I needs get to pee. Where is to go?"

"Come on. I'll show you." Tyler said, pulling me up as he stood. Naked, we headed to the opposite end of the house from the outdoor kitchen into a large open bedroom. "This is our room. The bathroom is through there.

When I came out, Tyler went in. I looked around the massive space. The king-size bed was centered in the middle of the room. Glass walls took up two sides, one facing the pool and the other a walled garden. Tyler had put our two cases on the bed, and I unzipped them and pulled out a pair of briefs before searching for the closet to put things away.

I was halfway done with my case when Tyler called me. He was standing in the walk-in shower, cock at full attention and wiggling his finger for me to join him. I don't even remember where I tossed my underwear.

Sometime later, we dressed and then put away our clothes. I was hungry and told Tyler. We had several options. One, there was a car in the garage, and we could drive somewhere to look for breakfast. Or, if I wanted to, the staff would be onsite in another thirty minutes, and we could have breakfast made for us.

I wanted to see the house and convinced Tyler that we should have breakfast at home, and later, he could drive us around so we could see what there was to see.

The tour started on the first floor. The ground level was smaller by a few hundred feet than the second floor. It housed the master suite, an expansive living room and dining room, a butler's pantry, and a kitchen set up to cook for forty or more people. A wide glassed fronted hallway ran the length of the second story. There were five bedrooms, which all faced the ocean and spilled out onto a deep balcony that overlooked the backyard.

The backyard housed the pool, the covered outdoor kitchen, an open-air cabana, and a pool house where the poolside bathrooms and outdoor showers were located.

A four-car garage housed the limo Rafi had been driving, a jeep, and a 1967 Lincoln Continental four-door convertible. Tyler told me the limo and jeep were for those renting the space. The convertible was his grandparents, and only he and Steve drove it. After breakfast, I was promised we could take the open-air Jeep or the Lincoln for our tour.

I thought maybe the Lincoln would be fun for another day, but the Jeep would be okay for my first outing. Unlike the big car, the Jeep had a canopy top that would provide me some shade to work with the SPF80.

After our tour was done, we returned to the cabana. Tyler pulled out a couple of water bottles from the refrigerator as I watched.

"You say staff that mean worker, corrected?" I asked.

"Yeah, there are four, sometimes more, depending on how many guests stay at the house. For us, while we're here, it's just the four. Moe and Lina have been with us for twenty years. Their two kids, who are in their late twenties by now, also work. Lina and Moe Tiu take care of the house. Lina cooks when I ask, and the kids take care of the outside. Also, Rafi Tiu, the oldest, drives the limo. He'll drive us the night of the New Year's party." That was a lot of information.

"They not happy you bringed husband?" That was my point to begin with.

"No, they're fine. I told Moe I was bringing my spouse, but they won't freak out or anything. Rafi's gay, so they're open-minded." Tyler leaned over and kissed me. "Don't worry."

Ten minutes later, four people walked out of the house and over to us. Tyler stood up and leaned down as Lina wrapped her arms around him and kissed him on the cheek. Moe hugged-slapped Tyler, and the two men, Paul and Makoa, followed their father's example.

I stood and waited.

The Tius were dark-complected, and Tyler was olive-complected. I was snow-white and must have looked alien with my white hair and ice-blue eyes, not to mention my ears, which I knew were sticking out from the side of my head.

"Moe. Lina. Paul. Makoa. I would like to introduce my husband, Jean-Philippe Roche. Mon chér, these are my Hawaiian family." They didn't move to shake my hand, but I watched as Lina said something to her husband in a language I didn't recognize.

"I am pleasure to meeted you," I finally said as the Tius didn't seem to know what to say.

Lina finally broke the silence by asking if I were a 'uhane,' a ghost.

I laughed, and everyone looked at me, "No. I albino. Very white! No am ghost."

"Are you French then?" Makoa asked, extending his hand to shake mine.

I told them I was an American but grew up in France as my parents were French.

Although everyone else seemed to relax, the men welcomed me with handshakes. Lina simply nodded, gave me a forced smile, and asked Tyler what we wanted for breakfast.

We went to the Pearl Harbor Memorial after breakfast. I didn't know the history as I hadn't learned it before I stopped going to school. I was honest with Tyler and told him I thought it was just a movie. As always, Tyler forgave my ignorance.

He had told me that the Tius would be gone when we got home and wouldn't return for a few days. Paul would come daily to clean the pool, but the rest, including Lina, wouldn't. I asked what he thought Lina's problem was, and he admitted he didn't know, but she was a native Hawaiian. Maybe there was some superstition, but Tyler had no idea.

We had dinner out, and when we got home, we locked all the doors, got naked, and spent the rest of the night making love, learning to swim, and raiding the refrigerator for snacks. At some point, we made it into the bedroom, although we left the doors open to listen to the sounds of the night and the ocean.

We drove back to Honolulu and Na Mea Huna Inc. the following day for a fitting with Alan and his crew. We were there for almost five hours. Alan provided lunch, but the rest of the time, we were part of creating something extraordinary.

Tyler's costume was basically a loincloth, covering most of his ass and all of his junk. The team provided samples of templates and drawings to illustrate the additional tattoos they would be adding or using to cover up Tyler's.

He was given a wig, styled to look like the barbarian had cut it himself.

My mouth watered at the sight of Tyler. He was incredibly sexy, and he wasn't even in full costume. We would have to be at the studio for six hours before we were delivered to the gala, but from what I could see, it would be worth it.

My outfit was a bit more complicated as I had two sets of wings attached via a harness to my back. The harness was covered with the material that was part of my clothing. Like Tyler, I was covered but just barely. Basically, my loincloth was material from the waist-band to my ankles. The material was light, sheer, and gossamer in its texture.

The top looked like strips of the same material woven together to cover as little skin as possible but to support the harness. The wings were fantastic, ethereal, and delicate. I had sleeves. Like the pants, they were strips of airy fabric from shoulder to cuffs. My hands were also covered. Built into the cover on my right hand was the mechanism for the wings.

The harness and the wings were surprisingly light, and Nils let us know the wings could be detached and reattached easily. That would allow me to be comfortable sitting in a car. Depending on how I moved my fingers, the wings would flutter, lay flat against my back, or spread out as if to lift me off the ground.

Unlike Tyler, all of my tattoos would be covered. Nothing could be done about the scars on my back. Sally said they added mystery to the character; I needn't worry.

We were exhausted when we got back to the house. Tyler fixed us something cold to drink, and after checking to make sure we wouldn't be bothered, I stripped and moved to sit in the shaded end of the pool. The afternoon and evening were spent naked and enjoying each other.

TYLER

I was just outside the kitchen listening to Jean-Philippe as he worked on the music Greco had suggested while on holiday. The sound of the classical guitar filled the backyard, and I smiled. As with everything he played, it was beautiful.

When the song ended, another was begun but abruptly halted. I started to get up to see what was going on but sat back down when I heard Lina's voice. "That is beautiful. It is a gift you have, Mr. Roche."

"I ams only Philippe. You calls me that, please." Philippe replied. "How are yous todays?"

"I am well, Philippe. What do you think of Hawaii? This is a beautiful place, no?"

"Everythings are beautiful. Tyler, he says for me it was yous and yous husbands who make this nice. Tyler, he says you as family. That nice for him." I could tell that Philippe was nervous as his speech was slow as he tried to find the words.

"I've known Tyler since he was a boy. He's a good man. I've also known his mother for a long time, Jean-Philippe." I didn't like what I was hearing, but I stayed seated. I needed to see how this was going to play out.

"Tyler, his mother, she no likes me. She has made bad things to happen. I know she loved her sons, but he is no child. He man. I do no bad thing for him. I loves him. He a good man!" Philippe's voice was firm.

"I'm not here to judge. I've seen how you look at that boy and how Tyler looks at you. I am happy for him, my Tyler. I think he's done well." There was the sound of a pot being put on the stove, and Lina said, "I heard you're a wonderful artist, and Mr. Trenton thinks you are the best man in the world for his son. That's all I need to know. What do you two want for lunch?"

Philippe told Lina to surprise us as we would eat anything, and music once again filled the air.

Over lunch, we decided to get a room at a hotel near the Gala. The hotel was across the street from the Gala's venue, and after we finished our lunch, I called and made reservations. I didn't want to feel rushed and didn't wish for Rafi to have to wait for us.

When we headed to *Na Mea Huna* Inc. this afternoon, we would check in at the hotel and leave a bag for tomorrow. Rafi would need to drop us off at *Na Mea Huna Inc.* after the hotel. We didn't need Rafi to wait as Alan promised we would be delivered to the Gala by nine.

Alan had asked Philippe to shave an hour before we were to be at the shop. They wanted a more ethereal look, and a beard wouldn't fit what they envisioned. He asked me not to shave on our first day in his shop. They wanted me as scruffy as possible and promised to fill in anything I needed.

Before leaving the house, I told Moe we wouldn't be back until late tomorrow afternoon or evening. We might even spend another night at the hotel. It just depended on how we felt.

Moe let me know that was fine. They would be here when we needed them.

It took about thirty minutes to check into our room. It wasn't fancy, but it did have a king-sized bed and a good-sized shower. Rafi waited for us, and once we were back down in the lobby, he delivered us to *Na Mea Huna Inc.* and made me promise to get pictures.

Philippe and I were not in the studio ten minutes before we were stripped down to our underwear. Philippe was given something that matched his skin to make him look naked but to cover his genitals. On the other hand, I was given a jockstrap matching my olive complexion. Once in our new undies, we were given robes and led to separate stations.

Everywhere I had a tattoo, I received body makeup. Once that was set, the tribal tattoos Alan and his team had shown me were applied. What amazed me was that I had one tattoo on my face, and when it was applied through the scruff, it looked as if it had always been there. The body makeup took several hours. While it dried, I was given a sandwich and a soda.

I asked how Philippe was doing and heard his voice from the

other side of the wall, letting me know they were turning the elf into a beautiful fairy.

We laughed.

It was funny.

Sally, who was in charge of my costume, told me what they were doing to Philippe. They wanted me to wait to see him until after his transformation and vice-versa. After the body artwork was done, I was dressed. I was certain the fabric wasn't animal pelts, but they looked as if I had killed a deer and used its hide to make the Tarzan-inspired loincloth.

Sally explained they wanted to emphasize the difference in our size and height; therefore, I was fitted with boots that stopped just below my knees. They were snug and added another two inches to my almost six-four frame. Philippe's sandals were flat, adding no height to his five-foot stature.

In addition to the boots, I was given a sling that held the sword. It must have been five feet long and deceptively light for something that looked real. Around my waist was a pouch, almost like a furry fanny pack, to which Sally had placed my wallet, keys, and a few other things inside and zipped it up. "We didn't give you any pockets, so this was our solution. Also, I put in the scabbard," Sally showed me a side pocket kept closed with what looked like bones, "a solution you two will need to wash off all the body makeup. It's not harsh, but you will have to scrub."

Finally, the wig was placed on my head, and I was posed in front of a covered mirror. With a flourish, Zeb pulled away the cover, and I stood looking at a cast member from *The Lord of the Rings*.

"Holy crap!" The words gushed out of me. I knew the *Na Mea Huna Inc.* team was good, but this was beyond anything I had expected.

"Yeah. We're good!" Sally said from behind me.

"Good isn't even close." I turned and looked down at Sally and her team. "Man, I hope you get a lot of publicity from this."

"Alan has that covered. Are you ready to see your King?"

I nodded and turned to face the end of the wall.

"Is the makeup waterproof? 'Cause I think I'm going to need it." I asked and was assured I would be fine.

Jean-Philippe was always beautiful. Even though his features were rugged, everything about him made him stunning. The being before me was not even human but a spirit.

It was The King of all the Fae!

With wings fluttering, the creature before me was fragile and, at the same time, fierce. Jean-Philippe's garments were as delicate as the four wings fluttering on his back. The scabbard sword was half the size of mine but looked as if it would slice a man in half with little effort.

Jean-Philippe's hair had been pulled up and back on his head and braided into a crown, with the gold filigree crown nestled in the strands. Makeup had been applied to his face to accent his cheekbones and the wideset of his eyes. When he smiled, small, pointed fangs brushed the top of his lip. His ears were prominently displayed, and he was as sexy as he was magical. It was weird to know this was my husband but not anyone I had seen before.

I had learned a line of French that I wanted to use when I saw Jean-Philippe in his costume, but the words I now said, with a bow, fit, "*Vous m'humiliez, mon Seigneur!*" 'You humble me, my Lord!'

"My servant, I am at your beck and call!'

Philippe's eyes lit up, and he gave me a regal nod before laughing and pulling me down for a kiss. "*Mon serviteur, je suis à votre entière disposition!*"[1] He said without translating and told me he would tell me later.

Alan came from somewhere and, after a final inspection, led us to a room in the back. "I need you two to sign these release forms. Unless you want me to, I'm not releasing your names. But these give me legal rights to use these photos."

As we had already agreed to Alan's terms, we signed the papers, and a photographer and his team spent an hour and a half photographing us. Some shots were individuals, but most were us together. I wasn't surprised when I saw the proofs on the monitor that Philippe looked terrific. He belonged in front of a camera and knew how to communicate what the photographer asked of him.

My pictures were also good, and the photos of us together were phenomenal.

Two hours later, Jean-Philippe and I made our entrance down the staircase. People stopped to watch, and flashes from cameras filled the ballroom. The team that put the Rainbow New Year's Gala together powered their way through the crowd to us, and we spent a good hour with them, having our photo taken.

There was enough time for us to have something to eat and a few drinks before the countdown for the New Year began. I had asked the bartender for a crate and, just before midnight, had brought it over so my husband could stand on it, even out the disparity in our height.

Our kiss started before the ball dropped and confetti rained down on us. "Happy New Year, Jean-Philippe." I pulled back long enough to say before resuming my kiss as his wings thrummed.

We danced for hours.

We crossed the street and entered the hotel lobby at almost six in the morning. A surprising number of people were in the hall at that hour, and many turned to watch the Elven King and his bodyguard as we strolled to the elevator banks.

"Sir! Excuse me, sir," a manager ran from the concierge desk with a newspaper. "I'm glad I saw you. You might want to have this. You two look fantastic. Have a good day."

He had handed the newspaper to Philippe, and once we were in the elevator, we looked at the cover of the Honolulu Star-Advertiser.

There were three photos.

One with us coming down the stairs. Philippe was in front of me, and I was off to the side. It looked like it was a photo from a scene in a movie. The other was the two of us standing with the Rainbow New Year's Gala committee. The first photo was captioned, 'Fae Royalty and Guard attend Gala.' The other caption announced the committee had been granted a Royal meeting. The third was the Fae King on a box being kissed by his warrior guard. That caption read, 'Fae King welcomes New Year with His Warrior.

Philippe laughed all the way to our room.

"I King, my husband. What make you?" He teased me as we started to undress, carefully placing the wings, the swords, and other equipment on the desk to be returned to Alan later in the day. It took me a while to unbraid the circlet out of Philippe's hair before we could get into the shower. Using the special soap that Sally had provided, it still took almost thirty minutes to get all the makeup off our bodies.

We were exhausted and fell into bed by eight. I hoped we would sleep until late in the afternoon.

JEAN-PHILIPPE

All three phones, Tyler's cell, my cell, and the room line, began ringing at once. I opened one eye and, seeing it was only ten-thirty, decided to ignore them.

"What the fuck?" Tyler's sleepy voice growled, and he rolled over to look at his phone. "Shit, it was Steve."

Before he could call back, Tyler's phone rang again. "This better be important!"

I watched as Tyler sat up abruptly and looked over at me. "When? The bitch! Did you talk to Dad? What'd he say?" At this point, Tyler got out of bed and walked into the bathroom.

I could still hear him. "He did. Okay. Are we supposed to call him? No, I'm sure Philippe has the number. Okay, when I get it...Oh, okay, let me look." There were a few minutes of silence, and then Tyler's big voice yelled and cursed. "I'm going to fucking kill her!" More silence. Steve must have been talking him down because when Tyler came out into the bedroom, he threw his phone across the room – thankfully, it landed in the chair – and gathered me into his arms. He was crying, and I could only imagine his mother had done something awful.

She had.

When he could speak, Tyler told me his mother had given the local 'rag mag' enough information on me for them to do a full-page story.

I did not know what a 'rag mag' was, and Tyler had to explain that to me.

The headline proclaimed, *"**City's Fine Orchestra Hoodwinked by Hooker!**"* The report went on to make me out as a horrible person who had taken advantage of innocent people.

My victims were Dr. Federico Greco, the city's award-winning symphony orchestra, and a police detective who lost his job because of his association with the prostitute.

According to Steve, Tyler's father had moved out of their home and taken up residence in one of the Braxton family's properties. Also, Greco had reached out to Steve via Trenton Braxton when he couldn't get ahold of me.

I was to call my teacher immediately.

Greco was livid.

The first five minutes of our conversation was calling Veronica Braxton every vile name in Italian he knew, and Greco knew a lot. "This is not right for her to do this, Jean-Philippe. But we are going to fix that. Listen, I've called in some favors, and you and Tyler must be ready...."

The phone was on speaker, and Tyler and I listened as Federico told me his plans to correct what had happened. He asked for and received my permission to use the footage of the Benefit Concert. We had one day to get everything set up on our end. I was to keep the phone near, and my teacher apologized for the time difference but promised it would be worth it when it was all done.

"You are more than a student to me, Jean-Philippe. You should already know this, but if not, I wanted to make sure you did. Tyler?" Tyler said he was there, and Greco ended the call with, "You take care of our beautiful angel. I'll talk to you two soon."

When the line was dead, I sobbed, telling Tyler I was so sorry for causing this trouble.

"This is not your doing, Jean-Philippe. She brought all this on herself. You did nothing." Tyler rocked me in his arms, and I tried to believe him.

We went back to bed and surprisingly slept until three that afternoon. Tyler had paid for an extra night, but we would not use it. We needed to return to the house and contact Moe, Lina, and the other Tiu family.

Tomorrow was going to be a busy day.

After we dropped everything off at *Na Mea Huna Inc.*, we headed home. From the back of the limo, Tyler called an interpreting agency and scheduled a French language interpreter for the entire day tomorrow, starting at six in the morning.

I would be doing an interview at seven-thirty a.m. that would be recorded by one of the local television affiliates. The nationally recognized and award-winning journalist reporter would conduct the interview via satellite. It would be shown on one of the national morning shows in three days. Like the television correspondent, the newspaper journalist, who was syndicated throughout the country, would be coming tomorrow afternoon. Federico Greco had pulled some heavy-duty strings to get these prominent people to come and interview me.

Greco called later that afternoon and told me to be honest. He would also be interviewed and tell his side of the story of how I became his student. "You have nothing to be ashamed of, Jean-Philippe. What happened was done to you. But you pulled yourself up and out of that life. It took you seven years, but you did it, and you should be proud of that. I know that Trenton Braxton is proud of you, and Tyler is too. Don't let one angry old bitch tear you down, do you hear me?"

"Si professore. Ti sento!" I answered in Italian. I did hear what he said. I just needed to wrap my head around it.

The Tiu family showed up later that afternoon and spent the night. They worked until after dark to make sure the property was clean and presentable. Tyler had given Rafi the information of the reporter he was to pick up around noon. He was at their disposal until they were delivered to the house on Hanapepe Loop.

The French language interpreter showed up at six the following day. He introduced himself as Richard Lambert. We spoke for a while after I got him to eat something and have coffee. I explained what we were doing and about my life as a prostitute. I didn't want him to stumble over any questions that were asked or how I answered them.

Lambert was professional and let me know he would do me justice. I showed him the article from the 'rag mag' and let him watch me at the benefit concert. Greco must have gotten permission from everyone but Elizabeth Grander's parents, as she was the only one whose face had been blurred out.

When he was finished, Lambert looked at me with wide eyes. In French, he asked, "You mean to tell me you have only been playing since you were fifteen. That's only seven years, and you then orchestrated an entire piece. Wow! You are amazing, and I hope that what you're doing today shows you are an incredibly talented and gifted man. Oh, by the way, I loved your costume from the Gala two days ago. I thought it was a lot of makeup. As you can imagine, I was surprised that it wasn't."

I got up, leaving the interpreter to finish his coffee, and went to look for Tyler. He was in the foyer with the television station's filming crew. They were discussing the best place for the interview. Tyler told them he was okay with them anywhere they wanted to set up.

Then, he introduced me to the crew.

As usual, there was a buzz of confusion and excitement when they saw me. The makeup team wanted to get to work right away as they needed to make sure I didn't 'washout' on camera. In the end, the team set up under the cabana with the camera facing the shrubbery wall and the sky's backdrop over the ocean.

It didn't take long for a frenzy to begin as the crew set everything up. I was given a microphone under my shirt and an earbud to hear the questions. Richard Lambert was also wired to listen to and respond to the questions. I was told my mic wouldn't be as loud as Lambert's. My voice would be background noise.

As it was being recorded and not live, I was told just to relax. If something needed to be reshot, it was easy to do.

Before the correspondent appeared on the screen, Tyler came over and kissed me, telling me he and our Hawaiian family would be there for me.

When the face of the reporter showed up on the screen, I was rendered speechless. How Greco could get this man to interview me was beyond my comprehension. But because he had, I would make him proud of me.

Mr. Emerson Conley spent a good ten minutes speaking with me to get me to relax. We had to get the rhythm of questions and answers as an interpreter was involved. Conley asked me if I had lived in the States since I was fourteen and why I didn't have better English. When I started in French, Conley asked me to speak English to get a sense of me.

"I no speaked good. I no have English when I kicked out home… of home. I learned English on street, other kids worked on street teached me. Most words bad, but I getted better. Same as French. Stepfather he no make me sure I go school. I speak French, but no read or writes." I could feel the blush under my creamy skin, but Conley just listened and nodded. When I was finished, he thanked me for sharing that with him and asked if there was anything I was reluctant to have asked.

I looked over at Tyler and smiled at him. "Yes. Once…one thing. I no want to say I married. Not for people! I want to keep myself…for myself. You wants meeted my husband?

Conley excitedly said yes, and within a minute, Tyler was wired and in front of the monitor.

"So, you're Tyler Braxton. Greco told me all about you. It's a pleasure to meet you." Conley said by way of introduction.

"Actually, it's Tyler Roche. It's my mother who's causing all this mess. I want to thank you for what you're doing." Tyler looked as humble as he sounded.

"Jean-Philippe. Tyler. No one should be the victim of bullying, not on any level. I hope what we are doing here today will stop this harassment." Conley said, and I watched as someone spoke to him off-camera. "Okay, we need to get started. Tyler, it's nice to meet you. Jean-Philippe and Mr. Lambert, are you ready?"

The interview took over two hours. Emerson Conley had asked hard questions. Asking me to elaborate on some and was happy with others. He asked about my stepfather and birthfather, which I didn't know. We discussed my history as a child prostitute, working the street and then at the agency.

The incident with Bernard was spoken of. Why had I let him use me in place of rent? I explained that I had no skills, and as I was working as a dishwasher to pay for food, transportation, and my lessons, I prostituted myself for a place to live. Like many kids in my situation, we didn't sell our bodies because we had a choice. Those choices were often taken from us by conditions we had no control over.

"What about social services?" Emerson Conley asked.

For many kids, especially LGBTQIA+ kids, that was not an option. That situation presented itself with little or no control over our actions. With no control over what happened to us, we were helpless. Having no control over our lives was what got people like me into the situation in the first place.

Foster care sometimes was worse than being a whore on the street. Of course, there were exceptions, as there were for everything, but many felt, as I had, that the streets were safer.

I reminded Conley I was a child, and I thought as one. Children don't often make the best choices, but we learn how to get by the hard way.

As for me, I explained when asked, Bernard allowed me to get off the street and get a job as a dishwasher. It wasn't ideal, as Bernard was brutal in his rent collection. But without the place, even with its high cost, I would not have been able to get off the street. I would not have been able to take my lessons with Federico Greco, and I would not have been able to perform as I did last month.

After the two hours, Conley thanked me and told Tyler and me that we would get a link for the edited version that would be shown on the network morning show in three days. Emerson Conley told me he looked forward to hearing wonderful things about me, and the next time he was in the Boston area, he would look us up.

Lambert and I were exhausted after the two-hour interview. We had about five hours before the syndicated newspaper reporter showed up. I showed the interpreter to a spare bedroom for him to use and relax.

When I returned downstairs, I thanked the crew for their time and the Tius for their support. After that, Tyler pulled me into the bedroom and made me lie down. As tired as I was, I was afraid I would sleep away for the rest of the day. Tyler, who laid down beside me, told me he had asked Moe to wake us at two if we weren't out before.

I relaxed in Tyler's embrace and fell asleep.

Like Emerson Conley, the newspaper reporter was someone I had heard of but didn't know. Our interview lasted almost three hours, and we were all exhausted by the time she left. I invited Lambert to dinner, which he declined. I thanked him for all his work today and hoped to see him again.

We waited for Rafi to return before the entire Tiu family, Tyler, and I went to dinner. While waiting, I texted my teacher to let him know how it had all gone. Surprisingly, he texted back, letting me know he had done his interview with Conley and the New York reporter. Like us, Greco would get a copy of the segment and the interview before it went live. Also, according to my teacher, our interview with Conley would be a weeklong segment.

Greco expected me to be in high demand when I returned home and for me to be ready. I reminded him about my class, and he promised me he would help me schedule around it.

I confided to Tyler that I thought Greco was being optimistic about the results but was trying to stay positive. I asked if he had spoken with his father, and he told me that he had and that Trenton was doing well. He was angry with Tyler's mother to the point he had moved out, which we already knew, as he just needed time to cool down.

Veronica Braxton didn't seem to understand that what she did had consequences. Even after the seven people, including the public defender, were fired, Mrs. Braxton still did something like this. From what I remember, she was on the orchestra board.

That probably was over.

TYLER

The interview by Emerson Conley was forty minutes long. We received the link the day before it was to air. Like everything that Conley did, the interview was informative and respectful. Greco's interview was weaved into Philippe's flawlessly.

Philippe and I thanked Conley for the great interview. A link for the article followed the next day; like Conley's, the piece was spectacular.

Philippe seemed to relax after watching the interview. My dad had called and spoken with Philippe. He apologized and told Philippe that he would do whatever it took to ensure he was not affected by Veronica's malicious behavior.

We went to the luau I had made reservations for, but that was the only thing we did. We stayed at the house. I taught Philippe to swim, and when we weren't relaxing near the pool, we were chilling with sex.

A lot of sex.

The flight back to Boston was long. Philippe slept most of the flight. I think it was his way of getting ready to face whatever awaited us in our hometown.

What was waiting was not what we expected. Reporters with cameras and microphones were waiting for us to leave the terminal's secure area. There was no way for them not to notice us. No one could confuse anyone else for Jean-Philippe, and my photo must have been plastered all over the place as they all yelled our names to get our attention.

Luckily, Dad had been prepared. A small army of men escorted us to a waiting limo from the terminal. Once inside, Dad laughed. "Well, that's a circus. Hello boys, did you have a good time?"

"It fun and crazy!" Philippe announced, and I leaned over to give my dad a hug.

"Thanks for this, Dad. How did you know this was going to happen?" I inquired as I accepted a soda from my dad.

"It's been a media frenzy since the first segment aired. The original article was retracted with an apology from the newspaper. I've been in touch with Federico, and he's happy with the results. Between Conley and Hwang's interviews, the orchestra and his reputations have been repaired." My dad told us. "Your mother did a lot of damage to a lot of people."

He looked really sad. I hadn't seen him this way in a long time. My mother was breaking my father's heart, and I could see it. "Dad, you want to stay for dinner?" I asked, not wanting him to be alone.

"Oh, son. Thanks. But you two must be exhausted."

"No. We fine. You come for dinner. We wants you to." Philippe said, moving so he could take my father's large hand in his.

"You're good kids. Thanks, and I will." Dad agreed, and we were quiet on the journey home.

Dinner was Indian; I knew it was Dad's favorite form of take-out. Dad relaxed in the living room while Philippe and I unpacked, showered, and put on fresh clothes. I was out first and offered Dad a choice of drinks. He opted for a red that I had several bottles of, and we drank a glass while we waited for dinner to arrive.

Over our meal, we talked about the house in Hawaii and the Tius. Dad was happy they were doing well and would be going to visit them soon. He had wanted to take Mom, but as it was, that wasn't going to happen.

He asked about our plans for the next few days.

Tomorrow, we were doing nothing but relaxing. Then, we both had things to do to prepare for our classes. I was expected to go to the Harvey Milk Academy, the Magnet School, for an interview. It would be the second interview, as I had Skyped with the principal before the winter break.

Philippe had a meeting with Greco. The Maestro wanted me to go with him, so we both had arranged our schedules to accommodate his wishes. Steve and his patrol partner, Olan, and his wife were coming over Saturday for a BBQ. We invited Dad to join, and he said he would consider it.

Later, we helped my rather drunk dad into the guest bedroom and got him settled before heading to our own bed.

"I've never seen him drunk before," I told Philippe once we were in bed. "Mom is really hurting him. That is even worse than how I feel about it all." I was sad that my father was so affected by my mother's behavior.

"He no thinked she be this ways. I thinked she maybe hurts him because he no hurt me." Philippe pulled me into his arms and held me. I agreed with his assessment.

"That could be true. I just don't understand what mom's trying to achieve." I commented and then explained what achieve meant.

Philippe pulled me up for a kiss, leading to a night of gentle love-making.

My interview went way better than I had anticipated. The principal, Mrs. Harrison-Becker, offered me a job starting the following week. They had already checked all my credentials. A position was open to teach high school world history and junior high American history. I would have six classes, three on each campus, and a free period after my lunch break. We discussed salary and benefits. Before I left, I was escorted to the small HR office to sign my contract and pick up insurance and other benefits forms.

I would still have to work on my alternative teaching certificate. However, Harrison-Becker assured me many teachers had been exactly where I was. She let me know the head of the history department and shared their name and contact information with me. She suggested I get in touch with them – their pronouns were they/them – at my earliest convenience. They would be waiting to hear from me.

I texted Cord Ross when I got into my car. I told them I would be the new history teacher and looked forward to working with them. If they wanted to meet before Monday, I would work my schedule to make it happen.

Cord texted back several minutes later. They suggested we meet for Sunday brunch. If I had one, I was to bring my wife, and they would bring their partner. It would be a relaxing way to meet. By the time I pulled into the underground garage, Cord and I had agreed on a place for brunch, and I let them know I looked forward to meeting them.

Philippe was home, practicing, when I returned with the good news. We had celebratory sex, and then I took us out for dinner.

To our surprise, people waved at us on the street. Once inside the restaurant, our local spot, people came up to the table to congratulate Philippe on the interview and wish him well. The manager kept people away after our food was delivered.

It was weird, all the attention. I was assured it would all blow over soon, but we would have to deal with it in the meantime.

Philippe told me over dinner that Greco had called. The Maestro asked if we could come earlier than we had initially planned and if we could have our attorney present. A lot was happening, which was all good, but some legalities might need to be addressed. Philippe told me he had already contacted Waldron, and Waldron had agreed to meet us at Greco's office.

"I tells him, no problems. Is okay?"

It was fine with me. I asked what Philippe thought was happening, but he wasn't sure. Greco seemed excited, but other than asking for us to come earlier and with Waldron, Greco hadn't said anything more.

We finished our meal, and Philippe wanted to know what we needed to do and to get so I would be ready for my first day of teaching. I told him about our Sunday brunch with Cord, the head of the history department for the Magnet School. I would find out what I needed then, and afterward, we could shop for what was required.

JEAN-PHILIPPE

We arrived at Greco's office at nine a.m. the following day. Waldron had been waiting in the parking lot, so we walked into the space together. Greco wasn't the only person in his office. There were four others, all but one dressed casually and all standing the moment I walked into the office.

Federico hurriedly moved to embrace me, speaking in Italian, letting me know he was happy to see me and excited to share this with me. He shook Tyler's hand and introduced himself to Waldron. While they were speaking, a man walked up to me.

In French, he introduced himself as the interpreter for the meeting, which is when I became nervous.

"Jean-Philippe. Tyler. Mr. Waldron." Greco started with the interpreter repeating the words softly in French beside me. "Thank you all for coming. I want to introduce Dr. Octavia Hall, Cade Evans, and Timon Campbell."

Dr. Octavia Hall was a tall African-American woman. Cade Evans was a foot shorter than the doctor and wore thick glasses, while Timon Campbell was so average-looking that you would pass him on the street and not even notice him.

We shook hands and offered our welcomes before Greco spoke again. "Let's start with everyone having a seat." Once we all were seated, he continued. "Timon Campbell, as you may or may not know, is a documentary filmmaker. He is in the final stages of producing a film about the murder and ritual slaughters of Albinos in Africa. He would like to work with Jean-Philippe. Precisely, Campbell would like Jean-Philippe to score the film. If you are interested, Jean-Philippe, you two will need to get together."

I listened to the interpreter's words and shook my head. I must be hearing them incorrectly. "What? I'm confused." I said in French, and my words were translated.

Federico laughed and told me he completely understood. But there was more I needed to listen to. Dr. Hall was the director of the city's Arts and Humanities Department, which was responsible for the city's performing art venues. She wanted to work with me on an event to fund awareness for homeless children on the streets.

Finally, Cade Evans was the individual who was looking for a guitarist for his quartet.

"It is many too much for my head." I said then spoke, *'C'est trop. Je suis accablé!'*

The interpreter translated, "It's too much. I am overwhelmed!"

Tyler took my hand, and Waldron began asking about contracts and what I would need to do if I decided to do any of them. They each handed a folder to Waldron, asking him to review the proposals and get with me. The only person with a time restraint was Campbell. He had a few more months of editing but wanted me to get the feel of the documentary so I would know what it needed.

Hall also wasn't in a hurry. But she needed to know before the middle of February if I was willing to participate. Evans would be touring in Europe and returning sometime in the fall...so there was no hurry.

They all thanked me and left, leaving only Greco, Tyler, Waldron, the interpreter, and myself.

"Fuck!" I said, causing everyone to laugh.

"He got that sentence correct," Waldron smiled at me and patted my shoulder.

Since I had the interpreter here, I used him. "Teacher. Is this all for real? It seems they are offering things to someone they don't even know." I paused to let the words be translated, then continued. "Scoring a film is a big task. Why would he want someone with no experience?"

Greco moved to me and sat me down next to him. "You orchestrated a beautiful piece in a month. Sure, you refined it and made adjustments a few months afterward, but you did the lion's share of the work before. Also, both Evans and Campbell have heard your music. They know talent when they see and hear it. So don't start doubting yourself now."

Tyler moved to sit across from me as Greco continued. "I think Dr. Hall and the city want to use you for PR reasons. Despite where you are now and how you worked hard to improve your situation, many don't, and the city might feel guilty about that."

The Elf Who Tamed A Giant

That was the only thing that made sense out of everything I was hearing. However, my teacher let me know that all three offers were good. There had been a hundred more, which Greco had thrown in the trash. Most were precisely that, trash, but these three would set my career path straight to the stars. Federico Greco had every confidence in me I could do each one.

His final words before we left were, "Jean-Philippe, you are brilliant and gifted. As is your wonderful husband, I am here for you on this journey. You are not alone, and you must remember that!"

I was shell-shocked as we drove to Waldron's office – he insisted – with the French Language Interpreter behind us. Once we were in the plush offices, Waldron called an associate, who was an entertainment lawyer. Waldron wanted her to review the proposals and then set a time for Tyler, me, and an interpreter to sit down and discuss the options.

"Tyler, he haves new jobs. He start works Monday. He no can missed works!" I watched the interpreter open his mouth and then pop it shut. It put a smile on my face.

Before we left, Waldron let me know how much Campbell was willing to pay me to score his film. I asked the interpreter three times for clarification before the figure stuck.

What would I do with such money?

Saturday, two days later, we were in Waldron's office at nine. Along with Waldron were the entertainment attorney, Emma Payne, and a French language interpreter. We spent two hours having the proposals explained, what the time constraints were, the responsibilities, and the dollar amounts being offered.

With Greco's input, Payne's recommendations, and Tyler's promise that I could do it and still go to class, I asked Payne to contact Hall, Evans, and Campbell. I would be happy to work with them. The only caveat I required was an interpreter to be present in meetings until my English improved.

Later that afternoon, I was still in shock. I was quiet throughout the evening as Tyler grilled steaks for Steve, Marie – Steve's girlfriend - and his partner Olan Rodgers and his wife, Shirley, and their three kids. I cooked the sides for the steak, but my body was on autopilot.

Over dinner, Tyler shared with everyone what had transpired over the last few days, including the three offers I had just accepted. Everyone congratulated me, but I admitted I felt way over my head.

They all agreed I was up to the challenge, and I smiled, nodded, and couldn't wait for everyone to go home so I could freak out in my bedroom with my husband.

I had a meltdown as soon as we were alone, but Tyler bolstered me with his love, and I knew I could do anything with him at my side.

Sunday, we met Cord Ross and their wife for brunch. Cord was surprised that Tyler had shown up with a husband, not a wife. They explained they had heard Tyler had been an undercover police officer and was as big as a house. They apologized for assuming that Tyler was straight from Tyler's descriptions. We laughed it off, and the meal turned out to be an informative and enjoyable time.

Cord welcomed Tyler to the school. They had a list of things Tyler might want for his classes, "I'm not saying you need any of this," Cord's voice was low but surprisingly melodic as they spoke, "for your classes, but I think you'll want them. Also, I already have the books you will be teaching from and a lesson plan for the next few weeks. I want to ease you into the curriculum and feel this is the best way to do it."

Bennie, Cord's wife, and I chatted as Cord and Tyler spoke. I had asked if she was a teacher, and she told me she didn't have the patience to teach. Bennie worked as a secretary for a construction company called GRC. She could put up with a room full of men way better than a classroom full of teenagers.

I thought she sounded like a reasonable person. I don't think I could teach either.

TYLER - SIX WEEKS LATER

Both Philippe and I started school the week after we returned from Hawaii. I, at Harvey Milk Academy, and Philippe to his English class at the Community College. The Alternative Certification Class wouldn't start until the summer. Cord and Mrs. Harrison-Becker assured me that wasn't a problem.

Since I didn't have to work on the Alternative certification, I signed up for an online French Class, which I thought I was doing well in.

I used Cord's lesson plans for the first few weeks and was ready to teach each day. I was surprised at how easy it had come to me. The kids warmed up to me once the students realized I wasn't an ogre. When they found out I had a husband and not a wife, the remaining walls crumbled, and I had six classrooms full of funny, warm, relaxed, and safe kids.

I couldn't imagine living my life in fear, as most of these kids had.

At Harvey Milk Academy, bullying was absolutely not tolerated, letting the kids be who they were in a safe environment. The group of kids that were the hardest for me was the kids in the housing. Those kids had been kicked out of their homes like Jean-Philippe. They had this school and the people who cared for them; that was at least something.

I'm sure he would have sought them out if Jean-Philippe had known about this place. Perhaps not, but I wished that for him.

"This is good." Cord had told me the start of my third week after overlooking the lesson plans, I had drawn up for the following week.

"I wanted to let you know that the classes I've sat in and then talked to the students have assured Harrison-Becker and me that we made a brilliant choice in hiring you. I want you to remember, Tyler, I am here if you have questions, and no matter how dumb you think it is, you need to ask me. Believe me when I say that during the first five years I taught, I asked some idiotic questions or questions I thought were stupid. They're not, Tyler."

Cord stood, their pregnant belly hitting a stack of books on the corner of my desk.

"You okay?" I asked.

"Why I agreed to carry this baby is beyond me. Bennie said it was my turn, and I agreed. But I feel like I have a wrecking ball attached to my stomach. I keep knocking things over with it." I heard the frustration, but I could see the happiness on Cord's face as they patted their belly. "This is the last one. Three is enough, and I'm not doing this again! You know where I am if you have questions or need something."

Cord waved goodbye as they waddled out of my room.

Each week had gotten easier, and I became more comfortable with what I was doing. In part because I knew that the kids were relaxed around me. Also, I hadn't been this relaxed on the job, ever. Sure, it could be stressful at times, but I didn't have to worry about blowing my cover or hoping the wire I was wearing didn't show.

The Monday Philippe began his classes, he started working with Campbell on the documentary. Philippe still had difficulty processing what he saw in the film but had almost finished the initial composition. I had heard some of what Philippe explained would be the soundtrack's foundation.

Philippe had flown to New York once and to Los Angeles twice. I had been able to go with him to New York and once to Los Angeles. The trips had been mini-vacations, and we had had enough time in LA to go to Disneyland. I had been before but watching my husband pure joy and wonder on his face, was better than seeing **Mickey Mouse** for the tenth time. Although, that was still exciting.

Come on...It's **Mickey Mouse**!

It was fascinating to me that while Philippe struggled with his English classes, he could sit down and write music for a full orchestra without breaking a sweat! When I asked, he told me he heard the music in his head, what each instrument should play, and then he wrote it down. Because he was a guitarist, the composition featured the instrument.

Unlike my husband, I didn't know music, but what I heard broke my heart. When I asked Philippe what Campbell had wanted, he said the filmmaker wanted something as dark and tragic as what was happening to the Albinos of Africa.

Campbell was going to get exactly what he asked for.

I helped him when I could with his English, and after a month, it improved. Philippe still struggled, especially when he was tired or frustrated. Still, while he didn't seem to see it, I noticed the improvement after each class.

History has always fascinated me. I wasn't one of those teachers who dressed up like George Washington or Winston Churchill, but I tried to do fun things that got the kids involved in class. It was an excellent way to learn, as far as I knew. It had always worked for me.

Working with the art teacher, the drama teacher, or even the American Lit teacher, I would come up with something to help reinforce what we were learning. As far as I was concerned, nothing was worse than a class taught by a teacher who droned on about a subject.

I checked with my supervisor when I had an idea, but Cord was usually happy and let me do my thing. Cord and the principal were impressed and encouraged me to continue. When they thought something wouldn't work or needed to be tweaked, they worked with me to explain why and helped guide me in the right direction.

Working with Cord Ross had been a godsend.

Over the last six weeks, Dad had spent a lot of time with us. We still hadn't told him we were married, but we didn't hide our matching rings. Dad was too sharp not to notice them, but he never said anything to Jean-Philippe or me.

Steve and Marie had been over almost every Saturday. Olan Rodgers, his wife, Shirley, and their three boys, Anand, Amir, and Arlo, joined Steve and me as we watched sports. We also threw a party for Rodgers, who passed his Police Officer Civil Service Exam and would soon leave his beat to become a detective.

Usually, Philippe, Marie, and Shirley would go off and do something. Philippe didn't understand most American sports except soccer; I typically didn't watch that.

Mom had been surprisingly quiet.

I had asked Dad, who was still living in one of the apartments they owned, what was up, but he just shrugged. He wanted to go back home, but as long as Mom acted like Jean-Philippe was the antichrist, that wouldn't happen.

"I'm really sorry about this, Dad," I told him one evening after dinner. I got up and wrapped my arms around him, and to my surprise, he tightened his embrace and cried on my shoulder.

It broke my heart.

Raj Lowenstien

Several weeks after we had returned from Hawaii, my cousin, Ashton, showed up. He told us that my mother was being charged with making a false report, for strong-arming several police officials and a public defender. She got a huge fine and community service, which would happen, as Ashton had told us. Additionally, she was required to attend anger management therapy for 100 hours. She was more embarrassed about being caught than what she had actually done – no surprise there – and was having her lawyer try to overturn the conviction.

Dad had tried to stand with her and wanted to support her. But she refused him as long as he didn't side with her about Jean-Philippe. Over the last month and a half, my dad had fallen a little bit in love with my husband, thinking he was the best thing in the world for me. I agreed, and it was nice our relationship hadn't suffered like Mom's and mine.

It was three, Friday afternoon when I got home. Usually, Philippe would be in bed taking a nap, and I let him sleep. Although he wasn't exactly burning the candle at both ends, Philippe often needed a catnap after his English and Guitar classes and working on the soundtrack. I had learned to let him sleep. Philippe was awake and moved in to wrap his arms around me. "I have bags packed." He pointed to the overnight and garment bags by the door.

We had a Braxton family event to attend this weekend. I tried to get out of it, but Dad had promised Mom wouldn't be there. He had wanted to get her to come, but when she found out Jean-Philippe and I would be there, she declined the invitation.

I took a moment to change, and then we headed to Woods Hole to take the ferry to Martha's Vineyard. The Braxtons had a summer home there that had been in the family for several generations. The party would not be there, but there were bedrooms enough for most of the family that would show up.

I had made reservations for Philippe and me at The Oaks Bluffs Inn for the weekend. As much as I wanted to see my cousins, aunts, and uncles, I didn't want to stress out myself or my husband.

It was almost a four-hour drive from our condo to the ferry. We talked about our week and what was upcoming on our schedules. Philippe slept for an hour, only waking when I pulled over to fill the tank and get something to drink.

Once back on the road, I asked about the score. I knew Philippe had finished it and was now fine-tuning it. Next week, he would start working with an orchestra specializing in movie soundtracks. They, the group in Boston, would be the musicians on the final work. Philippe had been told that the Premier would be done before a live audience in Boston. That would follow with a performance in New York and then San Francisco, Timon Campbell's hometown.

"When will you have the dates? I want to make sure I am off and can come with." I reached over and took Philippe's hand.

"They tells me will haved dates first April. But I thinked maybe the Premier will be June. It will be *'limited release,'*" Philippe said those words slowly and carefully, "then on a *doc-u-men-tary* channel after releasing. You out of school. I have go to California and NYC before to worked with orchestra."

I smiled. Philippe was working incredibly hard on his English, and I tried to do the same in my French. We each had our own personal tutors, so we were ahead of the game, at least in my mind.

"*C'est bon!*" I said and got a kiss on the cheek.

"*Vous vous débrouillez bien dans votre cours de français. Je suis fier de toi!*" Philippe told me then repeated it so I was able to figure out the words.

"I'm proud of you too, Babe," I told him after about five minutes.

We spent the rest of the trip talking about the weekend. We were celebrating my Dad's brother's birthday. Uncle Ben was twelve years older than Dad. My uncle wanted his siblings all together for the weekend. Most of my cousins and their families, at least the ones on the East Coast, would be there.

I had already heard from one of my cousins that the house on Main Street in Tisbury was overflowing with people. Most of the overflow had rented rooms closer to the house than The Oaks Bluffs Inn, which was fine with me.

We caught the second to the last ferry onto Martha's Vineyard. I had been coming here almost every summer since I was a kid. I spent my time between my Braxton family and the Hawthornes. Fifteen of us made up the Braxton grandkids. Half of us were married and already had children of our own. Steve and I were the only Hawthorne grandkids, and although I was close to my Braxton cousins, Steve and I were like brothers.

Philippe's reaction to things I took for granted still surprised me. He had never been on a ferry. The night was cold but bright with a full moon. I stood behind him, my arms wrapped around Philippe as he took in the brilliant night sky.

"It beautiful." I heard him whisper.

Kissing the top of his head, I murmured back, "It is." But I wasn't speaking of the view.

After twenty minutes in the cold, we returned to the truck. I turned on the heater to warm us up and asked if Philippe wanted to get something to eat before we got to the hotel.

"No. I no hungrys. Maybe a French fry and soda. No! Milked Shake." Philippe said, and I hoped there was a fast-food place open.

We ate most of the three supersized orders of fries and drank our shakes before we arrived at The Oaks Bluffs Inn. It took a few minutes to check in before we were in our room. Philippe carried the overnight bag and followed me in.

"What time we have to be at you family?" Philippe asked as he unpacked the overnight bag. "Maybes we sleep late? Yes?"

I was in the bathroom and could hear the worry in his voice. This was the first time we would meet family; Dad didn't count. After a discussion, we decided to leave our wedding rings on. Let people think what they want. We didn't care.

After washing my hands, I stepped out to find Philippe on the bed, wearing nothing but a smile. "You know that's not going to work, right?" I chuckled as I took off my clothes.

Philippe feigned surprise, "You no want sex with me?" He started to move to put on his briefs.

"Oh," I scooped him up and moved to cover his body. "I always want to make love to you, but we still have to have breakfast with the family and then go to the party at the country club tomorrow night. If it helps, I will attempt to sex you up three or four times between now and then."

Philippe reached up and ran his thumb along my bottom lip. "You old. Two time maybe. Four," he made a sad face, shook his head, and blew a raspberry in my direction.

Tickling was the best revenge I could think of. That and showing my husband I wasn't too old after all.

We showed up at the Braxton vacation house at nine. Breakfast was going to be buffet style, and I was in charge of providing enough eggs for twenty-five. I bought sixty eggs at the local market, hoping that would be enough.

Philippe had started mumbling in French once we got back in the truck. I caught a word here and there, but mostly, I just knew he was scared to death. Over the last six months, I learned many French curse words. I had explained to Philippe that those were almost as important as being able to ask: 'Where is the restroom?' 'How much for a hotel room?' and 'How much for a beer?'

How was I to know if people were speaking ill of me if I didn't know the dirty words? Therefore, I heard enough to know Philippe was cussing up a storm.

"It's going to be okay, Babe. If it gets bad, we'll leave. I promise. I already told Dad, and he agreed."

He cut off my words and looked over at me. He said slowly and with exaggerated care, "*I will not let them be mean to you!*" The words were heavily accented but grammatically correct.

"Damn, Babe, that was great. Anyway, I'm not letting anyone be mean to either of us. We got Dad on our side, and I know a few of my cousins, so all's good." I reached over and patted his thigh.

"That too hard. English crazy language. No maked logic. Rules *mystifiant. Estupid*!" Philippe snarled, and I barked out a laugh.

He was correct, and I told him.

I didn't know how people learned English. I also admitted that French was a bit weird as well. Philippe called me *'lourdaud,'* telling me he would write it down so I could ask my French teacher about it next week.

Dad met us at the truck when we pulled up alongside the twenty other vehicles on the private driveway. Dad opened the door and pulled Philippe out of the car, planting a kiss on his cheek. "Hey, son," I heard him say to my husband.

"Hello, Father. You good...Are you good?" Philippe said, correcting himself.

"I am wonderful. How's that man you're married to?" Dad said with a wink at me over Philippe's head.

"You knows?" Philippe asked, and I said, "You know?"

Like I had thought, Dad didn't miss a thing.

"Okay. I didn't say anything," Dad began as he moved around the truck to help with the eggs, Philippe in his wake. "Some are going to guess. Some are just going to assume you are 'partners,'" Dad air-quoted the last word. "I don't really care. If it gets too much, you get Philippe out. Do you hear me, Tyler?"

"Yes, Dad. We already talked about it. But honestly, I think, at least for now, it's going to be cool."

The kitchen was set up for a kitchen staff. Therefore, it was big enough for seven of us to work around each other as we put together the meal. An aunt and her daughter chopped up ten pounds of boiled potatoes, green peppers, and onions to make hash browns. I worked on scrambling the eggs while two cousins cooked bacon and sausage.

The other two, my dad's youngest sister and her wife, were on toast brigade. Others set the dining room table, while others set up folding tables to accommodate the Braxton hordes. Another table held pitchers of orange and apple juice, a pitcher of water, and two industrial-sized coffee pots, one with coffee and the other with hot water for tea. By ten o'clock, the chafing dishes were filled to over-flowing.

Before we gathered, Uncle Ben thanked everyone for coming and welcomed the new members to the family. Philippe and two new spouses, as well as three babies, were introduced. Uncle Ben announced Philippe as my boyfriend, which got me more than one shocked look from my family.

Those of us who cooked didn't have to clean up. Philippe was put on dish detail, but there wasn't much to clean up as we used recyclable and disposable plates, utensils, and cups. After telling him I would be out on the beach, I went outside and walked the football field's deep path to the Atlantic Ocean.

"Your mom told me about him, but I didn't believe it." I had heard the footsteps but hadn't turned to see who was following me. When I finally did, I was surprised to see my oldest cousin, Meredith Braxton Turner. Her gaze wasn't as friendly as I had hoped, so I straightened my spine.

"My mother shouldn't be speaking about him. She's done enough to make our lives miserable." I said as sweetly as I could.

"He used to be a whore. That's what I was told. Really, Tyler, you could do so much better. He can't even speak English."

I took a step back, then one toward her. "If you're just here as Mother's mouthpiece, Meredith, you can leave. I've heard all her shit already, and it hadn't changed anything but our relationship."

"I don't need to be your mother's mouthpiece, Tyler. Half of us know it to be true. Fuck, Tyler, look at you. You're a hot-looking guy. You could have any eligible woman from any good family you wanted. They'd fall at your feet. What the hell is wrong with you?" My cousin at least tried to look worried, but I had heard this all before.

"Meredith. I will say this one time. Please share it with your favorite aunt. Jean-Philippe is the best thing that ever happened to me. He's beautiful and kind, brilliant, and twice the person my mother will ever be. That goes for you too, cousin. You just illustrated you are cut from the same die as Veronica Braxton. That isn't something you should be proud of. Now, get the fuck out of my face!"

Turning my back on her, I stared out at the horizon. I would not let my mother or her minions ruin this weekend for us.

"It was a bad things she say. You mother...your mother, she can no leaved you along...alone." Philippe's voice was just barely audible under the crash of the waves.

I didn't turn around but reached behind me. Philippe took my hand, and I pulled him so he stood against me, my arms around his shoulders.

"She, you mother, her puppet. We knows she play this game." Philippe reminded me.

"I know, Babe. I was just hoping she would let us have this weekend. I'll tell Dad, but we're staying unless you want to leave." I leaned down and kissed his head.

We agreed that we would stay. Philippe reiterated that he had been through worse and name-calling was not even worth worrying about. He was a wise soul, my Jean-Philippe. Standing there looking out across the ocean made me realize that as much as they thought they were large, my family was small, grains of sand on a beach. Only if I let them could they hurt me, hurt us. Philippe wasn't about to let them break him, and I would follow in his footprints.

JEAN-PHILIPPE

We returned to the hotel around three that afternoon. Tyler showed me around the island and its many famous sights. Like most things, I was unaware of the history the island had. Not only was it renowned for its people, but it once had a sizeable Deaf population. There was even a sign language, Martha's Vineyard Sign Language, named for the people who had populated the island. Tyler bought me a book entitled *Everyone Here Spoke Sign Language: Hereditary Deafness on Martha's Vineyard*. I promised I would read it once I learned to read.

Tyler couldn't keep his hands off me when we were back in the room. I understood he was trying to make us feel better about this evening. I knew there would be things we would have to deal with, but I loved my husband, and we both needed the feel of each other. It wouldn't help the situation, but it would help us face it.

It had taken a while for me to get used to having money. I was still very cautious with my spending, but I had let Tyler convince me that I needed a wardrobe with nice clothes. I had the Tux I had made for the Charity Event in December. Since then, I have added two more tailored suits.

Tonight was semi-formal, but Tyler had warned me that to the Braxtons, that meant formal. We had had our suits steamed by the staff at the Inn, and they hung ready for us. We would arrive at the country club, picking up Father Braxton at seven.

There was an hour of cocktails, then a formal sit-down dinner. Tyler had let me know there would be about a hundred people there.

Half would be family, close and extended, while the other half would be friends and business associates of Uncle Ben.

Tyler's father had asked me to bring my guitar and prepare something to play. He told me he wanted to show me off, and also, there would be some people Trenton thought I would know or at least would know of me.

We discussed it. I didn't want to force myself on the party, but Tyler had spoken with his uncle, who seemed excited to hear me play. My guitar and sheet music were in the truck, and Tyler promised to bring them in when it was time.

Once he was in the truck, Trenton told us there would be a band during the cocktail hour and after the meal. I could go ahead and play just before dinner and get it over with if that worked for me, which it did.

I love movies.

I had seen many movies where a character entered a room, and everyone stopped. I always thought it was funny or exciting. But to have it actually happen was something I didn't enjoy. Tyler and his dad were as uncomfortable as I was. Trenton's sister and wife saved us from the awkward silence.

"All three of you look so handsome," Tyler's Aunt Trudy said as she wrapped her arms around Tyler and me. "I knew you were handsome already, brother." She leaned up and kissed Trenton's cheek. Trudy introduced me to her wife, Mercedes, and we were led to their table. Once seated, Trudy announced that the Braxton family was full of assholes and for me to take no notice.

"I hear you're working on the soundtrack for a documentary. From what I've heard, it's haunting and spectacular." Mercedes, who I supposed was now my aunt, commented over a glass of champagne.

"How you knows?" I looked at Tyler, who shrugged his shoulders.

"My company, the company I work for, is one of the backers of Timon Campbell's work. He is brilliant. The one thing we love about him is his ability to spot talent. We weren't exactly pleased when he pitched you to us, but after we saw the concert footage, we were sold. I expect a long and successful career ahead for you, Jean-Philippe." Mercedes patted my hand.

"*Merci*. Thank you." I wanted to say more, but Uncle Ben walked up to the table just then.

"Trenton said you would be willing to play for us. Can you do that now? I think it might help." He smiled down at me with a wink.

"I'll get your things, Philippe. You go to the stage." Tyler said, standing to go get my guitar.

I excused myself and headed to the WC. I needed a minute before

I got up on the stage, where everyone would stare at me.

After a moment to collect myself, I stood behind a wall. No one was there, and no one would see me until I walked away. But, like the pantry, I was privy to a conversation.

"Did you see her?" One woman asked another.

"Yeah. This is going to get interesting." The other commented. "You know, they dated for like five years. I had heard he even asked her to marry him. I wonder why she's here."

There was a snicker, then, "Amanda Pollack is a family friend. I think Uncle Robert and Amanda's dad work together. That's how Tyler and Amanda met. If you asked me, he'd be all over her once Tyler sees how beautiful she still is and that she is single. I heard Aunt Veronica told her to come and save Tyler from the monster."

"I don't see why he's so hung up on that little freak. First of all, I have never seen anything that white. Nothing that wasn't dead, anyway." There was laughter, which wasn't pleasant. It reminded me of the woman at the pantry on my birthday. "Then did you see his ears? I heard he had been a sideshow freak, and his parents pimped him out to make money for drugs." This was from a new voice, a man this time.

"I hear he's really smart and talented." Another voice added in my defense.

"Fucking anything for money doesn't make you talented. It just makes you a whore!" This voice I recognized, Meredith.

"Oh shit!" The first woman said, "Here comes Tyler."

The sound of people scurrying away was followed by Tyler walking around the corner.

"There you are. Are you ready?" He scooped me into his arms and kissed me. I smiled into the kiss.

"Just so you knows, Amanda Pollack is'ed here. It seemed as maybe you mother invite her. Be nice. She maybe understand, but maybe she not!" Tyler's eyes widened at my words, but his crooked smile let me know he understood the game.

Tyler walked me to the stage. The band had graciously set up a chair and a stand for the music. I thanked the conductor, letting him know the piece was five minutes long and I would be out of his way. He laughed and told me not to worry.

I took a moment to set out the music for "<u>Romanza</u>" and tune my guitar even though it didn't need it.

I mostly looked at my husband, Trenton, Aunts Trudy, and Mercedes. However, I noticed the look of surprise and shock on many of the faces. Meredith even looked a little green. Perhaps she was beginning to question some of what she had heard about me. Even if she didn't, I didn't care.

There was a thunderous round of applause after I was done.

Tyler came up on stage and helped me put away my things. I thanked the band members and followed Tyler back to the table. While he returned my things to the truck, I was congratulated and thanked. I recognized several of the voices from the discussion near the WC.

I smiled and thanked them. But I then noticed a bit of excitement over by Meredith. I looked in the direction she was facing and saw Tyler as he wrapped his arms around a tall, beautiful woman. He smiled at her and kissed her chastely on the lips. Eyes turned from them to me, and more than one face wore a smug smile as if to say I had this coming.

Tyler took the woman, Amanda, I was sure, out to the dance floor and took two turns as the band played slow music. From the table, I could see the gleam in her eyes. Someone had promised her that Tyler Braxton was on the market, and she had the correct currency to lure him away.

Veronica Braxton was a cruel bitch.

I watched as the two moved from the dance floor to the table where another uncle, Robert, was. They sat and spoke for about thirty minutes before there was an announcement that dinner would be served in fifteen.

While I watched Tyler and Amanda, the four people at my table watched me. Trenton looked as if he was going to be ill. I leaned over to him, patting his hand. *"Mon père. Nous savions qu'elle était ici. Nous pensons que peut-être Veronica l'a fait venir. Tyler est un homme bon. Mais il sait que c'est un jeu. Je ne suis pas inquiet. Vous n'avez pas à vous inquiéter."* Then, I repeated the words in my broken English to ensure Trenton understood. "We knows she is here. Wes think maybes Veronica get hers to come. Tyler he a good man. But he know this a game. I no worries. You no worries."

"He's not the only one who's a good man, Jean-Philippe." My father-in-law smiled at me, and I saw the love for Tyler and for myself in his eyes.

Trenton and I stood when Tyler approached the table with Amanda on his arm. Trudy and Mercedes looked alarmed, as did a cousin whose name I had forgotten.

"You all remember Amanda Pollack. We dated for about five years. That seems like a lifetime ago," Tyler said, looking down at Amanda and kissing her cheek. I felt sorry for her as she leaned into the kiss, closing her eyes for a second. "Amanda, you remember my dad, Trenton Braxton. This is my Aunt Trudy and her wife, Mercedes. You might have met Landon before. He's Uncle Trevor's son."

Amanda nodded to each as they were introduced. She had met Landon before, and they seemed to know each other rather well. But during the introductions, Amanda's eyes kept drifting back to me. Living and working the streets had taught me many things, and reading expression was one of them.

Amanda Pollack was jealous and was at the birthday bash for a reason.

That bubble soon vanished. "Amanda. I want to introduce my husband, Jean-Philippe Roche. Philippe, this is Amanda."

As I was still standing, I reached over, offering her my hand. Amanda looked at it as if I had some horrible disease but shook it before excusing herself.

"Wow!" Landon exclaimed. "That will be all over the place before dessert is on the table."

"Married?" Aunt Trudy looked surprised but couldn't hide the smile on her face.

"It was a quiet affair," my outed husband commented.

"That is the understatement of the year!" Mercedes added.

"When?" Trudy asked, and Trenton let them know just before Christmas.

Tyler and I both looked at him. "How?"

"When I came to your place to give you your Christmas gift, you had on the rings." Trenton laughed, and our salad was served.

Before the salad plates were off the table, Trenton's cell rang. With a glance, he told us it was Veronica and asked us to please excuse him.

"She is going to be so pissed," This was Landon.

"Good," Trudy commented over a gulp of wine.

"She do not like me," I added.

Mercedes burst out laughing. "She thought I was the spawn of Satan when Trudy and I married. Your mother is a serious homophobe, Tyler."

"I realized that after her first little attempt to break up Philippe and me." Tyler began, then followed up with the things she had done. First, she tried to get his dad to buy me off, and then his mother getting me arrested and almost deported.

"It didn't work out like she hoped. I'm afraid of what she will try to do next. At this point, anything is possible." Tyler shared with the table.

I was sorry to hear the sorrow in Tyler's voice. Like Trenton, Veronica's actions were hurting Tyler.

When Trenton returned to the table, he only said that it hadn't taken long to get to her. "I was hoping the therapist would help her. I'm not sure it will. She doesn't want to let go."

I reached over and took his hand. Like Tyler's, it was large and calloused. "You are a good father," I told him, ensuring I said the words correctly.

"You are a good son," Trenton patted my hand and turned to his sister, "Where are the kids?"

Amanda was not detoured even after learning I was Tyler's husband. After dinner was cleaned up and the band played for the next four hours, she pulled Tyler to the dance floor several times. I watched my husband dance with his hand on her waist and the other holding Amanda's. He laughed at her comments, to which I could see she was pleased.

Her attempt to engage Tyler was evident even from across the room. Each time Tyler returned Amanda to her table, he would come back and take me out to dance and tell me everything they had discussed.

The jest of the conversations was always the same. Amanda simply couldn't believe that Tyler could be happy *pretending* to be married to a former prostitute. Not for one minute did she imagine he let me actually have sex with him. He was the man, and I was the woman. It was the only way she could comprehend our relationship. But if Tyler wanted a woman, she was there. She and Tyler had such an extraordinary sex life when they were together. Amanda was sure she could fix him if they spent time together.

Tyler didn't even try to explain to her that he wasn't broken. "There's no point. All I hear is what I've already heard from my mother." Tyler kissed me and smiled.

I wasn't worried; I let him know. And whatever Tyler needed to do to see this to an end, do it.

But Amanda wasn't done. On our way back to the hotel, Tyler reached into his shirt pocket and pulled out a keycard. "What is this?" I asked.

Tyler was laughing. After a moment, he told me that, obviously, Amanda had slipped a keycard into his pocket. Attached to the card was a sticky note letting Tyler know her room number at The Oaks Bluffs Inn and that she would expect him soon. The message was signed with her name and five tiny hearts.

I wanted to laugh, but what Veronica was doing to Amanda wasn't right. "Your mother, she is evil. Amanda is maybe bitch, but she no deserved this."

"You're right, Babe. She doesn't. She'll get the hint when I don't show up tonight. I'm not going to worry about it." Tyler squeezed my hand. "We are set up for an express checkout so we can leave early in the morning and head back home. We'll stop for breakfast along the way."

I couldn't be mad at Amanda, not yet, anyway. Amanda was under Veronica's evil thrall like all those people at the 4th Precinct. If she didn't snap out of it soon after getting the clear message that Tyler wasn't interested, I would allow myself to be pissed. Until then, I just felt sorry for her.

We stripped out of our suits, throwing them over the chair before brushing our teeth and crawling into bed. As tired as we were, we still found time to make love before falling exhausted to sleep.

TYLER

The week was busy.

We arrived home Sunday from Martha's Vineyard around three, having taken our time and stopping at a few places along the way to sightsee. I had seen these places before, but Philippe had not. Like our trip to Disneyland, almost everything was a new experience for my husband.

Monday started our classes. I was teaching, and both of us attended language classes. Philippe was still doing his biweekly classes with Maestro Greco but had added a crash course in conducting an orchestra on Wednesdays and Fridays.

Luckily for us, Spring Break for Harvey Milk Academy and the community college was the same week, the third week of March. We weren't going to be able to go anywhere, but Philippe had promised me he would take some downtime. Maybe we would take a few days, lock the door, turn off the phones, and just veg.

It would take some convincing, but I was going to try. We had dinner plans with Javier and Lola, but that was always relaxing.

On Tuesday, Cord popped into my class during my free period. "Got a minute?" They asked, sitting down and staring at me with a half-smile on their lips.

"Yeah." I knew this look. They wanted something. "What are you up to?"

"We, the department heads, are asking teachers and staff to take a kid home for Spring Break. These are good kids, Tyler. But most of them are starved for a family. The house parents do a fantastic job, but...." Cord sighed. "It's the young ones we are looking to place. We have some kids who are just babies. Sixth graders are only eleven or twelve."

I lifted my hand. "I'll talk to Jean-Philippe. We're staying at home. He'll be working, but we have room for one or two. I can't promise, but I'll ask. I'll let you know tomorrow."

When I got home that afternoon, Philippe was taking a nap, so I turned on the television, the volume low enough not to bother him. I was going to take him out for Sushi and a drink. I wasn't buttering him up, exactly, but I really didn't know how he felt about kids.

The idea of having my own had always been in the back of my mind, but Jean-Philippe and I had never talked about it. He was such a loving, caring person, but having to be a parent might not be something he desired. I supposed I would find out.

Dinner was leisurely. We were halfway through our meal when I broached the subject. "Philippe, Cord stopped by my classroom today." I began.

Philippe put down his chopsticks, "Yous okay. Not havings troubles?"

With his nerves, his freshly acquired English skills flew out the window.

"I'm fine and not in any trouble. You remember the Academy has dormitories for the kids who had been kicked out of their homes when they came out?"

Philippe nodded.

"Well, some of those kids are as young as eleven. The older kids are easier to keep entertained. The school wants to find homes for the little ones during Spring Break. The younger ones are so new to being without family; they have a hard time at the holidays."

"We can haved one or two. Enough rooms for them. I knows how they feel. My hearts breaking for them. *Oui mon cher*! Yes," Philippe jumped out of his chair and moved to wrap his arms around my shoulders. "You are good...a good man. I loved you!" He kissed the top of my head, well, the back, as he still couldn't reach the top of it even with me sitting.

Over the rest of our dinner, we discussed what we might do, and Philippe insisted that we would have kids in the house over the winter holidays. This conversation prompted me to ask about having children of our own someday.

"You want?" he asked.

"I always thought I would. What about you?" I reached over and took Philippe's hand.

"I no have family. Same like kids at school. I want to have…to give home for them. One maybe older, like me, for *adopter*…." Using the translation app, Philippe got out his phone and searched for a word. He laughed, "Is almost same. For *adopting*. But I want one that is me and one that is you! Oh, I say that good!" He gave a small fist bump to the air and smiled at me.

Philippe's smile was like seeing the sun for the first time.

"Really?" I wanted to make sure I had heard him correctly. "You want to adopt and have a few of our own."

Philippe nodded, held up a finger, and pulled out his cell. "I's cheater." He informed me as he typed something. I watched as he mouthed the words a few times before looking back at me.

"We have money." His words were slow. "I know adoption is expensive, and so is sur-ro-ga-cy. But we have money for suchs thing. Yes? If you no want, I fine. I understanding."

It was my turn to get up and hug and kiss my husband. I hadn't realized I wanted to hear those words. "*Je t'aime, Jean-Philippe!*" I told him.

"*Je sais, Tyler Roche!*" I knew enough French to understand what he had said. Of course, Philippe knew I loved him.

Wednesday, I was able to corner Cord, who was busy, to let them know we had room for two kids if that was doable. "Two? Are you sure, Tyler?" They seemed confused, but I assured them Philippe and I had spent hours discussing it, and we had the room.

"I don't have time today, but tomorrow or Friday, why don't you two meet Bennie and me for dinner, and we will talk about it. What you need to do. I'm craving meat, so let's go to a place I know that is not far from where you guys live. It's a steakhouse. I'll send you the address. Let me know if that works for Philippe, and I'll get Bennie to start looking for a babysitter." Cord waved goodbye and disappeared down the hallway.

It ended up being Friday when we met Cord and Bennie at Heinrich's Steakhouse for dinner. We spent most of the meal discussing everything but why we agreed to meet. The school knew of Jean-Philippe's past but also understood that the past was the past.

Already, news that he would be working with the city and Dr. Octavia Hall on an event focusing on the young homeless population on the streets was circulating in the LGBTQIA+ community. Also, the school board felt that Jean-Philippe was a good role model as he had been where all of the students in the boarding school facility had been and survived.

Philippe looked uncomfortable at this praise, but I assured him what Cord was saying was true. If Philippe could go through what he had and still be where he was, he was someone to look up to. I looked up to and respected him immensely.

He lifted his hand as if to push away the words. Philippe started to speak but shook his head. "I just want to live. I want more for me. I...." He shook his head again and took a drink from the wine glass that was still almost full.

Cord leaned across the table. "I get it, Philippe. But many kids don't have whatever you have. We've been talking about having some sort of assembly at the Academy. Asking people in the community to come and talk about their experiences. I'm not sure this is something you would want to do, but you could always open the assembly with music." Cord smiled and changed the subject.

He was quiet all the way home. When I asked Philippe if he was alright, he assured me he was just thinking about everything that had been said. I didn't push the issue, and when we crawled into bed, Philippe wrapped his arms around me and spooned against me.

Sunday evening, all hell broke loose.

It was almost ten, and we were winding down for the night. Both of us had busy weeks ahead, including dinner with the Gutierrez. Philippe was in the kitchen, and I was brushing my teeth after showering. I moved into the living room and behind Philippe when the doorbell rang. On the monitor was Amanda Pollack.

"What?" Philippe looked at me, and I just shrugged.

"Let her in. I'll go get some pants on." I told him as I was standing naked.

Pulling the bedroom door closed but not closing it all the way, I could hear the conversation.

"Amanda. What can we do for yous?" I had to smile at Philippe's careful diction.

"You dirty fucking whore. What have you done to him? Are you blackmailing him because there would be no other reason for him to be with you! We'll do whatever we can to save him from you." I peered between the door and door frame, watching a moment longer. "Do you have him drugged? Is that why he didn't answer the door?"

I had all of this I could take. I stripped out of my flannel pajama bottoms and called out. "Hey, Babe. I need you to get back in here and fuck me again." Stepping into the open space, I froze as if I hadn't known she was there.

Feigning shock, I grabbed a dishtowel from the kitchen island, barely covering my dick, as I moved closer to my husband. "Amanda. What are you doing here?"

I moved to stand behind Philippe, dropping the dishtowel and using him as my cover.

"We know this sick bastard has something he's using to blackmail you. Maybe even drug you so you won't leave. We're going to do everything we can, Tyler, to save you." Amanda was so sincere that I felt sorry for her for just a second. "Whore!" she spat the word at Philippe and back-handed him.

"Amanda. That was an assault. I'm giving you to the count of one before I call the police and have you arrested. I do not ever want to see you again or for you to come near Philippe and me. If you do, I will make sure your life is ruined. You need to remove yourself from my mother, or she will drag you down." I leaned down to gather the towel and cover myself.

"We love you, Tyler. We just want to save you." She pleaded, tears streaming down her face.

"Amanda. You tell my mother I don't need saving. Jean-Philippe has already done that. If I have to, and I'm rather sure I do, I will get a restraining order against you and Veronica. Do I make myself clear? Get the fuck out of my home, Amanda. Do not come back." I didn't touch her but moved to open the door as wide as possible.

She glared at Philippe for a moment, then gave me a look of pity before walking out the door.

I took Philippe into my arms and held him, telling him I was sorry.

After a while, I moved away to get my cell. I called Waldron's office and left a message detailing what had just happened. I asked him to file whatever papers were needed for a restraining order on Amanda Pollack and Veronica Braxton.

It was another night of holding each other. I was afraid it was going to get worse before it got better. I would call Dad in the morning and let him know what happened. Maybe he could do something, but I was relatively sure he was at the point where my mother had done too much damage, and I wasn't sure Dad cared anymore to try and save her.

JEAN-PHILIPPE

Thursday evening, Tyler's father came over to fill us in with the information he had regarding Veronica. A lot had happened since Sunday evening. Veronica had given Trenton an ultimatum: either he supported her in separating me from Tyler, or she would divorce him.

Veronica had already moved all of her legal matters to a new firm. She had already begun the separation process before even speaking to her husband of thirty-five years.

"I don't know who she is anymore, Tyler," Trenton had sobbed into his son's arms.

On Monday morning, Trenton told Veronica on a phone call that Tyler was happy. I was a friendly and loving man, and he would not do anything to jeopardize what Tyler and I had. Tuesday, Trenton had been served divorce papers.

Tyler was worried about his dad losing everything he had worked decades for, but Trenton assured us that his legal team was on top of it. Also, Tyler's parents signed a prenuptial agreement before marriage and updated it over the years.

The house where Tyler grew up would be sold, and the profits would be divided between Trenton and Veronica, each getting 40% of the money and Tyler the remaining 20%. Trenton's company was 80% of his alone.

There would be no alimony or support payments as Veronica was the one filing for the divorce. She was using "Irreconcilable Differences" as her reasoning.

Trenton was brokenhearted but, at the same time, ready for it to be over. He and Tyler spoke of where Trenton would live. All the properties were jointly owned, so Trenton would have to start looking for something soon. He was leaning towards a flat. He didn't want to mess with a yard as he had done that already.

Tyler was just as shocked as his father. No one understood why she was behaving as she was. However, I remembered what Aunt Mercedes said about Veronica being a raging homophobe. When I brought this up, Trenton had said he knew she was conservative in her thinking. Most of the time, their ideas didn't clash. This was something he had never seen or ever expected. He had actually just assumed Veronica didn't like Mercedes, and her sexuality and the sexuality of Trenton's sister, Trudy, hadn't been the issue.

"Do you thinks if me...I not...I was not a prostitute, she will be okay. Or no?" I asked, not looking to make excuses for Veronica Braxton but offering something.

"We originally thought, and I have to admit I did too, that you were just some hooker after Tyler's money and taking advantage of him." Trenton started.

"Dad. I'm not a ten-year-old!" Tyler objected.

"I don't care. You are my son. My only child, and I wanted to protect you if someone were hurting you. Doesn't matter if you're ten or sixty. My point," Trenton looked at me, "is that it didn't take me long to realize you had something special after watching you and Tyler together. You could see the love for each other on your faces. I used to look at your mother that way, and she at me." Tyler's dad cleared his throat, closing his eyes momentarily before continuing.

"Anyway. Once I realized you weren't trying to rob him blind and you loved him, I let the idea go. Also, especially after what Veronica did to get you arrested, I knew, without a doubt, I would love and support the two of you no matter what. I mean it, boys." He reached over with his hands and took one of ours.

I got up and moved to hug him. "Thank you, Dad." I kissed his cheek and returned to my chair.

We finished off a couple of bottles of wine discussing next week and the two junior high kids we would be hosting over Spring Break. I will be working and meeting with Greco. However, one of the kids had already asked if they could tag along. It seemed they played the clarinet, and meeting Greco would be 'so cool.' Tyler and I had already made plans for two nights out, one just for a casual meal and the other at Heinrich's

Steakhouse, which we had fallen in love with.

That brought up the topic of grandchildren. We let the future grandpa know we were interested in having a family, but not just yet.

Friday, we had dinner after a class on how to make tamales at Javier and Lola's. It was after midnight when we tumbled into bed. Next week was Spring Break, and we would pick up our two kids tomorrow around two.

Donny, a twelve-year-old seventh grader, was tall and lanky. Freckled-faced and redheaded, his dark brown eyes looked up at Tyler when he came into the Common Room with his house parents. The house parents, a straight couple, introduced themselves and handed us a paper with contact information, insurance, and medical information. We signed a few documents, and once over the shock of my giant husband, Donny began to chatter.

Tyler listened to him as if he was telling him the most exciting thing. "Donny is starved for a strong male role model. I know Mr. Roche doesn't have Donny in any of his classes, but if he pays that much attention to the description of a new video game, Mr. Roche will have a friend for life."

I smiled and turned as another set of house parents walked in with a slight figure following them. "Hello, everyone. I would like to introduce Syl. Syl," the house mother turned to look at the androgynous teenager, who blinked wide blue eyes. "This is Jean-Philippe Roche."

I offered my hand, and Syl, who was only a few inches taller than me, accepted it. "I know who you are. I've heard you play. You're amazing. My pronouns are they/them." They told me, still holding my hand.

"Mine is he/him/his," Donny called out as he and Tyler joined me.

Like we had done with Donny, we signed and accepted documents.

Donny had been in the dorm since starting this school year, but Syl had been housed here since they were eleven and had come out to their parents as non-binary and gay. Syl was short for Sybil, and we had been cautioned beforehand to make sure that wasn't used. It wouldn't be a problem as Syl had been introduced as Syl.

Easy to remember.

Each of the kids brought a small overnight bag. We placed the bags into the back of the truck and headed to the condo.

Syl would get the guest room, and Donny would sleep in the office with a Murphy bed and its own bathroom.

Donny chattered all the way to the condo. Syl added a comment here and there but didn't say much. Once in the house, I showed Syl their room while Tyler took Donny into his space for the next week. We told them to take some time to unpack, get situated, and meet us in the living room.

I hoped they liked Mexican food because that was on our agenda for this evening. Steve, Marie, Olan, Shirley, and their three boys would be over for a BBQ tomorrow. Marie had a little sister near the ages of Donny and Syl. Hopefully, the five would get along and have a good time.

As it turned out, the teenagers did like Mexican food, and we walked the four blocks for dinner. Tyler let them know they could order anything off the menu they wanted. They hesitantly checked out the offerings before asking if we were sure. Donny's plate was as big as Tyler's, and both all but licked them clean. Syl, like me, chose a smaller entrée, but we left nothing behind.

We talked about the upcoming week.

Syl would come with me on Tuesday and again on Thursday if they wanted. Greco had been excited by the idea, and when I told Syl they needed to bring their clarinet, which I had seen the case with their things, they almost turned as white as their napkin.

"You don't have to play if you don't want to. Maestro wanted you to bring it, just in case. Wednesday if you want you can come with me. I'm working on how to conduct an orchestra as I have to do that for a project. Maestro Greco is teaching me, and I will conduct a rehearsal performance. You're welcome to come. I already got permission." That's what I wanted to say and what my husband translated.

Syl and Donny stared at me when I started to speak, and I explained I was still learning English and they needed to be patient with me. Up till now, everything I had said, I had rehearsed in my head over and over again.

Syl smiled for the first time. "I didn't start to learn English until I was six. My parents moved us from Slovenia. We spoke Slovenian at home. I still dream in that language. I get it."

I reached over and patted their hand. "It is not easy. I haved to think rely difficult...hard."

"Really hard," Tyler corrected me and kissed me lightly.

TYLER

It took only one day for the kids to relax. Well, I should say for Syl to relax. Donny did relax, which meant he stopped talking a mile a minute. Philippe and I slept with our bedroom door open Saturday night, just in case one of the kids cried out.

It didn't happen.

Sunday, after breakfast, we got ready for the BBQ. I hooked up my PlayStation, which I had purchased just before I married Jean-Philippe, so the kids, if they wanted, had something to do. Once everyone arrived, it didn't take long for all six kids to run off into the office.

The weather was nice, so all the doors that led from the house to the balcony were open. The kids ran in and out but were told not to run on the balcony. I wanted to add that there was no running in the house, but there wasn't anything so valuable it couldn't be replaced if it was broken.

Over a late lunch, Steve announced he was preparing to take his exam to become a detective like his former partner, Olan. Everyone was excited for him, and Olan promised to help him however he could.

It was almost ten when the Rodgers loaded up their three and headed out.

Philippe and I were pleased with how it all went and were thrilled when we got hugs from both kids when they wished us goodnight.

Over the week, we enjoyed our little family. Donny and Syl were bright kids. According to Philippe, Syl was a talented Clarinetist. Donny loved math and was already ahead of his grade level. By Wednesday, both kids had opened up about their families.

Donny's folks had left Boston after kicking him out. Before leaving, they signed him over to the state, letting them know they never wanted to see him again.

Fortunately, someone in Social Services who had an association with the Harvey Milk Academy had the file land on their desk. Within a week, Donny was at the academy and back in school.

Syl's story was the same and different. Their dad and mom were divorced. Neither wanted the responsibility of a child who didn't fit their criteria of a perfect daughter. Syl heard from them occasionally, but their first and only question was whether Syl had decided to be a girl. Each time, Syl let them know they were still who they were, and the parent would sigh, shake their head, and walk away.

"I know they'll never accept me, and I'm getting better at accepting it. One of these days, they might get it and want me in their lives, but that isn't going to happen. I told my *mati*, my mother, that last time she showed up. She didn't seem surprised or even hurt."

Donny asked Philippe about his story. Donny had heard, and Syl agreed they wanted to know. Philippe told his story, cleaning it up a bit. Both kids were in tears by the end but were happy everything worked out.

By the end of the week, we were all sad. Philippe and I promised to keep in touch, and they could always come to see me in my classroom if they needed or wanted to. I promised Donny, a big football fan, that I would take him to a few games once the season started. Maestro Greco had given Syl season tickets for the orchestra that could be collected from the Will-Call Window. They were for the nose-bleed section of the theatre, but there were ten, and Syl could bring anyone they wanted.

The week had been such a revelation that we spent the next month working with Waldron's law firm to fill out and register to become foster parents. We weren't there yet. Philippe needed to finish his work with Timon Campbell. But after that, we would be more flexible.

Philippe and I flew to San Francisco the second weekend of April. Like LA and New York, I had been to the '*City by the Bay*' several times. I had taken off the Thursday before so we could settle in San Francisco before it was late evening. Friday and most of Saturday morning, Philippe would be with Campbell and his team checking out the layout for the premiere in a few months.

As San Francisco was Campbell's home, he was excited to show Philippe the historic Golden Gate Theatre. Not only that, but Campbell had pulled a few strings, got us on a dinner cruise Saturday evening, and provided a car/guide for a trip to the wine country on Sunday.

We had a redeye flight booked for early Monday morning, but I could sleep on the plane and be ready to work. If nothing else, I would hit the sack as soon as I got home from the Academy Monday afternoon.

I accompanied Philippe to the Golden Gate Theatre Friday morning. It was originally a vaudeville house and opened its doors in 1922. Later, it was a theater that showed movies. After a decline, it was reopened in 1979 as a performing arts theatre.

Like many old theatres, it was a stately Grand Dame of a building. I took a seat a few rows up from the stage. I watched as Campbell, Philippe, his interpreter, and several others to whom I had been introduced walked around the stage and the pit and disappeared backstage, only to reappear twenty minutes later.

They moved to an aisle and watched as a massive screen was lowered from behind the curtains, filling the stage.

After lunch on Friday, I returned to the hotel and waited for Philippe to return. I knew he would be busy, so I brought a few things I could work on. I also checked in with Dad. After the week with Syl and Donny, Dad moved out of the apartment and into our guest bedroom. Dad had promised Philippe and me he would move out as soon as he could, to which we assured him he needn't rush on our account.

To make him feel more at home, we rearranged the office – taking out my exercise equipment – and turned it over for him to use as a home office. I found a folding screen we had placed in front of the hallway leading to the back bedrooms. The screens looked like a Japanese Silk print but were actually a one-way mirror. The screen allowed you to see who was in and what was happening in the central part of the condo from the hallway.

From the other side, you only saw the beautiful landscape. We promised Dad we would not walk around the house naked or do anything that would traumatize him. He had laughed, telling us he remembered when he was our age, but thanked us for not traumatizing him by having sex on the kitchen floor.

Philippe was mortified at Dad's words, but Dad laughed for a full five minutes at Philippe's horrified expression. I just smiled. We had done just that the night before Dad moved in.

As far as I was concerned, Dad was doing surprisingly well. At least, as far as I could tell.

Mom, who I was now only calling Veronica, had really damaged Dad. I think he felt as betrayed by her behavior as I did. The thing was, Dad and I talked about it. I felt so awful that my actions, which I wouldn't amend, caused this.

Dad promised me the divorce was a long time coming. As much as he had tried to keep the marriage going, over the past decade, Veronica had become more challenging to live with. "I'm surprised this hadn't happened as soon as you went off to college," He confessed during one of our late-night *tête-á-têtes*.

That had been a surprise to me.

My afternoon call was a pleasant one. Dad was at the condo, watching television and waiting for Steve and Marie to come for dinner. He was fine, and I was not to call him again but to have a good time with my husband.

A car picked us up on Saturday to deliver us for the three-hour San Francisco Premier Dinner Dance Cruise. The views were as spectacular as the three-course meal. We drank, well, I drank a few cocktails, and after dessert, I whisked Jean-Philippe out onto the dance floor for a spin around the postage-sized cleared area. After that, since we were reminded to bring our jackets, we stood up on the deck until we docked.

Another surprise from the trip was Campbell had booked us at Meadow Wood B&B in Napa Valley. The car, with the driver who would ferry us from place to place, drove us to the B&B outside St. Helena, California. The B&B had expected us and were pleasant even though it was almost eleven when we were dropped off.

Ken, our driver, handed us a printed itinerary for tomorrow and let us know that it could be switched around if we wanted.

The Cottage Room was rustic and elegant. The King-sized bed was between a large fireplace and a small outside eating area. I took a moment to light the fire as Philippe pulled out our toiletries for the evening.

Once the fire was lit, we stripped down to our briefs, put on the thick robes that the B&B provided, and sat outside. However, the cold night air didn't take long to chase us back inside.

Philippe stripped out of his robe and briefs and lay on his stomach facing the fire. "This very nice. We needed fireplace in out... our home."

Following his example, I moved to cover him with my body, keeping most of my weight off him. In his ear, I whispered, "Should we start looking for something?"

Philippe wiggled his perfect ass against my dick and suggested that was a topic we could discuss at a later time. Then he, my husband is very limber, twisted around and pulled me down to his mouth. And as I had been a very good man, I got one of his 'bendy' surprises!

The score for ***Albinism: A Death Sentence in Africa*** had been completed for over a month. I had to put it away, or I would find something that needed to be changed. Campbell and Greco both assured me the composition was perfect. I had already recorded it at a studio in Greater Boston.

It was a unique experience to have the movie on the screen and conduct the small orchestra, adjusting the speed and volume to match what was happening on the monitor. The process had taken three days. The first day and a half focused on getting through the movie itself. As we played, I made notes, so by the third day, it took two takes to get it to everyone's satisfaction.

My schedule was now open to begin work with Dr. Hall and the benefit the city wanted to have to draw attention to the plight of teenage homelessness and prostitution. I would be the main attraction for the concert, but I also knew I wanted to bring in others, and that was what I was working on now.

Cade Evans was currently on tour in Europe, so I had until September before I would be able to become part of his group.

I had thought I had bit off more than I could chew, but it all seemed to work out better than I had hoped.

As for Tyler, he had adjusted to teaching as if he had been born into it. The students loved him, and the school was already trying to get him more involved with the board. Tyler had told me this was in part because of who his family was.

"Is this somethings you want?" I had asked one night after the lights were out.

"*Peut-être, mais il faut y penser.*" Tyler had answered in rather good French.

"Why you thinks about it?" I said in English.

He pulled me against him, Tyler's chin resting on the top of my head. "I'm really enjoying teaching. If I sat on the board, that's a lot of responsibility I'm just not sure I want right now."

"So, tells them." I shrugged, and Tyler corrected my words. That put a smile on my face.

We had begun speaking more French in the house. Well, Tyler and his father spoke French, and I spoke English. It was nice that Trenton could help with my language immersion. I let them correct me, but only if I wasn't tired. When I was exhausted, usually by the time dinner was finished, they let me be.

Mostly!

I was still working with Greco on Tuesdays and Thursdays but had finished my crash course in conducting. We were currently working on an upcoming performance. Elizabeth Grander, Leroy Kilgore, and I were all asked to perform with the city's orchestra in October. According to Greco, Grander's parents weren't sure they wanted her to be on stage with me. Still, Greco assured me that Grander could be replaced as incredible as she was. I needn't worry about her closed-minded parents.

Thursday, I got home later than my usual time. I picked up the ingredients to make a Bouillabaisse and a loaf of French bread. Tyler would be home after four; if I started the stew now, it would be ready by six. The longer it simmered, the more flavor it would have, so I wasn't worried about overcooking it.

It was five when the house phone started to ring. I didn't answer it because I never answered that phone, and if Tyler or Trenton needed me, they had my cell phone number. I was surprised, however, that it was five and Tyler wasn't home. I stopped practicing and called his cell. It went straight to voicemail, which was unusual.

He sometimes forgot to charge it, so I wouldn't worry, not yet anyway.

The phone rang six more times, but there was nothing when I checked the messages.

At six-twenty, there was a banging on the door. Steve in his uniform, Olan in a suit, Ashton Braxton, and a woman I didn't recognize stood in the hallway outside the condo. I threw the door open, and Steve reached for me first.

"We need you to come and sit down, Philippe." Steve's words

were difficult to understand as I was terrified.

I was maneuvered to the sofa, Steve on one side of me and Olan on the other. Assistant Deputy Police Chief Ashton Braxton stood in the same place he had all those months ago.

"Jean-Philippe, as far as we know, Tyler is alive," Ashton spoke, and the woman translated into French.

I shot off the sofa and ran into the bathroom, emptying my stomach of my lunch in between sobs. After a moment, I felt a hand rubbing my back and another handing me a cold, wet cloth. "You need to come back into the living room, Philippe," Steve's voice was unnaturally calm as he pulled me up and back to the sofa.

Once I was situated, Steve held my hand, and Braxton began again. "This is what we know. At two-thirty today, someone called the school office and told them you were injured and were outside and needed Tyler to ride with you to the hospital." Ashton paused to allow the translator to finish.

"Once outside, he was tased and thrown into the back of a van. We were able to read the plates from the outside CCTV. The van was old and reported stolen yesterday."

Before Ashton could continue, a red-faced Trenton burst into the apartment and scooped me into his arms. After a minute, Ashton told us to have a seat, and I sat with Tyler's dad's arm, holding me tight against him.

"Right now, we have only one working theory, and I need for both of you to keep it together. We think this might be payback. Ted Collins, the man who had had Tyler beaten and stabbed, got out of jail on a technicality two days ago."

I don't know who was sobbing the hardest, Trenton or me.

"This isn't a sure thing, Uncle Trenton. We're working on locating Collins now."

"Whats if Tyler he is...he has...Collins haved him?" I tried to ask, then switched to French. "What happens to Tyler if this Collins has him?"

Ashton's face told me everything I needed to know. If Ted Collins had Tyler, he was dead. Trenton understood this, too, because the cry that came from him was devastating.

Trenton, Steve, and I sat on the sofa, too stunned to think or speak. After ten minutes, Olan told me the stew had been removed from the burner and placed in the refrigerator.

I needed to gather my wallet, phone, and whatever else I needed as I was required to go down to the station for questioning.

"What the fuck for, Ashton!" My father-in-law bellowed at his nephew.

"Uncle Trenton, we just need to ask him a few questions. We already know he had nothing to do with this, but we must follow protocol. The questions need to be asked." Ashton tried to soothe his uncle.

Trenton turned away from the men in the room after asking which precinct I was being taken to. Then he called Waldron to let him know what was happening.

"Dammit, Uncle Trenton. Jean-Philippe doesn't need a lawyer. He isn't a suspect."

Trenton's shock had become a steel façade. "Be that as it may, Waldron will be in the room with him when you question him. Do I need to call my lawyer?"

"No," Steve spoke, trying to take some heat off the Assistant Deputy.

"I'll drive over, and when this bullshit is done, Jean-Philippe, I'll drive you home." Trenton leaned down and kissed my forehead.

It was almost midnight when we got back home.

I was exhausted but unable to sleep.

The questions were more about Tyler and if he had said anything unusual or spoken of anyone following him.

A different detective came in halfway through the process. He asked me the questions I knew would come.

"Mr. Roche. Tyler Braxton recently changed his Will so that you are the sole beneficiary if something were to happen. Are you aware of this?" The detective accused without accusing.

"Oui. J'étais dans le bureau de M. Waldron lorsqu'il les a signés." I said and the translator said, "Yes. I was in Mr. Waldron's office when he signed them."

Robert lifted his head and looked across the table at the officer, "Mr. Roche asked me to change his will. Mr. Roche, here, didn't know about it until it was signed. He, in fact, tried to talk Tyler Roche out of making the changes."

"That's convenient for him, but we're talking a lot of money. Maybe you got greedy and wanted the money for yourself?" The detective sneered at me.

"Detective Loomis, I will not have you use that tone of voice with my client. His husband is missing." Robert Waldron growled.

"Just doing my job. We've already checked your financials. There have been no unusual activities on your accounts. Nothing to show you would have paid someone to murder your husband."

At that, I burst into tears, and Loomis left the room.

Ashton stepped in a moment later, apologizing for Loomis' behavior. However, I was relatively sure my cousin, by marriage, had been on the other side of the one-way mirror the entire time.

The bed smelled of Tyler, and I finally had to get up and go lay on the couch. Sometime around two, exhausted, I fell asleep.

The aroma of coffee woke me, and I looked over the back of the sofa to find Trenton, still in his pajamas, making coffee. He had thrown a blanket over me at some point, and when I stood, I folded it up and left it on the couch.

"You sleeped…you sleep?" I asked, accepting the coffee mug.

"About as well as you, I would think. Why did you come out here?"

"The beds its smell of Tyler. Too hard." I didn't even try to keep my voice from breaking.

Trenton wrapped his arms around me and rocked me for a few minutes. He was hurting and just as afraid as I was.

"Do you called Veronica? She maybe need to know." I questioned, sitting at the kitchen island.

He looked shocked at my suggestion. He hadn't even thought to call her. Trenton pulled out his phone and dialed her number. Like Tyler's, Veronica's cell went straight to voicemail. "That's odd." He commented, getting up and refreshing our coffees.

My phone rang shortly after I had finished my coffee. It was Mrs. Harrison-Becker, with Cord on the line, wanting to know if I had heard anything. I shared with them what I learned, which I admitted wasn't much. I promised to keep them posted. Mrs. Harrison-Becker asked me to write her number and call her and/or Cord if I needed anything or had any new information.

At ten, Steve showed up. He let us know Ashton appointed him as the go-between between the police department and us. As of now, they did have some good news. Ted Collins had been arrested almost as soon as he got out of jail for drunk driving. The police department had obtained a warrant for his cellphone, and the calls he had made were not out of the ordinary and weren't to anyone who might need to be worried about. "What that means is that there is a good possibility that Collins has nothing to do with this."

"Have you checked with Veronica? Her cell goes to voicemail, which is completely unusual for her." Steve seemed stunned at Trenton's comment.

"Do you think she would do something like this?" he asked.

"To be honest, Steve. I wouldn't be surprised. She's just as dangerous as this Collins character. I can't imagine she would, but I also didn't imagine she would do what she did to Philippe in January." With each word, Trenton Braxton seemed to shrink.

Steve looked at his uncle for a solid minute before pulling out his phone and placing a call.

TYLER

"So," I began after turning off the computer. "Dr. King's speech was a monumental event. We have to look at the time to understand its context. However, everything that Dr. King said can be applied today. Yes, it was about equal rights for African Americans in the 1960s, but it was also about more. Can someone tell me why it is?"

I still felt chills hearing Dr. King's *I Have A Dream* speech. It was important for this upcoming generation to understand why it was made and its impact on African Americans and for other minorities.

Did it, in fact, even have an effect on others?

Hands flew up, and I was about to call on a stud[1]ent when I was called to the office over the class intercom.

"Oooh! Mr. Roche's in trouble." One student laughed.

"Going to the principal's, Mr. Roche. What did you do?" Another called out.

"You discuss among yourselves what you think, and as I am not in trouble, I'll see you in a few minutes." I teased back, hoping I was indeed not in trouble.

Halfway between my classroom and the office, Cord was waiting for me. "What are you working on with your class?" They tried to smile, but I saw right through it.

"What's going on, Cord?"

They didn't answer as Mrs. Harrison-Becker came sprinting down the hallway. "Mr. Greco said he was okay but needed to get to the hospital."

That froze me mid-stride, and then I started to take off. Harrison-Becker grabbed my arm. "Listen and walk. Mr. Greco said Jean-Philippe fell and broke his leg. They had one of the other members of the orchestra – I think – put him in a van. They have to pass this way, and your husband wants you to go with him to the hospital."

The three of us stopped in front of the office. I looked out the glass doors, and there was an old van parked at the curb, its sliding door open. I could see legs on the floorboard and a hand waving for me. It didn't look right, but I needed to check if Philippe was out there.

"Dr. King's *I Have A Dream* speech." I turned to Cord, then to the principal. "I'll call you when I know something, but I'm assuming I'll see you tomorrow."

We all walked out of the school. Cord and Harrison-Becker stopped at the top of the stairs as I headed down. When I realized what was happening, I had enough time to turn to the two horrified people and yell, "Get the fuck inside!" before someone tased me.

Three large men shoved me into the van, and it sped off. I was aware enough to know that Philippe was not in the van. I was grateful for that.

"Give him the drug before he comes around," A deep voice barked out, and I felt the sting of an injection in my leg.

After that, I remembered nothing.

I didn't move as I regained consciousness. I listened. There were voices, but they were not nearby. I was aware of the restraints on my wrists and ankles. I had been stripped and was in some sort of gown, like the ones you get in the hospital.

With effort, I just felt. I had an I.V. in my arm. The place smelt like a doctor's office, not having the pungent odors of a hospital.

"Good, I see you are awake. We're happy to have you with us, Mr. Braxton." I opened my eyes to see a man dressed like a doctor. He was as unassuming as you could get. Nothing about him drew your attention to him. "I'm Dr. Mandelsen, and you are in my clinic. The next few days will be hard on you. I apologize for that, but it can't be helped. We have to get all the toxins out of your system you have been given by your captor. After that, we will work on helping reprogram you. We see this often with people who have been seduced by the homosexuals. It's a shame, but we will make you better."

I let him speak, but now I had a few things to say. "Please understand, Dr. Mandelsen, when I am able, I will break your fucking neck and anyone else who gets between me and the door."

His smile sent a chill down my spine. He was one unhinged man. "They all say that, but in the end, they are all as normal and compliant as good straight people should be." Mandelsen nodded, and a nurse added something to the I.V.

My guts were on fire. I was sitting on the tiny toilet in the cell with my head in the sink. Nothing was left in my system, but I still had diarrhea and was vomiting. Over a speaker, someone let me know just a few more hours, and they would let me clean up and have some liquid. They didn't want me to become dehydrated.

I was naked in a cell when I was woken several hours ago. The cell had three things: a bench attached to the floor, a small toilet, and a deep sink with a wide-mouthed drain. The lights in the high ceiling were recessed, and the door had no visible handles.

A large drain was centered in the floor, and the floor sloped to it, allowing easy drainage. It was my nightmare vision of a horror movie prison cell.

As soon as I woke, the cramps started, and then everything I had eaten or drank over the last forty-eight hours came up or out. I hadn't moved from where I sat for so long that I feared my ass was becoming part of the stainless-steel toilet.

"Mr. Braxton," Mandelsen's monotone voice called out from a window that opened in the door. "How are you feeling?" He didn't wait for an answer but droned on, "I know you feel a little weak, but in a few minutes, we will move you to a room and start a few bags of saline to help you feel better. Now. Are you going to cooperate?"

"Fuck you, asshole!"

"I thought so," He said, not sounding surprised.

I didn't look up but heard the pop before a dart lodged into my shoulder. "That will help you relax so we can clean you up and get you settled."

The drug took effect quickly, and I had enough forethought to get off the toilet and move a few feet to lie on the floor. The last thing I wanted was to get a damn concussion from falling off a toilet.

"How many days have I been here," I asked the orderly who had brought me what looked like breakfast.

Whatever they were giving me made me feel like a zombie. I was aware of what was happening around me but didn't seem to have the energy or the will to do anything about it.

They appeared to have reduced the dosage today, as I almost felt normal.

"You've been here two days, Mr. Braxton. Today is Saturday. After you eat your breakfast, we are going to move you into the 'visitation room.' You have a visitor coming at about ten. They are so excited to see you. I'm going to step out of the room and release your restraints. Please eat then shower. While you're cleaning up, I will lay out a fresh gown for you." The orderly was just as creepy as the doctor running this place.

I waited. The man stepped out of the room and closed the door. I heard a buzz and then a click as the restraints snapped open. Like the cell, this room had a window in the door, and the orderly was watching me. I smiled and threw the plate of food. It hit the center of the window.

That made me laugh.

They really loved their dart guns in this hellhole. Because I refused to get out of bed, the orderly, or someone, shot me with another dart.

"Dr. Mandelsen tells me you are being very belligerent, Tyler. You need to cooperate so you can get better, and we can get you home," Veronica's voice seemed concerned.

It had taken me a few minutes to get my bearings. I was in a room resembling a parlor in an elegant home. Veronica was sitting across from me on a sofa. A tea service with petit fours on a delicate plate was on a coffee table between us.

Across from her, I was strapped at my wrists and ankles into a chair.

"Veronica, what the fuck have you done. You realized this is kidnapping?"

She actually tsked at me. "When you remove someone from a cult and have them deprogrammed, it isn't kidnapping, Tyler dear. I'm just doing what needs to be done. Your father doesn't have the backbone to do it, but I do. Dr. Mandelsen has had some success in reprogramming people like you. I know you don't want to live your life as you have been. Amanda will be waiting for you when this is all done. You are going to have such beautiful children together."

Who was this crazy woman?

"Veronica…"

"Dammit, Tyler. I am your mother, and you will address me as such. This is another thing that evil, disgusting pervert has taken from me, and I will not have it." She screamed at me, spittle hitting my face.

This is a game I knew how to play. Four years working undercover had to account for something. I put the blandest expression on my face with just a hint of a smirk, "You, Veronica, lost the privilege to be my mother in January. You will never be more to me than a sick, twisted, hateful bitch who threw away her husband and son. Nothing, bitch, nothing will make me ever call you mother. Well, maybe 'motherfucker' but you will never be my mom again. Do you understand that, Veronica Hawthorne?"

My ears rang from the force of the backhanded slap she gave me. She smoothed her skirt and smiled down at me. "I know what you just said was part of the brainwashing that whore did to you. But don't worry, my love, I won't hold it against you."

"You need to listen, *Veronica*!" I sneered her name. "When I am out of this place, you, Mandelsen, and everyone who helped you will be in jail for a very long time. I'm going to play along, but when I am out, you had better be somewhere where I can't find you. One more thing, Veronica, if I hear you call my husband a whore one more time, they are never going to find your body. Do...you...understand...me!"

There was a flash of fear in her eye, but just for a second. The smile was replaced with one as evil as I had ever seen in all the times I dealt with cold-blooded murders.

Veronica was not a healthy woman.

A few minutes after she left, the orderly came and wheeled me into a surgical theater. "Electroshock therapy has come a long way since it was first used." He spoke as he moved me under an operating light and proceeded to attach electrodes to the side of my forehead. After he was satisfied with their location, he forced a bite-guard into my mouth, strapping it tight behind my head. "Don't want you to bite your tongue off, now do we?"

Mandelsen came in, and the orderly stepped out. "I was not happy to hear how you spoke to your loving mother. She's worried about you and is doing everything she can to help and protect you. This will help start the process of putting your mind in the right place. We'll talk more tomorrow. You'll sleep most of the day away."

Shaking my head, yelling 'no' around the rubber in my mouth, I watched as the maniacal doctor moved over to a control panel and made a few adjustments. He looked over his shoulder at me with a smile before hitting a red button and sending electricity through my brain.

We didn't speak on Sunday.

Instead, the orderly wheeled me into the room with the electroshock equipment twice that day.

I wasn't a religious man, but I prayed to whoever was up there to send some help and to keep my beloved Jean-Philippe safe.

JEAN-PHILIPPE

Friday and Saturday were a blur. Trenton never left the apartment. The only time we were not in the same room was when we tried to get some rest in the evening. I gave up sleeping in our bed. I had moved to the living room, and on Saturday, Trenton had two rollaways delivered, and we had set them up in the empty space of the living room.

Neither one of us wanted to be alone.

We ate and drank, not for enjoyment but for sustenance. We needed to keep up our strength.

Saturday evening, Ashton came by to inform us that Veronica had been located. She was in the Hamptons at a cottage she had leased a month ago. From what they were able to find out, Veronica had been there for a week. She had procured a new cell phone, which is why Trenton hadn't been able to contact her.

The police had obtained a warrant for her cell phones. They determined the calls Veronica had made did not raise any red flags.

"We've been able to use the CCTVs to track the van. It pulls into a warehouse north of the city, but nothing ever comes out. We worked with the police in Middleton, but the van had been wiped clean. The only thing we could find was a syringe with Tyler's DNA on the needle. We determined that the drug Midazolam was in the syringe." Ashton informed us.

"Whats is it, Mid-a-zo-lam? It hurted him?" I asked, reaching over to take Trenton's hand.

"No. It just would have knocked Tyler out. That's actually a good thing, Uncle Trenton. Philippe. That means that whoever wanted him wanted him alive. We know for a fact that Ted Collins or the group he was associated with isn't behind this. We've been looking at other cases Tyler worked on while undercover or as a beat cop. Word on the street is there is no word on the street, and that's also a good thing." Ashton finished and sat watching us.

We were quiet after what we had heard.

Ashton told us that he, Steve, Robert Waldron, and maybe Detective Rodgers, Olan, would be coming over tomorrow for beer and bringing pizza. We needed the distraction, and they needed it too.

I thought it was a good idea, anything to help keep my mind busy. Trenton wasn't as sure but finally capitulated when his nephew told him it wasn't an option.

It ended up being Steve, Ashton, and Olan. They brought over two six-packs and called for pizza once they were in the condo. Steve had brought two bottles of the stout that I liked, which I nursed on for most of the evening.

Surprisingly, we had a good time. I hadn't seen Trenton this relaxed in a while, and even though I was still freaking out inside, I was able to go along with the crowd. I wasn't much for sports, but I was learning to enjoy basketball. Tyler had worked to educate me. He was an avid fan and had season tickets to the Celtics and his alma mater. Tyler wanted me to go along but, more importantly, to enjoy the game.

It was getting late. Everyone helped clean up, and Steve walked the empty pizza boxes to the end of the hallway and into the garbage shoot. He returned, and everyone chatted for a few minutes before they started towards the door.

The loud banging on the door froze everyone in place. I looked at the monitor and turned to the men, my family. "Get into hallways. Don't comed out. I waited and sees whats happens." I whispered. They did as I had asked, and I rumpled through my hair to look like I had been sleeping.

"Whats you want?" I snarled as I threw open the door. Veronica wasn't alone. A man who made Tyler and Trenton look small came around behind her and grabbed me by the neck, moving me across the room and against the far wall.

Veronica closed and locked the door, then turned to the man, telling him to keep me still. When I was in front of him, my arms pulled back behind me; Veronica pulled something out of her purse and swung it. I was hit twice in the face and three times in my chest.

I tasted blood but didn't make a sound. It wasn't the first time I had been beaten. I knew how to hold back the cries of pain.

"What you do to Tyler?" I said, spitting blood at her feet, which garnered me a backhand across the face.

"He's safe and away from you. Dr. Mandelsen will fix the damage you have done. Amanda is ready to make him a nice wife. I was going to just put your ass on a plane and send you overseas. You would be surprised how much I could get for you. Someone like you on the market is worth enough that I could buy that Bentley my spineless husband wouldn't get for me." She was pacing now.

"Who you sell me for." Damn my English, but Veronica understood me.

I was worried that someone would come out from behind the screen. I added, "You needed to stay where you ares," I looked directly at Veronica but hazarded a glance over her shoulder. No one came out, so I knew they understood.

"Some prince in the Middle East. From what I understand, he has quite the harem." She hit me again. "But I've decided to buy the car without selling you for a handsome profit. Rollins, what can we do to make his death as painful as possible but make it look like an accident?"

Rollins, the man behind me, chuckled. "I have a few ideas, Mrs. Braxton. We could break all his limbs, then I could snap his neck and throw him down the stairs. Or better yet, we could have him write his own suicide note, and then I could chuck him off the roof. I still would break his arms and legs first."

"I like the last one. Let's find something to gag him; don't want him waking the neighbors. I'll look for some paper first," Veronica turned and headed to the back office just as Steve, Ashton, and Olan came around the screen with their guns drawn.

"Freeze. Rollins, let go of Mr. Roche and put your hands up. NOW!" Ashton bellowed.

Instead of freaking out, Veronica went ballistic. Calling the men every disgusting name, telling them she was only protecting her son. Nothing any of them had the balls to do.

I had moved to the kitchen and watched Steve handcuff Rollins and, Olan, Veronica. Ashton was on the phone calling for a few squad cars and an ambulance to take me to the hospital to be checked out.

My eyes drifted to Trenton, who was moving slowly into the space. "We have it all on video, Veronica. Everything. What happened to you? What kind of woman has her own son tortured and traffics someone just because you don't like them. Make me understand, Veronica." With each word, Trenton Braxton was breaking into a million pieces.

I stepped around and wrapped my arms around his waist. "The woman I loved is gone, Jean-Philippe." He sobbed, and despite the pain of his arms around me, I didn't let go.

Veronica continued ranting as we waited for the police and ambulance to arrive. Rollins was already letting Detective Olan Rodgers know he would tell them everything. He wouldn't have killed me; Veronica hadn't paid him enough for that.

Listening to the Assistant Deputy Chief of Police as he spoke on the phone, I finally had hope that Tyler would be alright. Ashton disconnected and turned to Trenton and me. "Dr. Mandelsen is a wackjob who has a clinic, in of all places, Shutter Island. He works almost exclusively with evangelic groups and provides 'gay conversion therapy.' From what I've heard, it's rather severe stuff."

I started to cry, adding my tears to Trenton's. Ashton continued, "Because he was transported across state lines, the FBI's involved, and they will be raiding the place in the next few hours. They'll take Tyler to a hospital in Manhattan. Philippe, we'll head that way as soon as we get you checked out."

We didn't speak more as backup poured into the condo.

I was taken to the emergency room, Trenton at my side. I remembered to put on my sunglasses even though it was night, as I knew the lights in the hospital would be bright.

Four hours later, I was released. I had deep bruising and a few stitches inside my mouth and on my cheekbone. Veronica had used a sock filled with soap to deliver her punches. It was very effective.

While I was being treated, Trenton had arranged for a plane to take us to Manhattan. Between doctors and nurses and a few people looking to see the elf, he had told me that the FBI had raided Mandelsen's clinic and located Tyler.

He was not in good shape but expected to recover.

At six a.m. the following day, Trenton and I stood just outside Tyler's hospital room. Trenton requested a French Language translator for me, and we listened to the doctor describe Tyler's injuries.

"As far as we can tell, he had at least four electroshock therapy treatments. You'll see the discoloration on his temples. The electroshock equipment Mandelsen was using was antiquated at best. The orderly, who was assigned to Mr. Roche, provided us with his chart. We know every drug that he was inflicted with. Mr. Roche. Mr. Braxton. Tyler is going to seem disoriented when you speak with him. We anticipate it will take a few days before he recovers from the electroshock." The doctor paused every few words to allow the translator to catch up, but I didn't need the time lag. All I wanted was to get to my husband.

"Mr. Roche has lost about twenty pounds, but he will put that back on once he gets some nourishment. Just take it slow with him and for yourselves. Any questions?"

"When can I take him home?" I heard the woman's voice repeat my words in English.

"Maybe three or four days. It depends on how long Mr. Roche's system takes to get rid of the heavy narcotics he was given. Three or four days," the doctor repeated.

"He's asleep, not unconscious," the nurse at Tyler's bedside told us as we entered the room. "He's going to sleep for most of the day, and that's a good thing. I'm Lavern, and if you need anything, let me know." Lavern walked past us and squeezed my shoulder before leaving the room.

I wasn't sure if it was FBI policy or my father-in-law's influence because Tyler had a private room. There was a sofa and two over-sized recliners in an attached sitting room. Trenton pulled up a chair, the type generally found in a hospital room and moved to take his son's hand.

That wasn't good enough for me. I checked to ensure no wires, tubes, or other paraphernalia were on the other side of the bed. Finding none, I climbed up next to my husband and breathed him in.

I didn't move when the doctor came in to check on him, not the three times Lavern returned. Only Trenton, forcing me up to go get something to eat, was able to move me.

While we ate, Trenton made hotel reservations for us nearby. An FBI agent found us in the cafeteria and questioned us.

We regurgitated what we had already told the Boston Police, which seemed to satisfy the agent. His one concern was Trenton Braxton. He was worried that Trenton would side with his wife in her defense.

"I can assure you, Agent Salah, what my soon-to-be ex-wife did to my son-in-law here," he pointed to me, "and my son was totally and completely unforgivable." Trenton Braxton was an intimidating man when he was all puffed up. "I will in no way be used by her or her legal team to defend what she did. Veronica Hawthorne is a sick woman."

"I understand, Mr. Braxton." Salah turned to me, "Mr. Roche, we have seen the video of your assault. We would like to take it further and see if we can track down the trafficking connection Ms. Braxton mentioned. Is that alright with you?"

"Do what you needed to does," I told the man, who looked at me for a second, then switched to French. "Will you be willing to testify against Ms. Braxton?"

"*Oui!*" I would testify in a heartbeat.

"*D'accord.* Okay, that's all I need for now." Agent Salah stood.

"If you need us, we will be here until we can take Tyler home." Trenton shook the agent's hand, and I followed suit.

When we returned to the room, I crawled back onto the bed, and Trenton stretched out in one of the recliners, falling fast asleep.

219

TYLER

This was a different place.

The smell was distinct, and the incessant beeping of a monitor was nearby. The other thing, unlike where I had been, was the small, warm body pressed against my side. I carefully opened my eyes and turned my head. The room was dark, but there was enough light to see my beautiful, magical Jean-Philippe curled up around me, an arm resting on my chest.

I looked around and saw Dad sleeping in a recliner, then I could separate his snoring from all the other sounds in the room. Closing my eyes, I let the tears finally flow. I had been terrified that I would never see Jean-Philippe or even Dad again. The last thing I remember was being taken back into that room, where they shocked me.

My mind was still fuzzy. One moment, everything was clear, then the next, I couldn't recall what had happened. I was surprised I could even remember my name between the drugs and the electroshock.

The feel of Philippe's fingers on my cheek, wiping away my tears, pulled my gaze back down to him.

"Hey, Babe," I croaked out.

"I missed you." He told me, moving up to brush his lips over mine.

"Where am I?"

"Manhattan. You was in place called Shutter Island." Philippe moved so I could see his face, and it was my turn to sit up.

"Philippe, what happened. Who hit you?" I lightly brushed my hands over his face, stopping only when he flinched.

"Your mother did that and a lot more." I turned to find Dad standing at the bedside. Like Philippe, his eyes were full of tears. He leaned over and kissed my forehead before breaking down and telling me how sorry he was that Veronica had hurt Philippe and me.

"Dad. Dad." It took a minute to get him to calm down, "You didn't do any of this, and I can tell you there would have been nothing you could have done to stop her. Veronica is a sick woman, Dad. I'm sorry. I know she's hurting you too." It was my turn to sob over what my mother had done.

The night nurse came in and threatened to kick them out if they didn't stop crying and let me rest. I promised we would stop crying for now, but I couldn't guarantee it would last.

"Well, at least your sense of humor is back," She snickered and left after adding something to my I.V. line.

"Damn, I'm going to go back to sleep. Dad. Take Philippe somewhere and put him to bed. You too. You both look like you haven't slept in days." I instructed.

I was surprised that they didn't argue, and after more hugs and kisses, I watched the two men I loved most walk out the door.

Sleep engulfed me within minutes.

It was two days before I had it explained to me what Dr. Mandelsen had put my body through. It would take a month or so for my system to return to where it had been. The medical team at the hospital assured me there were no lasting effects.

Philippe and Dad were at the hospital each day.

On day three, I was able to call Mrs. Harrison-Becker and catch her up on what had happened.

School was almost out for the year, and my classes had been covered. She wanted me to come by when I returned home just to check in but assured me my job was waiting for me when I got back.

Cord called me later that afternoon and let me know my kids were doing well. However, it had been hard on them when the news of my abduction circulated around the Academy. If I was feeling up to it, they wanted me to come by before school ended so the students could see me.

It would be two more days before they would release me. During my stay in the hospital, Agent Salah and his partner stopped by and questioned me once a day. I learned what happened to Philippe through the FBI, not Dad or Philippe. Also, they shared the charges against Veronica Hawthorne with me.

Kidnapping.

Assault.

Conspiracy to commit murder.

And a grocery list of other charges....

Veronica was claiming innocence. She was telling anyone and everyone who would listen it was a conspiracy. Despite the rhetoric Veronica was spewing, Salah explained that a team of Psychiatrists examined Veronica and assured the FBI and the legal teams that she was sane enough to stand trial. Since the charges were Federal, she would do a considerable amount of time.

Through the FBI, Veronica's request for me to visit had been delivered and categorically denied. I would be happy to see her once her trial had begun. Other than that, I had no desire to ever lay eyes on her again.

Dad had us flown back to Boston. He didn't come with us to the condo but told us he was going to Uncle Ben's for a few days.

We stood in the open space between the door and the living room. I was looking down at Philippe, who was looking up at me. We didn't speak, but Philippe offered his hand after a second, and I took it. Then, I pulled him to me, lifted him off the floor, and carried him to our bedroom.

We didn't remove our clothes but curled around each other on the bed.

"I was afraid!" Philippe's voice trembled against my chest.

"I was too," I pulled him tighter against me.

"I am sorry! I did this things to you." Philippe attempted to move out of my arms, but I held him tight.

There was no way this was his doing.

"My love, you did not do anything. This is all on Veronica. Don't you know I would do it all again if that meant I was with you? What you've brought to my life is so much more than that hateful woman could ever take away. Please don't cry," Philippe was sobbing.

I moved so I could pull him up to look into his face. I pushed his hair behind his ears, Philippe's beautifully pointed ears, and kissed his lips. In French, I told him he was my life. He was my love, and nothing would change that.

"You sure?" The fact that he doubted me hurt me more than anything the woman who had been my mother could do.

"I'm sure."

I undressed my husband, then myself, and pulled the covers over us. The feeling of Philippe's hairy body against mine was a balm to my soul. Philippe let me hold him for a while before turning into me and scooting up so we were face-to-face.

"*Vous êtes mon coeur*! You are my heart!" he whispered against my lips. "Whats do you needed for me. How I make you safes."

I didn't answer, not with words. Rolling Philippe over on his back, I kissed him, then took my time making love.

It was almost noon when we woke up the following morning. We showered and dressed, then went out for a late breakfast. It was Sunday, and the corner diner was packed when we arrived.

Philippe had changed so much since I first met him. He rarely covered his ears, although he always wore sunglasses. However, they were stylish and cool, unlike the cheap ones he had before. His English was improving.

I had seen the confident man hidden deep inside Jean-Philippe. He had been there when he played his guitar for the first time for me. It had been there each time he had given me all the food he possessed. His sewing had been praised, and I knew my husband could take care of it if I ever needed stitches.

However, every once in a while, I saw the scared little boy who thought no one wanted him. That frightened child had been in bed last night. It had broken my heart to think he would blame himself for Veronica's actions.

Philippe, I think, was surprised that I loved him.

Even if it took the next sixty years, I would do everything I could to prove he deserved everything. More importantly, I did too.

JEAN-PHILIPPE

Opening night in Boston was just a week away. ***Albinism: A Death Sentence in Africa*** would be released the following day after the gala event for a limited time. It had been explained to me that, although the documentary was destined for one of the streaming channels, showing it in a theatre would allow it to be considered for an Oscar.

Tyler had recovered, although occasionally, he would have a spell where he just zoned out. They were becoming few and far between, but we still worried about it.

He was speaking more French now than English in the house, and I was speaking more English than French. My English classes were done for the semester and would pick up again in August. I was still working with Greco.

The event planned by the city took place last week and went well. There had been a lot of media coverage, and I had given so many interviews I lost count. As much as I didn't like the interview process, I had gotten better with them. I was still using a French Language interpreter but was getting to the point where I might not have to.

Evans had reached out to let me know he was staying in Europe. I was relieved but also disappointed. Maestro Greco assured me I could do well on my own and he could make a few recommendations when I was ready.

As crazy as it seemed, I had actually had to hire an assistant to help with my schedule. Leslie came and worked out of the office in the condo five days a week for five hours a day. It worked for her as she was going to college. Her organizational skills were phenomenal, and she spoke French.

We had the office again as Trenton bought a condo near his offices. Tyler and I had dinner with him at least once a week.

The divorce had been quick as Veronica was in jail. Her trial was scheduled for later in the year. Because the FBI considered her a flight risk, she was housed in a minimum-security Federal prison. She still reached out to get Tyler to come and visit, and he always refused.

Javier had retired, and as a retirement gift, I had gotten him and Lola plane tickets to Hawaii and two weeks at the house on Hanapepe Loop. Javier had protested that it was too much but getting him to agree to the gifts with Lola on my side hadn't taken much.

As it was already the third week of June, Harvey Milk Academy was done for the summer. Tyler had visited his kids the week before the school year ended, and I had gone with him. It was nice to see how much the kids loved him. I watched as my husband returned the kids' love lavished on him. Tyler would be a good dad if we ever had our own children.

Cord and Benny had their third and, according to Cord, final child last week. The baby was beautiful and a boy. His two sisters were both pleased and slightly jealous of all the attention.

So much had happened since I had gotten Tyler back home from New York. I sometimes couldn't believe it. Right now, I was standing looking out the glass doors. I did my own zoning out occasionally, and this was one of those times. The view used to be of the park two blocks over, but now a new building was going up, and soon, the view from our balcony would be a forty-story office building.

"What you thinking about?" Tyler's voice came up from behind me, and his arms wrapped around my shoulders.

"The trees will soons being gone." I was sad about that.

"Maybe we should start looking for a house somewhere. I know we said we would wait, but maybe it's time." Tyler kissed the top of my head.

"Maybes. Where you thinked a good places to looking?" I was tired.

"I think a good place to look is something we need to think about. You can work anywhere, but I don't want to move too far from the school. How about we pull up a map and start checking." Tyler turned me around and took my hand.

We started towards the office. The laptop was in there, but I had other ideas. "How about we go to the bedroom," I said, pulling my shirt over my head.

Wednesday, the following week, we started rehearsal for Saturday's Premiere.

The Wilber Theater had already sold out tickets, with part of the revenue going to charity. I had gotten enough tickets so my family could come. Tyler would be with me in New York and San Francisco, but I wanted the rest to be able to come if they desired, and they all did.

Wednesday, we just watched the documentary. It was still hard for me to sit through it. I needed a break ever so often as the subject hit too close to home. I hadn't understood that Albinos in Africa were hunted and murdered like trophy animals. As difficult as my life had been, at least no one wanted to chop up my body to make charms.

The movie was ninety minutes long, so we divided the time into forty-five minutes with a twenty-minute intermission. Campbell already knew where we would take the break, so we watched and listened to a recording of the score.

It took three times watching and listening before we decided where to break that fit the best, not only for the documentary but the music. Tomorrow, we would have the orchestra in the pit and spend half a day and half a day Friday pulling it together.

As the movie-making process was new to me, I was mesmerized by how it all fits together. I just assumed the soundtrack would be embedded, which it was. However, the score for the three events was removed to allow the orchestras to play.

Thursday and Friday went without a hitch. Campbell and his team were thrilled at how everything flowed together. Unlike the orchestra that would be performing in New York and again in San Francisco, the orchestra in Boston was the same one I had performed with. Greco was there, backing me up, encouraging me, but allowing me to shine.

I would never be able to repay him for what he had given me.

Greco denied he did anything unique or different, but he had helped me put my life together in a better place. He had believed in me, like Javier and Lola. He had given me love and guidance without looking down on me for what I did to have food and a place to sleep.

Not many people had done that, and I would be forever grateful to those who had.

"I think I'm going to be sick," I told Tyler's reflection in the mirror in French.

"No. You are going to be wonderful." Tyler smiled back at me, straightening the bowtie to my tuxedo.

We were in one of the dressing rooms at the Wilber. In less than two hours, I would be standing on a podium before one-thousand and ninety-three paying theatre-goers. Timon and Greco had both stopped by and wished me to break a leg. At least Timon was just as nervous as I was. He told me that he had to change his shirt twice already and would probably have to do it again before he took his place on stage.

"Remember Jean-Philippe, this is how you felt in December. But you did great. You worked hard with Greco to be able to do what you are about to do. Your score is breathtaking. Just as breathtaking as you. You got this." My husband told me, turning me around to look directly at me. "I love you. I'm proud of you. Your mom would be proud of you...is proud of you. Be proud of yourself, Jean-Philippe. You are truly amazing."

Tyler wiped the tears from my face before telling me he was leaving. He would be sitting five rows behind the orchestra pit with the rest of my family. Javier and Lola would be there, having returned from their vacation. My father-in-law, Steve, and his new wife, Marie, Olan, and Shirley Rodgers, sat with Tyler. We had invited Cord and Bennie, but they weren't ready to leave the newborn with a sitter.

"Je t'aime, Tyler. Merci pour tout ce que vous m'avez donné! " I said. He had given me so much, and I would always let him know how much I cherished him.

Tyler leaned down and kissed me. "Je vous aime aussi."

I knew he loved me.

Tyler showed me every day. It was the one thing I never doubted.

TYLER

I was so nervous I felt like I was the one who was going to be sick. I smiled and assured Philippe he would do great, which he would. All the while, I was trying to find a way not to hurl all over my handsome husband.

"You look like shit," Steve thoughtfully said.

"It's going to be okay. Philippe's going to do wonderful, and we all know it," Dad patted my arm, but he looked as pale as I felt when I turned to look at him.

Lola, who was sitting two seats down, passed me a tissue. "It's going to start soon, and you'll forget how freaked out you are." She offered.

"After seeing what the documentary was about," Shirley was speaking to Marie, "we decided the boys could stay home. We got Olan's sister, Mary, to take them to a movie."

I listened to the conversations around me as the majestic old theatre started to fill up. Listening to everyone around us reminded me of Jean-Philippe's work on his speech over the last few weeks. Campbell wouldn't come out until the documentary ended, so Philippe would start the event.

We had practiced what he would say, doing our best to keep his English as understandable as possible. Philippe had been offered an interpreter, but he wanted to do this. So, we repeated the words over and over again.

The lights dimming made my breath catch. Dad squeezed my arm but left his hand there. We both needed the connection.

A spotlight lit up the podium. My beautiful elven husband stood there with a smile on his face. His smile grew even brighter when his eyes fell on me. I mouthed, 'I love you,' and got a slight nod.

"Welcome to the Premier of Timon Campbell's documentary, ***Albinism: A Death Sentence in Africa.*** I am Jean-Philippe Roche, and along with the Boston Orchestra, we will be providing the soundtrack for the movies…movie. Let us begin." Philippe nodded to the audience, including those in the balcony, then turned to the musicians.

I watched as Philippe's shoulders rose at the deep breath he took before lifting his baton. The music played for a few minutes before the large screen flickered to life, and Campbell's documentary began.

The screen could have been showing a Disney movie, for all I knew. My eyes were only on Philippe. Every movement, as he directed the men and women before him, was like magic to me. When he used one hand to bring up the volume of the violins or had the percussion section beating like a terrified heart, I held my breath.

I knew the music. I had listened to it as Philippe had cobbled it together. I had even heard the recording, but this was different somehow.

It reminded me of the first time I had gone to Philippe's guitar lesson with Greco.

I had been bowled over, humbled, and brought to tears.

This was more.

That this heart-shattering sound, the music lifting two thousand people up and holding them as it shattered their hearts, came from the man I loved. He had kept this magical gift safe deep inside him, even with everything he had gone through.

There was a standing ovation at intermission and an even longer one when the documentary ended.

Campbell came out after people had returned to their seats and thanked everyone for coming. He made it a point to thank Philippe for this breathtaking score and thanked the Wilber Theater, Maestro Greco, and the Boston Orchestra for their time.

There was a brief question-and-answer period. Most of the questions were for Timon Campbell, but a few were for Philippe, who answered as best he could, taking the time to form each word as he spoke. One reporter asked a question in French, and the relief on Jean-Philippe's face was almost comical.

Philippe and I met Dad and the rest of the family at a restaurant near the Wilber Theatre. The restaurant had a private dining room, and we could relax with a few drinks and a glorious meal. It took an hour before Philippe was able to stop shaking.

Everyone gave him hugs and kisses, Javier and Lola adding tears to the mix.

"The first one is the hardest," Dad was telling Philippe. "The next will be a breeze." He assured Philippe, but I was almost sure Dad was including himself. Dad was just as freaked out as I had been.

At one in the morning, we tumbled into bed.

We would have one day before we had to be in New York. Philippe was scheduled to be on several morning shows along with Campbell and Late Night by himself.

We would be in New York for three days before the Gala there. The following morning, we would be on a plane to San Francisco.

After that, we planned a week's worth of doing absolutely nothing.

JEAN-PHILIPPE

We had been home only one day after an extended week in San Francisco. Leslie had cleared my schedule and had promised not to plan anything for another week when we got home. Trenton had stopped by briefly to let us know he would be in the Bahamas for a conference and, if we wanted, to come and spend a few days. He had a villa rented for two weeks, and there was enough room.

Tyler and I thought about it and had planned to buy tickets, but that never happened.

Tuesday morning at one-thirty, Tyler's phone rang. It was never good when your phone rang early in the morning, and Tyler woke almost immediately as he answered.

I listened, watching his expression to see if this was terrible news.

"Yeah, I know it's early. What's up? Yeah. Okay. Now? Can't it wait? Okay. No, I understand. We'll be ready. See you soon." Tyler disconnected his phone and looked at me. "We need to get up and get dressed. Steve will be over in a few minutes. They, the police, need us to meet someone. Olan said it was important. Nothing to do with Veronica, and Dad is fine. Come on."

I followed Tyler into the bathroom. We took turns using the toilet before washing our hands and faces and brushing our teeth. I put on the jeans I had taken off when I went to bed and pulled a clean T-shirt out of the closet.

It was too early for coffee, but I fixed a pot of tea. Tyler was still in the bedroom when Steve knocked on the door. "Whats happened?"

I asked as he closed the door behind him.

"It's a weird situation. Olan and his captain wanted you to come to meet someone. I can't really say more. Olan will explain when we get to the station house."

In ten minutes, we were following Steve in our truck.

Detective Olan Rodgers was waiting for us when we were shown into the squad room. "Thanks, you two for coming. I know it's early, but this is important. Steve told me you two are set up to foster. Is that correct?"

I looked at Tyler, who was nodding his answer, and I nodded.

"Why?" I asked.

"I want you to come meet Simone Ngoro. She's eleven." Olan didn't say more but suggested I go by myself before Tyler came in.

It was an interrogation room, but someone had tried to make it comfortable. Simone Ngoro lifted her head when I walked in, then stood staring at me as if I were a ghost.

"Are you a real elf?" She said in French and shook her head before asking the same question in broken English.

In French, I answered. "No, just look like one. I'm Jean-Philippe Roche."

Simone seemed to relax just a bit at my French. She was tall, taller than me. As white as I was, Simone was as dark. Her hair was cut close to her scalp, and she was stunning. When she noticed me looking at her, she lifted her chin defiantly.

Still in French, I asked if she was hungry or thirsty. I didn't wait for her answer but took a chair opposite where she was standing.

She returned to her chair and let me know she was okay. The police officers had been taking good care of her.

I nodded.

"Why are you here, Simone?" At my words, she started to cry. I was torn between reaching for her and not touching her, but I covered it with mine when her hand slid out.

"I am gay. I told my cousin this, and she told my father. My father tried to sell me to a man because he didn't want me around anymore. The man was a police officer, and my father is now in jail. I have no place to go. I wouldn't go back to my father's house even if he wasn't in jail."

Now I understood why they called us.

"My father kicked me out of the home when I was thirteen. I'm gay too. Unlike you, I had nowhere to go." Our conversation stopped when Tyler, Olan, and a woman walked into the room. Tyler sat next to me. Olan stood at the head of the table, and the woman sat next to Simone.

"Simone," I was still speaking French, "this is my husband, Tyler Roche. Tyler, this is Simone Ngoro."

"It's nice to meet you, Simone," Tyler offered his hand, speaking in French. Simone looked at me and then accepted the handshake.

Simone looked over at the detective. "He is the man my father tried to sell me to."

"Detective Rodgers is a good friend of ours, Simone. You were lucky he was on your side." Tyler's French was choppy, causing Simone to grin.

"Here's the deal, Simone," Olan began, and the woman translated the words into French. "Jean-Philippe and Tyler are foster parents. That means, if you want, you can go and stay with them. Or, if you prefer, we can send you to a foster home where there are other children. It's up to you. Mrs. Mason works with the Department of Children and Family Services and will do whatever you feel is best. Just know you will not be going back to your father. He has already signed paperwork to release you into DCFS custody."

I watched as the words hit Simone. She was a tough kid, but I could see the heartbreak.

Tyler touched my arm. "We can do this, Babe. I know I didn't ask, but...."

"Yes. Simone, if you want to come, you are welcome. You will have your own room. Whatever you want." There was nothing else to say. The decision had to be hers.

"Do you speak French at home," Simone asked?

"Yes, and English too. Tyler is learning French, and I am learning English. So, we both help each other."

"I don't have anything to bring." Simone didn't wipe the tears away.

"Don't worry. We will work it out."

She turned to Mrs. Mason. "What if I don't like it?"

Mason smiled and said that they would find another place for her.

"What if I like it too much?" That was Simone's next question.

I answered that one. "Then you have found a home."

At six, Tyler and I lay on the bed looking at each other.

"We have an eleven-year-old in the guest bedroom." Tyler looked shell-shocked.

"Yes. I guess we will find out if we are parent material. Did we do the right thing?" I snuggled against my husband.

"Time will tell, I suppose. We'll have to go shopping when we get up." Tyler said with a yawn.

"Seems like you did this before. It worked out well." I said in French and waited to see if Tyler understood.

"Yes, it did." He kissed my neck, and soon he was asleep.

I got out of bed. I would sleep later.

I walked down the hallway. I had closed the door, but Simone had opened it back up. She was sound asleep, the ebony of her skin beautiful against the jade of the sheets.

I knew as I stood there, I would not be able to let her go.

Tyler and I had just found our first child.

EPILOGUE
TYLER, JEAN-PHILIPPE ET SIMONE ROCHE

The Christmas tree seemed out of place against the lushness of the backyard. Moe and Lina had the tree up and decorated when we arrived at the house on Hanapepe Loop. Dad would come later in the day with his girlfriend, whom he had met in the Bahamas. Steve and Marie were with him. The rest of the Tius would join us in two days.

"Dad," Simone called down from the balcony. "Can we go swimming now? You said we could once we got settled, and I already put my stuff away." Simone still spoke her native tongue most of the time, but like me, her English was improving. "*Grand-mère Lola* wants to swim too."

Lola stepped out of her room and called down, agreeing with Simone.

"Yes, go swimming. What's the point of being in Hawaii for Christmas if you don't swim?" Tyler called up to our daughter, and I wrapped my arms around him.

"This was a good ideas." I rubbed against him after making sure no one was around.

"You better quit that." Tyler chuckled.

"If everyone is in the pools we have time to sneaked away." I offered.

"Dad, Papa, you two need to behave." Our daughter of one month shook her head as she headed to the diving board.

"Go swimming." I teased.

Lola and Javier, both in their swimsuits, came out, and we watched as they got into the clear water. "Oh, this is nice," Javier smiled over at Lola.

"We're going to go get our suits on," Tyler called out, taking my hand.

"Sure you are," For a twelve-year-old, Simone Roche was too smart for her own good.

She knew her fathers too well.

I had a family.

More than just Tyler.

All the people who would be here with us had become a family. So much had changed since I discovered a bloodied Tyler freezing on a Halloween night last year.

My mother would be happy for me. She would have loved the people who loved me and I loved back.

Most of all, she would have loved her granddaughter.

My life had been filled with the most beautiful music ever created.

Tyler had been the parchment on which the notes of the rest of my years would be written.

"How about you come and let me show you how much I love you, Jean-Philippe," Tyler whispered into my ear as he lifted me up and carried me to bed.

He could show me, but I already knew.

Jean-Philippe's Music & Other Things!

Rodrigo's Concierto de Aranjuez

https://www.youtube.com/watch?v=bhwbQBgXLy0

Waltz' from Opus 59 by Matteo Carcassi.

https://www.youtube.com/watch?v=VdsQ8_pNh4o

237

Bach's Toccata on One Guitar – Marcin

https://www.youtube.com/watch?v=nUtTfjq7CyU

Spanish Romance Classical Guitar (Romanza)

https://www.youtube.com/watch?v=YJEarbgTlO8

Everyone Here Spoke Sign Language: Hereditary Deafness on Martha's Vineyard

https://www.amazon.com/Everyone-Here-Spoke-Sign-Language/dp/067427041X

I Have A Dream – Dr. King

https://www.youtube.com/watch?v=smEqnnklfYs

www.ingramcontent.com/pod-product-compliance
Lightning Source LLC
Chambersburg PA
CBHW040902010826
48978CB00013BB/1116